THE

STO⚡
GIRL'S
SECRET

BOOKS BY CERI A. LOWE

The Rising Storm
The Girl in the Storm

THE
ST⚡RM
GIRL'S
SECRET

CERI A. LOWE

Bookouture

Published by Bookouture in 2018

An imprint of StoryFire Ltd.

Carmelite House
50 Victoria Embankment
London EC4Y 0DZ

www.bookouture.com

ISBN: 978-1-78681-529-3
eBook ISBN: 978-1-78681-528-6

This book is a work of fiction. Names, characters, businesses,
organizations, places and events other than those clearly in the
public domain, are either the product of the author's imagination
or are used fictitiously. Any resemblance to actual persons, living or
dead, events or locales is entirely coincidental.

For HB

Prologue

A solitary hawk wheeled across the sky as the late afternoon sun melted behind the last of the clouds, and a quiet dusk settled over the Community. Everything was calm. As the two leaders walked together through the main square, rows of Industry guards that lined the edges of the space saluted mechanically. Dark glasses covered their eyes, rendering their faces featureless. Controller General Elizabet saluted back, while Controller General Ariel watched them, captivated by how they no longer even seemed like people to him. He tried to count them but each time he reached around fifty, he forgot where he'd started. No words were spoken, but the deference of the guards was apparent. He nodded at the people of the Community who walked by and they returned his nod silently.

Unity Square bustled with groups of people who had gathered to get a glimpse of the Controller Generals as they walked through the Community. The old-style buildings in the streets beyond cast dark shadows as the day prepared itself for evening. The small stage that stood at one end had been strengthened and a large FreeScreen broadcast dangerous images of the Deadlands. Scattered around the square, the few trees that had survived the Storms all those years ago, wavered in the wind.

Ariel smiled as a small child with long dark hair and olive skin darted from one corner of the square, running backwards and calling to her friend who stood mute, holding the hand of her parent, her other hand covering her mouth. The child, unaware, continued to run until she backed into the pair of Controller Generals. She screamed in shocked surprise and then started to cry. Ariel bent down to comfort her, but his companion pulled him back.

Elizabet glared at the girl. 'Who does this thing belong to?' she said looking around at the people gathered around them, most of whom kept a respectful distance.

A woman at the edge of the square put up her hand, gingerly. 'She's my daughter, Controller,' she said, in a nervous tone. 'She didn't mean anything, she was just excited and…'

'Why is she not in the Academy?' Elizabet called across the square. 'Hours have been extended until after sunset. Every one of our children are required to receive the fullest education at all times.'

'I'm s-sorry, Controller General,' stammered the woman. 'She didn't mean anything by it, it's just that it's her birthday and—'

'Oh, come on!' shouted a man from the crowd. 'She's just a child, she didn't hurt you.'

Elizabet turned to one of the guards and nodded in the direction of the woman. The guard narrowed his eyes and Elizabet nodded again, this time more forcefully, and gestured towards the man who had spoken.

Ariel stepped aside as two of the guards retrieved weapons from their holders and marched away both the mother of the child and the man who had spoken out. The remaining guards shuffled across to bridge the gap they had left. The captives struggled a little, but made no sound as they were removed from the square. The rest of the crowd remained silent as the little girl sobbed on the immaculately swept concrete.

'Someone collect this,' said Elizabet, offhandedly, pointing at the infant. 'Immediately, please.'

A flutter of whispers came from the crowd as a young man edged forward to pick up the crying child. He backed away quickly and moved out of the square, the little girl whimpering in his arms. Elizabet performed a final salute towards the guards, a slight smile crossing her lips.

Ariel felt a chill run down his spine as they walked on. 'Do you really think that was necessary?' he hissed. 'They didn't do anything wrong. It was her birthday.'

Elizabet shook her head and looked at him closely. 'I have much more experience than you in managing these kinds of people. Those creatures were rebels and I know what damage a rebellion can do – we need to deal with them effectively. You should know that well enough yourself; just look at your father. You're lucky you've been given a second chance, and you need to act quickly when incidents like that occur. Unless, of course, you still have sympathies…' Her voice tailed off with an edge of menace.

'I don't,' Ariel replied quickly, watching Elizabet's eyes flicker a darker blue than he had seen before, like the rip tide of a dangerous sea. He bit his lip, a dark cloud of uncertainty forming in his stomach as they walked on in silence.

The journey back to the Industry Headquarters was undeniably tense. The buildings that edged the roads were mostly dark inside – some inhabitants pulled the window covers tight as they marched through the unlit streets, the last edges of the sun giving them just enough light to navigate the shortcuts they both knew so well: although the roads now seemed different to the boy, untrodden and less familiar.

Ariel watched as some people slunk back into the shadows as they passed while others greeted them almost reverently, their eyes never quite meeting them and their words short and clipped, keen to move on. Ariel watched them – his friends and peers – as they drifted past.

'Things out here are really strange,' he said, nervously. 'That woman who just went by us used to be a friend of mine – I've known her all my life and yet she acted like she didn't really recognise me.'

'With power comes great change,' said the girl officiously and with some disdain. 'Your friends and colleagues will act differently now that they know you're about to become one of the most powerful leaders that has ever existed. People *should* be afraid of us. Especially the rebels.'

'But I don't know any rebels.' Ariel thought of his sister, Lucia, who had died recently after multiple infractions against the Industry. And his father, Carter, who had been killed trying to escape the Community. 'Not any more,' he added, a sadness in his voice despite his attempts to hide it.

We are at a turning point in our evolution,' continued Elizabet, smiling tightly with a strange look on her face that made her look significantly older than her teenage years. 'There are great plans for us to implement,' she continued. 'Much change is to come.'

The boy looked thoughtful as they arrived at the building, nervous heads turning as people scuttled past them. Guards stood outside, dark glasses reflecting the sunlight. They looked almost identical, manufactured.

'I agree about the need for change,' said the boy, finally, raising a weak salute. 'Everything, seems, well, a little different since we've become Controller Generals.'

'It's your perception that is different,' said the girl, coolly. 'You are no longer part of that great mass of people who serve the constitution and the law – you are one of the two people who govern it.'

They strode into the Industry Headquarters. Large FreeScreens projected scenes from the past – devastated landscapes of uprooted trees and smashed buildings. Part-erect church spires poked up in marshy town landscapes strewn with bones and debris. In the midst of the destruction, a boy and girl stood, their eyes wide as they each filmed the chaos.

'… London is unrecognisable as the city it was before. My name is Alice Davenport and this is the Deadlands.' The voiceover of the girl on the screen echoed through the main hallway as Industry workers filed through the foyer and back out into the corridors on their way towards the Food Plant, Censomics Labs and down into the other levels of the Headquarters. Each kept their heads down and their stride march-like. The video screen started again, this time with views of the Community, the rebuilding work and proud proclamations of the Original Scouts.

The two Controller Generals stopped to observe the scene. 'We need some more footage,' said Elizabet, her voice curt. 'This is all old and uninspiring. Most of it is from almost a hundred years ago. We need something that will drive forward the next generation.'

'But it's part of the constitution,' replied Ariel, his eyes on the screen. 'It's what was agreed by the Original Scouts.'

'They are all dead and it's their Descendants – you and I – who are in charge now.' She guided the boy into the tunnels, saluting at the guards as she passed them. 'I have plans,' she said, almost fiercely. 'Big plans for how this place is going to be run and I won't have the legacy of Alice Davenport floating like some half-breed ghost above my head.'

The boy looked puzzled as they entered the maze of underground tunnels. 'But Alice and Filip saved the Community,' he said. 'They were the ones that sacrificed everything so that we could…'

The girl cut him off. '*We* are the future now,' she said. 'You are *with* me, aren't you, Ariel?' Her words were threatening but she spoke in a calm, almost light-hearted way that filled Ariel with dread.

He frowned. 'Of course I am,' he said. 'But some things will be the same, won't they? We're not going to change everything.'

'Not everything,' said the girl, running her fingers through her short, blonde hair. 'But most things. My plan takes care of most of that. That was enough to get us established in our new positions.' She smiled dangerously. 'I explained that we had worked on it jointly.'

The boy shook his head. 'But we didn't.'

'We did.' The tone in her voice was decisive and silencing.

Ariel nodded slowly. 'Of course,' he said. 'But this plan of *ours*… you need to share the details with me. And you need to do it soon.'

'All in good time,' said the girl. 'But not now – we must get back down into the Catacombs.'

'Why does Anaya Chess want to meet us there?' The boy glanced up at the flickering lights that illuminated the darkness of the tunnels. It was traditional for the former Controller General to meet privately with the incoming rulers. 'Why couldn't we have completed the final part of our handover in the Control Room? Or up in Unity Square.'

'Because there's something she wants to show us,' said the girl, lowering her voice as they passed the last of the guards. 'And if it's what I believe it is, it will change everything.'

Chapter One

The Injured

At times, the weight of her on his back became too much and he fell to his hands and knees, hauling himself through the darkness of the forest on all fours like an animal. His breathing was shallow – hers was almost non-existent – but they pushed forward in the near blackness, following the trail that he knew by heart.

He knew the smells and the sounds of the wood like he knew himself. He'd spent most of his life moving through the branches and the grasses without being seen or heard.

She made the noise again. The one that reminded him of the many people he'd witnessed losing their lives to the hardness of an existence in the Deadlands. The noise that was almost final – almost the last breath. He rubbed one hand against his forehead and brushed the sweaty hair from his eyes. Through the fading light he could just make out the silhouette of the moon, high above the trees.

'We'll make it,' he said through gritted teeth, but there was no response. He pushed himself upright and picked up the pace. She didn't have much time left.

'Not long now, Elvira,' he repeated. 'We're going to make it, okay?'

The woman on his back made a low groaning sound but didn't speak. A small trail of blood leaked behind them as Samuel half-walked, half-crawled like an animal through the darkness of the evening. Tiny white-diamond stars glittered in the sky above them but neither of them looked up to appreciate them. The thin light of the moon cast a thread of yellow across the path as Samuel inched them forwards towards the thick-poled stockade with torch flames that shone in the distance. He watched the orange glow blur in front of him, getting seemingly closer and then further away. His back throbbed and his arms were numb – exhaustion coming over him in waves of pain.

The agony in his limbs distracted him from the fear of returning to the place where he knew he would be unwanted and unwelcomed. He had, after all, been responsible for the death of one of the people of the Township. They had made an agreement that had gone terribly wrong. Samuel had tried to use the man to work against his brother, Carter, but when the man had panicked and killed his friends, Samuel simply had no choice.

He'd had no choice.

He repeated it to himself over and over on the journey. As much as he had hated his brother at that point, the guilt had been overwhelming. He'd been so wrong about his brother Carter. And Samuel rarely, if ever, admitted he was wrong. He'd shot Saul, one of the Township, and they had buried him, miles from home. He'd pretended not to know who he was, pretended that they hadn't had an agreement. He had plotted, he had lied and now Saul was dead.

The two of them hadn't eaten in a long time. Elvira was weakening by the hour. Their last hope lay with the mercy of the Township, and their leader, Frida. He remembered her with some fondness, even though she'd been so angry when she'd found out the truth about Saul.

But she was a fair person, a kind person and she would understand. She had let them leave the Township to continue with their mission. She would get some help for Elvira and save her life so that he could go back to help Carter. If he could speak to her first and not one of the others. One of the others who wanted him dead.

As they approached the gates, Samuel's legs gave way beneath him and he collapsed, face first, into a messy heap in the foliage, Elvira sprawled across his shoulders. She groaned loudly. Samuel was thankful she was, at least, still alive. In the distance, the lights danced in a careful, linear progression towards them and he could hear low voices.

'Someone's coming,' whispered Samuel over his shoulder with an element of relief. 'Someone's coming.'

He breathed heavily, pain wracking his bones and his eyes heavy with a gritty tiredness. He felt the weight on his eyelids bearing down until he could see nothing except the blood-dark inside of his mind.

'Someone's coming,' he tried to whisper but before Elvira or anyone else could answer, exhaustion had overcome him.

When he finally opened his eyes, the voices had grown much louder as a small group of people holding torches came closer. One man stood towards the front and waved a hot, smoky flame in front of Samuel. His voice was all too familiar.

'Well, look what we have here,' said Eli. 'You don't look in great shape.'

He kicked Samuel's shoulder lightly with the toe of his foot before he noticed Elvira strapped to him. He motioned to the group of people with him and they gathered around in a circle.

'We need your help,' said Samuel, gritting his teeth. 'My friend is hurt.'

'What happened to her?'

The group drew closer and walked around the pair, examining them from every angle. Eli continued to hold the torch close to Samuel's head while the others rummaged underneath him, looking through his pockets.

'Don't think he's armed,' called one of the women. 'But we should tie them up anyway so they can't escape.'

'We're not going to try to escape,' Samuel gulped desperately. 'I can barely walk and my friend here is hurt, I told you. Please – I know what I did to Saul was wrong and I'm so sorry, and so ashamed…'

Eli crouched down next to him, the flames dangerously close to his hair. Samuel could feel the heat and thought he could smell burning. The weight of Elvira on top of him as well as the aching in his muscles inhibited any movement he may have wanted to make. He blinked in the torchlight.

'Where are the others?' demanded Eli. 'And no lies.'

'Please help her,' said Samuel. 'There are no others. It's just us. She had an accident and I've brought her here for medical attention.' He paused. 'I can't get her back to our Village alone. It will take at least another two days – three with her weight – and…' his voice trailed off in exhaustion. 'We've not eaten nor drunk any water in the last day and she needs help.' He could hear the desperation in his own voice. 'I thought you were peaceful people,' he added, letting his head fall back into the mud.

Eli walked around him, his disdain at the situation clear in his voice as he spoke. '*You* want *my* help?' he sneered. 'After your betrayal?'

'Can you believe it?' said one of the men, raising his voice. '*He* wants *your* help!' Another stamped his foot on the ground, dangerously close to Samuel's head, scattering light dust that coated his face.

Samuel started to cough. 'Stop that,' he began, desperation turning to anger, and he tried to lift himself and Elvira up off the ground. But the weakness in his arms didn't allow him the leverage and they slumped downwards again.

'What does this mean for us, Eli?' hissed one of the men, turning his face away so that Samuel could no longer hear him. 'He shouldn't be here. He's not one of us. Should we kill him now?'

'No,' whispered Eli, suddenly thoughtful, pulling the man aside. 'We may be able to use him to our advantage with the others here. As long as we play this right, they'll soon realise that I should be leading this Township and Frida is no longer fit to represent us. We need a stronger, more forceful person in charge, now that things are in motion. We need to make the right move this time and oust her once and for all. Killing him now would be a waste.'

The man nodded. 'We *encourage* him to stay until the time is right?'

Eli looked serious. 'Yes,' he said. 'We need to play this carefully and get the result we need.'

There was a cold, mindful silence before a woman's voice rang clearly through the night air.

'Eli, what's going on here?'

The group stopped and turned back towards the entrance to the stockade of the Township. The woman, Frida, stood with a large torch in her hand, glaring at the scattering of men and women that stood, open-mouthed, around Samuel and Elvira. She stood tall amongst them, her warrior-like authority casting a dark shadow across the trees. The lines and patterns that covered her face seemed to glow dark in the moonlight and her very presence filled Samuel with some relief.

Eli scowled at her and stepped backwards, away from Samuel.

'Get away from them,' snapped Frida, pushing her way through. She shook her head at Eli. 'You should know better than this,' she spat at him. 'All of you,' she continued. 'All of you!'

A thin sheet of white-grey cloud had unrolled itself across the sky and, through it, the tiny stars blinked over the Township. As Frida knelt down next to Samuel, the men fell silent. She called to them as she checked over Elvira's injuries.

'You can all go back to whatever you were doing. This is the Township leader's business. So, I'll handle this.' As the group turned to leave she stood up again. 'Not you, Leanor, you can stay and help me. You too, Astor.' A boy of about fourteen and a girl just a few years older left the small crowd and knelt down next to Samuel.

'Astor – go and fetch the stretcher from the medical unit, and Leanor, you untie the woman,' said Frida. 'Carefully, she looks badly injured.' She glanced at Samuel who was spitting dirt fragments from his mouth and scowling. The girl, Leanor, took a knife from her belt and slashed at the pieces of fabric and rope that bound Elvira to Samuel. The rope was knotted in thick strands but Leanor cut quickly, gently slicing through the cords until Elvira lay balanced, but unattached to Samuel's back.

As Leanor worked, Frida shook her head slowly. 'Oh, Samuel,' she said in a disappointed tone. 'What are you doing here?'

'I had to come,' Samuel pleaded, relieved that everyone else had disappeared. 'I didn't want to come to you, but I need help for Elvira. After the unforgivable things that I did, I knew that I would not be welcome but for Elvira's sake, I had to come. I don't expect your forgiveness but I hoped for your help, at least for her.'

Astor reappeared with the stretcher, which was made with thick poles of wood, woven with branches, leaves and old fibres. Between the three of them, Frida, Leanor and Astor carefully lifted Elvira onto it as she moaned in pain. One of her legs was twisted and her face and arms were badly bruised. There was a deep gash on the side of her head and her clothes were bloodied and tattered.

'Easy,' said Frida as they laid her flat. 'We don't know what injuries she may have.'

'How are we supposed to help her?' said Astor, creasing his forehead. 'We don't know much about medicine.' He held a small cup of water to Elvira's lips and she gulped it down messily. Her eyes flickered open as Frida sat on the ground next to her and touched her cheek gently. Samuel crouched on the other side, rubbing mud from his mouth and eyes.

'Where does it hurt?' she said, quietly. 'Are you able to tell me?'

Elvira moaned and started to speak. 'My arm,' she whispered slowly. 'My head and my arm. And I can't feel my left leg.'

Leanor took her knife and slit the length of the ragged trousers Elvira was wearing. Underneath, they could see one of the bones protruding wildly from the lower part of her leg, bruising already forming a dark flower underneath the skin, and blood caked along the length of her shin. There was a sharp intake of breath from Astor and Samuel looked away.

'Bones, we can reset,' said Leanor, bravely. 'And the cuts we can stitch.' She looked at Elvira. 'But the head… if there's anything internal we might not…'

'Sssh,' interrupted Frida, turned towards Elvira again. 'You're going to be all right,' she said softly, her words reassuring. 'We just need to get you to our infirmary. It's not as well equipped as your clinic in the Village, but we will be able to help you better there.'

'Thank you,' said Samuel, nodding. 'I hope that—'

'You will have your time to speak later,' snapped Frida. 'For now, you help these two to carry her into the Township. Straighten yourself up and take the front of the stretcher.'

With Leanor and Astor supporting the rear of the structure, Samuel helped lead the stretcher through the torch-lit gates and into the main circle of the Township. A group of children sat around a small fire and spat into the flames as they walked past the low, brick-built buildings that lined the clearing.

Towards the back of the open tree space, he could just make out the grain store and shivered. The night was cold and his mouth was dry. An unnerving silence fell over them.

'Is it much further?' he called to Frida, parched. 'I need something to drink.' He paused. 'Please.' As his voice echoed against the buildings and through the clearing, he saw heads rise in the darkness, several pairs of eyes fixed on him – watching. The lights of the large, domed building in the centre of the clearing were dimmed. There was a murmuring from a couple of women, sat in the shadows with their backs against a huge oak, almost empty of its leaves.

Frida threw them a glance. 'Just here to the left,' she said to Samuel as they reached the edge of the clearing and passed down through an alleyway between two brick buildings. The alley widened out into a broad courtyard with torches lashed to large gateposts, illuminating a large building set back into a copse of trees that had grown thick around the edges.

'This is it.' Frida directed them through the courtyard and into the building. 'This is where we bring our sick.'

They carried the stretcher up some stone steps, through a hallway and into a large room. Between them, Astor and Leanor lifted Elvira onto one of the many beds that lined the walls – all the others were empty. Leanor removed the remaining rags that covered Elvira and placed a clean sheet over her.

'Fetch some water,' she said to Astor. 'And get the supplies from upstairs – splints, bandages and whatever pain medication we have that's already mixed up. I'll get to work immediately.'

Frida turned to Samuel then nodded towards the door. 'We will leave them to it,' she said definitively. 'And you will come with me.'

'I want to stay with her and make sure she's okay,' Samuel protested. 'She's my responsib—'

'You'll come with me, clean yourself up and get a meal,' interrupted Frida, pushing him towards the door. 'You have travelled here for our help, you are weak and you are also obliged to tell us what has happened. Letting you in here will place a great strain between me and my people and therefore I want answers.'

He nodded, but inside a deep guilt for what he'd done worried him as a tight knot formed in his stomach.

'You should never have come here,' Frida continued, exhaling deeply. 'You have done a brave thing, bringing your friend as far as you have alone. But coming here was a mistake. It really was. You have placed yourself and your friend in grave danger.'

Chapter Two

The Awakening

For the first time in over eighty years, sixteen-year-old Alice Davenport breathed deeply and opened her eyes. Her head was aching and her body stiff. Her vision was blurred, but she could make out two figures standing before her, wide and open-mouthed. She looked around at the smooth grey walls and the single, dull light that illuminated the small, cell-like room. Her stomach felt empty and hollow; there was an emptiness that filled her completely. Her baby was gone.

Something about the boy with the short blond hair and piercing eyes looked familiar, although she didn't know him. The girl with him had a smooth, blank expanse of skin where one of her eyes should have been. Alice blinked the sleep from her own eyes, confused and afraid, and tried to back away from them. Her whole body ached and an overwhelming dizziness filled her head. Her first thought was to her child – the baby that had been inside her, the child she had never felt leave her. And then her mind turned to the people, her friends, who had put her there in that room.

'Where is my daughter?' she whispered, feeling her stomach. 'I was pregnant; they froze me down here – they must have taken my child from me.' Outside in the corridor there was silence and an uneasy quiet settled in the room.

'And who are *you*?' she added, eyeing them both as the blurriness subsided and the pair in front of her sharpened into focus.

The last thing she remembered before going to sleep was Filip's face emblazoned in her mind. An unparalleled anger coursed through her as she recalled the betrayal – by him and by her friends. She had spent months creating the new world and leading the survivors of the Storms in the new Community after five years underground for them to turn on her and condemn her to a forced cryonic sleep. But for how long? She had no idea. And now, in front of her were two strangers who looked at her as if she were an alien.

The boy spoke first – his voice calm and clear, while the girl looked nervous and a little restless.

'Alice,' he said, softly. 'My name is Carter Warren and this—' he pointed at the girl '—is Angel Stanton. You've been asleep for over eighty years.'

He paused for a moment – how could he explain to her what had become of her world? The one, he imagined, she had worked so hard to build. He exhaled deeply. 'The Community that you created after the Storms has gone badly wrong – very badly wrong. I don't think it's what you intended it to be.' He watched as a confused disappointment clouded her face. 'And that's why we're here. We're here to put an end to this. To make things right.'

Alice felt her whole existence implode like shards of glass. Eighty years.

Carter put his hand on her arm gently, and she flinched. 'I don't know why this happened to you,' he said. 'And I don't know exactly how we're going to put the world back together again. But I do know where your daughter is. Or at least I did.'

Jescha had been the first of the next generation. The first true Descendant. Everyone knew she was the daughter of Filip Conrad and Alice Davenport. Jescha's daughter, Samita, was the mother of Carter's children, making Jescha their grandmother. She had been in the house when he had first gone to visit Ariel, his son. He'd not seen her but he had heard her. She was still alive – at least she had been then.

The room fell silent again before Alice's eyes became hard and bright with angry tears. A thousand questions raced through her mind and she couldn't pinpoint the one she wanted to ask first. She opened her mouth to speak and then closed it again.

Eighty years. Her daughter was no longer a child – hadn't been a child for decades. She would have had her first birthday without her, learned to speak and walk. She imagined her – dark brown eyes, her skin the colour of soft, milky coffee and her smile wide and happy. Or perhaps she had taken on Filip's genes – green-blue eyes that would have reminded her of the sea. Had she been happy?

'Eighty years?' she said, her heart sinking. 'How is that even possible?'

Her mind tracked back to that night in the house in Morristown Row when she lay there in the bed while Filip performed the procedure. It had been so cold, so perfunctory but, somehow, they had made a child. One that had developed inside her for months. And even though she had been confused and unprepared, she had grown to love the baby that she had known in her heart would be a girl. A daughter. She felt the thick scar that ran down her middle bite into her skin.

'My little girl,' she said, finally. 'She's still alive?'

'Yes,' said Carter, slowly. 'She's an old woman now, but she's still alive. Her name is Jescha.'

Alice's heart lifted at the sound of the name she had chosen for her but then immediately sank and she placed both of her hands over her stomach, tears forming in her eyes. Her daughter made her think of her own childhood. Of her mother; the dark days in Prospect House, then the Ship. And Filip.

After the Storms, when they had come above ground, things had been so very different. The new world brought with it a very different set of rules that at first had simply unsettled her, but then had destroyed her belief in everything she had thought was ethical and real in the world. Paradigm Industries had enforced a repopulation plan, and ordered the destruction of art, music and, above all, choice. The memory with Filip and the syringe; the first time she realised that her baby would be born into a world of control. The worst part for Alice was that she herself had been part of their plans – she had been part of the Industry, had believed in these sick ideas at first. She had escaped with Richard Warren, a boy she'd met who'd somehow managed to survive the Storms without the Industry, and she'd returned to the Community in order to make things right.

But she hadn't. The people she'd trusted – Filip included – had frozen her in the Catacombs. For eighty years.

She pushed back her tears, the very core of her sick with pain. But at least Jescha was still alive. She would find her. As the realisation sunk deep into her bones, in a second, it struck her. Warren.

'Carter Warren?' she said, slowly.

'Yes.'

'Are you any way related to Richard Warren?'

The boy looked surprised but then smiled a little. 'Richard Warren was my great-grandfather,' he began. 'He was one of the Descendants.'

'He saved me,' interrupted Alice, a slight waver in her voice. She remembered with a shiver how she and Filip had found Richard in Prospect House, sick, and had taken him back with them into the

Community. She'd thought at the time they had been saving his life but she had placed him in the greatest danger possible. She remembered the kind, serious look in his eyes when he'd convinced her that 'Doctor' Barnes – and Filip – were a threat to her. Alice had never trusted Barnes, with her constant interfering, insistence that Alice focus on having a child, and mysterious experiments in her lab that no one was allowed to question. Richard had told her the awful truth: Barnes had plotted the murder of Kelly, one of Alice's best friends, when she'd deemed that Kelly had been asking too many questions. Barnes had infiltrated every element of Alice's life and destroyed it from the inside outwards.

Alice recalled how she and Richard had fled the Community together and how he'd shared his family with her. She thought fondly of his brother Joe, the boy who'd loved to surf and how they'd shared a meal and listened to music – a brief reminder of how life could be different. She shook herself from the reverie.

'Tell me more about my daughter.'

Carter looked through the grille in the door and out into the corridor.

'We're not safe here,' said Angel, nervously. 'We need to get out of the Catacombs – or at least out of this room. They could come back at any time.'

'They?'

'The Industry, the Controller Generals,' said Angel, her voice shaking.

'Things have changed a lot since your time,' said Carter, mindful of the decades Alice had been incarcerated in the cold, dark cell, asleep.

Alice stretched out her arms, feeling the weakness in her muscles tense. 'What's it like up there?' she said nervously. 'Is it… are people happy?'

He wondered how much to tell her about the cruel way in which they stratified society into Descendants, First Generation and the Lab Mades – created underground and treated like a lesser species. How much could he let her know about the total control of the Industry and about the lies the people had been told about their past. Even for someone as strong and determined as Alice, he was doubtful how much she could take. The look on his face told Alice the answer to her question.

'Who is left? Is Filip still here?' Alice's heart started to beat fast. 'What about Barnes? And Quinn?' She felt the air around her chill at the thought of those who had betrayed her. If she had been asleep for as long as the boy said she had, there was a fair chance they would all be gone. Everyone she had ever known or cared about. All dead. She wondered, after everything that had happened, whether she had ever loved Filip. When they had emerged above ground, after five dark years sheltering from the Storms in the Ship, everything changed. The plans they had made for rebuilding their drowned world that had seemed so simple and yet so far in the future became terrifying real. One of her best friends, Kelly, had died at the hand of Alice's adopted daughter, Izzy. Her adopted son, Marcus, a sweet and innocent boy, had been sent underground, and the terrible betrayal by Filip, Quinn and Barnes made her blood run the coldest shade of pale.

'Is Filip here?' Alice repeated, more loudly this time.

Carter looked confused. 'Filip Conrad?' he said. 'No, I believe he died many years ago. And Quinn?' The confusion turned to disbelief. 'You mean Quinn Fordham?'

'Yes,' said Alice, quickly. 'Did you know her?'

'No,' said Carter. 'But I believe Richard Warren did. Quinn Fordham gave birth to his child, my grandfather Milton.'

Alice shook her head in disbelief. She remembered Quinn's face, evilly joyful when Alice had been tied to the chair in the Control Room and she and Barnes announced they were having Richard's child. That was just moments before she was forced into the Catacombs by Kunstein – the woman who had been her mentor and friend, who had first saved her from the Storms and taken her into the Ship to be raised by Paradigm Industries. Her teeth started to chatter; she pulled the sleep suit around her and started to shiver.

'Get me some clothes,' she demanded. 'I need to get out of here. I need to find my daughter. And I need to tell someone – everyone – what's been going on.'

Angel took a turn looking through the grille in the door. 'I don't know where we're going to get anything from,' she said despondently. 'Most of the rooms are locked.'

Carter pulled his own, ragged clothes from the previous day out of his bag. 'Put these on,' he said. 'They're not clean but they're better than nothing. We need to get you out of here.' There was something about the guts of the teenage girl before him that he admired – so much more than when he'd seen her on the Industry films as a child.

Alice took herself over to the corner while the other two turned away. As she pulled the sleep suit off she ran her hand down her shallow belly; a long thin line, cleanly stitched, ran across the width of her lower stomach. It had healed perfectly, leaving the hard, ugly smile as the only reminder of the daughter that had been stolen from her. She lifted the top over her head and down low, covering the carved lip in her stomach. She pulled on the trousers and turned around.

'I don't suppose you have any shoes?'

Carter smiled awkwardly. 'Just the ones I'm wearing, but I don't think they'll fit you.'

'We need to go,' said Angel, an urgency in her voice. 'Remember what Elvira said?'

Carter cast his mind back to the conversations they'd had with the friend who had told them about the secret place in the Catacombs. The woman who once lived in the Community but had escaped, risking her life to go back and help them. Carter turned to Alice. 'A friend of ours told us that what's in this chamber is a secret that only Controller Generals know about. And they could be here at any time.'

'Why would anyone want to come down here and see me?' said Alice, confused. 'And if people *have* been down here, why has no one let me out before?'

'Because their whole society is built on a lie. On the lie that you gave your life to bring your daughter into the world and that every woman should be prepared to be like you.' Carter paused, watching the colour drain from Alice's face. 'When the news was announced that you had died as a result of an attack on the Barricades, the Industry started to create new life down here in the Catacombs. They called them Lab Mades and they were considered 'less' than those born the traditional way. It was the excuse they needed to play God and continue their experiments. If they knew you were still alive and that the Industry had silenced you, people would see them for what they are – they would see their lies and deceit and start to think for themselves.'

Alice felt sick, deep in her stomach, remembering how Kunstein had tried to defend her in the Control Room. How she had walked her down the stairs to the room where she had spent the next eighty years. After they had taken her baby from her, had Kunstein convinced Filip to keep her alive? Had she hidden her from Barnes and the others? Had she bargained for her life? She shivered. 'We need to tell them,' she whispered. 'People need to know what's really been happening.' She stood, pulling the loose trousers around her thin waist. 'And I need to find my daughter and tell her the truth.' She made her way to the door.

'No,' said Carter, kindly but firmly, reaching his arm out to stop her. 'Not yet. We need to figure out a way of getting out of here safely and letting everyone know that what they thought was the truth is very far from it. That's why we came here.' He paused for a second. 'We want the same thing, Alice. We want to destroy the Industry but we need to be careful – the future of many civilisations depends on what we do next.'

'I can get us out,' Alice insisted. 'I know the tunnels down here better than anyone else. I used to go down through the vents and—'

'That's what we did,' said Angel, interrupting nervously. 'But we went into one staircase and it triggered an alarm.'

Alice laughed, fiddling with the cuff of the shirt she had borrowed from Carter. 'If they thought anyone was down here, you'd have been captured already.'

Angel breathed a sigh of relief. 'So, no one knows we are here?'

'Probably not. Can we go now?'

Carter shook his head. 'There's still the issue of Ariel and Elizabet. They will be making their way down here at some point today as part of the handover ritual for becoming Controller General. They must see you here otherwise they will come looking for you – and they *will* find you. Getting out of the Community might not be as easy as it was for us to get in.'

'I don't plan to get out,' said Alice. 'Not without taking this place down. And not without my daughter.'

Carter rubbed his forehead. 'My son is here too,' he said. 'He's one of the two people we expect to come down here.'

Alice's face brightened. 'Isn't that good news?' she said, almost excited before her face darkened. 'Your son? Your *son* is about to become Controller General?' She thought for a moment, confused and looked at Carter. 'How old is he?'

'He's almost fifteen,' said Carter. 'Around the same age as me. And if my history lessons served me correctly—' he almost smiled '— just a year or so younger than you.'

Alice shook her head, unsure whether her sixteenth birthday had passed. Or her seventeenth even. 'That's… isn't that… how the hell…?' She exhaled deeply. 'That's just too weird,' she concluded. She looked the boy in front of her up and down. Whatever his journey had been, it had led him here to her and it couldn't have been easy. And he was the father of a teenage boy the same age as him. There was something about him that reminded her a little of Richard – his bravery and confidence. And to her, it had only been yesterday that they had been together in the Deadlands. 'Weird,' she repeated, shaking her head.

'Weirder than having an eighty-year-old daughter?' said Angel, deep lines forming in her forehead. They all laughed, somewhat awkwardly, before Alice returned to her previous thought.

'So, if your son is the one coming down here, and he's about to become Controller General, surely we can explain this all to him and he can help us? He can help me find my daughter, we can explain to him who I am and then we can get out of here?'

Carter wished it could all be that simple.

'My son is loyal to the Industry,' he replied. 'And if it was just him, maybe we'd have a chance.' There was a moment of hesitation before he continued. 'But there's a girl with him, another candidate for Controller General – we overheard them talking and this time, for some reason, they are both going to be initiated and will take the position jointly.'

'Who is this other girl?' said Alice earnestly. 'Maybe we can talk to her, and with the support of your son…?'

'No,' said Carter, firmly. 'She's… she's different. She's more Industry than anyone I've ever met.'

'You've met her?'

'It's a long story,' said Carter, 'But yes, I've met her. And she's not someone who would help us. She's got a lot of history with the Industry, from the old times – she's related to someone you know. Filip Conrad.'

Alice shivered again at the sound of his name. And then, the horrifying reality of what Carter had said slotted into its ugly place.

'What is her name?'

'Elizabet. Elizabet Conrad.'

Alice ground her teeth hard and placed her hand over her mouth in shock. Izzy. Her adopted daughter. The Industry had insisted on young families forming after the Storms, and fifteen-year-old Alice had been more than willing to take in the ten-year-old girl who had been brought up with her partner Filip before the Storms. She thought back to the girl who she had mothered and taken care of, but who had taken great pleasure in destroying anything she'd touched. The girl who had threatened her stepbrother Marcus with a gun. The girl who had shot and killed Kelly, one of Alice's best friends. The girl who had betrayed her. Her mouth filled with a sick, acidic taste.

'How old is she now?'

'About fifteen, sixteen. The same age as us.'

Alice closed her eyes tightly and shook her head. 'She has got to be stopped. That girl is evil. Whatever terrible things have been happening here, she will only make them worse. I will not fail again. Are you going to help me stop them?'

Through the silence of the room, Carter could feel the undeniable hatred and tension that had built up in Alice. Her arms were folded tightly across her chest and the nails on her fingers were digging deep into the palms of her hand. The tight line of her mouth was white against her light-brown skin. Carter could see that she was more than angry – she was heartbreakingly furious.

'How well did *you* know her?' asked Angel. 'Is there any way you could speak to her and she could help us? I mean, if you know her and Carter knows Ariel…' Carter shot her a glance and narrowed his eyes.

Alice spoke clearly but she couldn't stop her voice wavering. She repeated her earlier words. 'That girl is a killer,' she said, angrily. 'It is because of her, in part, that I am here in the first place. She'll never let me out of here alive.' She laughed ironically. 'I raised her as if she was my own child and she murdered one of my closest friends.'

Angel looked bewildered. 'So, Elizabet is like your daughter and Ariel is Carter's son. And this is who we're up against?' She shook her head. 'And you're all the same age,' she added. 'It's really quite unbelievable.'

Alice and Carter looked at each other.

'And technically, we're all related,' said Carter, solemnly. 'Your granddaughter is the mother of my children.' He paused. 'Which makes Ariel your great-grandson.'

Before Alice could respond, a dull noise from outside the door stopped the conversation dead. It was faint and came from a long way down the corridor but it was definitely the sound of voices. Carter looked up at the air vent.

'We need to get out of here,' he said urgently. 'If they find us in here, we'll all be arrested and most likely killed.'

Alice nodded, pulling off the clothes and getting into her sleep suit. 'Get into the vent,' she said in a whisper. 'And I'll get back in here.' Her fingers were shaking as she fumbled with the plastic covering. Carter leaned over and pulled up the zip, touching her gently on the arm.

'We'll come back for you,' he said. 'We'll be just up there, okay? You might have to give us a hand though. And don't confront her, however much you want to.'

Alice nodded and tried to calm her heartbeat to a steady pulse. She watched as Carter lifted Angel up to the vent and they pulled it outwards from the wall. It came away easily and, with a push, Angel climbed onto the thin ledge and through into the ventilation shaft. Alice interlocked her fingers and Carter thrust his foot into the basket of her hand, Angel hauling him in and behind the vent. Alice locked the vent cover back into position and lay back on the bed, her heart pounding in her chest, pulling the sleep suit around her. The sounds came closer, now clearly voices. And then, from the corner of her eye she saw the crumpled trousers that Carter had loaned her, balled in a small heap in the corner of the room.

'Shit,' she whispered under her breath. The voices were louder now, just outside the door.

'So, this is it then?' said the boy. 'This is the big secret we get to find out now that *we're* Controller General, Chess?'

A woman's voice came through the door. She sounded weak and tired. Worn and exhausted. Alice glanced over at the trousers.

'Before you go in,' said the woman, Chess, 'there's something you should know.'

Alice took her chance and flitted silently out of bed, grabbing the trousers and dived back onto the rester, pushing the trousers underneath her body. She held her breath.

'Did you hear that?' For the first time in almost eighty years, Alice heard the girl's voice. It sounded a little less childlike but it was unmistakeably her. Izzy. She shivered uncontrollably within the sleep suit.

'Probably just the ventilation systems,' said Chess. 'I remember the first time I came in here there was…'

'Can we just get in?' said Elizabet, impatiently. 'I know what's in there already. I just want to see her.'

A cold bead of sweat formed on Alice's upper lip. If they discovered she was awake, there was no way she could take on all three of them, especially in her weakened state. She thought of her daughter, Jescha, and tried to keep herself calm. Her mouth felt dry and there was a tickle in her throat that she attempted to stifle by swallowing hard.

'You can't possibly know what's in here,' said Chess. 'This is classified information.'

'I do know,' said Elizabet, with self-importance, 'because I was there when she went to sleep.'

There was a brief rush of air as the door opened and Alice closed her eyes tightly. A deep, wrenching pain knotted itself in her stomach as she worked hard to slow and regulate her breathing. She tried to think of nothing, to clear her mind, to make herself almost invisible. And then her voice came again.

'You're still here then?' Elizabet's voice was quiet, but cutting.

'Who is she?' said Ariel. 'It just looks like another Sleeper to me and there are thousands of them down here.'

Alice heard Chess cleared her throat as if she were about to speak.

'Actually,' said Elizabet, 'you can leave us now, Anaya. Thank you for the escort down here but we no longer need your services.'

'My services include ensuring you are both safely returned to the Control Room for your next briefing,' said Anaya, a bite in her voice. 'These tunnels can be quite complicated to negotiate, especially after an absence.'

Elizabet smiled tightly. 'I'm quite capable of finding my way around here,' she replied.

'I also need to provide you with the background to this room,' said Chess. 'That's part of the handover process.'

Alice heard a deep sigh come from Elizabet. 'I think you know that I don't need the history behind this room and I will ensure that Ariel gets the true story. So, now that I... we... are Controller Generals, I don't believe we are required to have your supervision. Leave us, Anaya. And ensure the door is closed, I have my own card to move around the Catacombs as I please. Now leave.'

There was a frosty quiet before Alice heard the door close and there was another brief silence before the boy spoke from the corner of the room. She was desperately glad she had moved the trousers that were stashed uncomfortably beneath her.

'Who is she? And what is she to you? How do you know her?'

There was another rush of cool air as Alice felt Elizabet walk towards the side of her bed. She was so close Alice could feel the warmth of her presence standing next to her.

'This,' she said, running her finger down the outside of the sleep suit, 'is Alice Davenport.'

'Alive Davenport? You mean...' The boy sounded surprised.

'Yes, one and the same. Our first so-called Scout. The pioneer that you all learned about in school. Except you learned it all wrong. That's not how it happened.'

'What do you mean? How come she's still alive?' Ariel, moving into the room. 'I thought she died during the birth of her first child; she went into labour in the Infirmary where she was recovering after an attack from outsiders, near the Fringes. That's why we had to build the Barricades so high and why the Industry had to start creating the Lab Mades – because natural birth was too dangerous.'

'Two very good stories,' said Elizabet, 'but neither of them completely true.' She laughed again. 'There was a threat from a group outside, but we dealt with that quite effectively. And natural birth is dangerous but – more than that – it was too slow. With the Lab Mades, we could create human life much more quickly that the usual birth cycle – in less than half the time. But, like most things, it wasn't perfect.' The laugh came again, this time there was an evil, almost demonic sound to it.

Alice felt the irritation grow in her throat – she desperately wanted to cough. More than that, she wanted to grab Elizabet by the throat and shake her like a doll. She dug the nail of one finger into the tip of another to steady herself. The girl sounded more like the doctor, Barnes, every time she spoke and it disgusted Alice to the core.

'You were there right at the beginning?' said Ariel, in awe. 'Right at the very beginning?'

Alice felt Elizabet poking at the sleep suit. 'Yes,' she said, proudly. 'I was there. With her.' She pressed down on the sleep suit around Alice's face. 'And Filip Conrad, Ellis Barnes, Quinn Fordham and the rest of them. But if it had been left to Alice, we'd all have been dead.'

Ariel shook his head. 'But that's not true – Alice was a pioneer. She gave us our first new resident of the Community. She was a hero.'

'She was a coward,' whispered Elizabet.

Alice could feel her walking up and down the length of the bed. She desperately wanted to open her eyes, to jump up and attack the girl she had once cared for, but instead practised hard breathing in and then breathing out again.

'She was a coward and a fraud,' repeated Elizabet. 'And I intend to expose her for what she was so that our Community can honour those people who *really* saved us. And who continue to save us.' She pulled the creases of the sleep suit out flat and Alice felt Elizabet's face close to hers through the plastic. For a moment, she thought the girl might pull the suit tight and squeeze the breath from her.

'Hold on, what do you think you're going to do?' Ariel's voice sounded concerned as he remembered the way Izzy had reacted with the girl in the square. 'We haven't discussed the next steps for our plans in detail and we need to consider what that would achieve. What you're talking about would change the way everyone feels about their history and about how the Community was created. We need to talk about this, Elizabet.'

Alice could hear the shock and unease in his voice.

'If,' he continued, 'we tell them everything they were ever taught about Conrad and Davenport was a lie then it could create absolute chaos.'

'I'm not going to do anything right now,' said Elizabet as Alice felt her fingers push against her and then a sharp pinching sensation that pushed into her shoulder. 'But when the time is right, life in the Community will never be the same again.'

Alice fought against everything inside her not to cry out in pain.

'Don't,' said Ariel, annoyance in his voice. 'Come on, we should go. I don't like being down here with all the Sleepers. We need to get to the Control Room.'

'She can't feel it, she's frozen. And she deserves it.' Alice felt another sharp pinch to her shoulder and she gritted her teeth hard.

'Did she move then?'

She heard Ariel's voice come closer.

'I saw her move. Her face moved.'

Alice felt her heart stop for the briefest of moments. She held herself completely still, cursing herself for the reaction. She wondered whether Carter and Angel were still above her in the ventilation shaft watching – whether they would come to her aid if the Controller Generals realised she was no longer frozen. There was another sharp jolt, this time a shove to her legs.

'Probably just a muscle shift,' she heard Elizabet say. 'They do sometimes react or twitch.' This was followed by a slight clip to her head. 'We'll deal with her later.'

There was a shuffling sound and then the door closed. Alice exhaled deeply and opened her eyes, fury, relief and terror all spliced into one emotion. She looked up at the vent – there was no sign of the others. She lifted her head from the bed.

'Wait, Ariel, I've got one more thing to do.'

Alice lay still, her head back on the hard mattress and she froze, motionless as the door opened.

'Don't think for one minute you're going to come out of this alive,' she heard Elizabet say, close to her face. 'When I unfreeze you, everyone is going to know the truth about how you tried to destroy us and how I saved the Community by having you put down here. My only regret was not having you killed with Kelly at the time. If I'd been in charge then and not Kunstein with all her sentimentality, you'd be dead already.'

There was a pause and a dark laugh.

'But actually, it was a good thing you were kept down here. Because now I can use *you* to expose everything that is wrong about letting those creatures roam around alive outside our walls – outside our Community.' Her final words came out in a whisper, so terrifying they made Alice's blood run cold. 'I'll be back for you soon and I can use you to start to put my plans into place. They are good plans, Alice. You'd be impressed with what I intend to do with these people and how I'm going to use them. I've been a *good girl*, Alice, just like you always wanted.'

The door closed again and Alice heard footsteps move away from the door and along the tunnel in the distance, until they faded away into complete silence.

Chapter Three

The Return

In the dim light of her house, Frida handed Samuel a large cup of water and a bowl of lukewarm vegetables. He dug into them quickly, shovelling spoonfuls into his mouth, taking a second to gulp the water before returning to the meal. When he had finished eating, Frida took the bowl away and replaced it with another cup of water.

'Now tell me what happened today,' she said. 'And where is your brother?'

'Carter's still in the Community,' said Samuel, draining the glass. 'And so is Angel. I had to leave, to bring Elvira somewhere she could get medical attention. She'd have died otherwise. We made it down into the Catacombs before the accident happened.' His speech was fast even though he was exhausted and his eyes were heavy with sleep.

Frida looked thoughtful. 'This is not good,' she muttered when he finished speaking. 'They alone will not be successful. Although your brother is resourceful.' She paused for a moment. 'But your presence here last time caused us great trouble and there is discontent between myself and Eli about how the Township should be governed – and what to do about those people inside the Barricades.' She paused, looking

Samuel deep in the eyes. 'What you did – he was Eli's brother and he's not going to forget that.'

Samuel felt the cold dread of shame creep over him – tinged with fear. 'So, he wants to kill me in revenge?'

Frida shook her head. 'It might be worse than that,' she said softly. 'I will do what I can to protect you but, for now, just do as I tell you, okay?'

A sharp slam of the front door and a shout indicated Eli's arrival. Frida put her finger to her lips. 'Get some sleep,' she said, quietly, pushing him into a small room at the side of the house. 'You've had a long day and you're exhausted. Let's talk more tomorrow.'

Samuel tossed and turned on the hard bed. Although his body was wracked with exhaustion, he couldn't sleep. He could hear Eli pacing the floor of the room next to the one he was in. His voice came in sharp bolts of anger through the dirty stone wall.

'He is back in our custody. Now what are you proposing we do with him? Do you have an effective plan for his punishment for what he did? Or are you going to just let him walk out of here again?' The voices were raised. Irritated and taunting.

'Eli, his punishment is my business. I will not have you challenge every decision I make. You and I both know that what he did was wrong. I am not saying there's justification for it, but both Carter and Samuel have important work to do.' Frida's voice was calm by comparison but Samuel could clearly hear the annoyance in her tone.

'So you're going to let him go? Let him leave unpunished? It goes against who we are as a Township. Antagonising those animals behind the fence will make things even worse. We've stayed away – as our people agreed to do all those years ago. And they have left us in peace.'

'Like I said, Eli, I will handle it. Times are changing and perhaps they are right to challenge the Industry and the Community.'

Samuel could hear the exasperation in Frida's voice. 'The Villagers have already told us that the Industry kill the children they don't want. They poison the water at will. Maybe that brother of Samuel's is right to take his argument to them – whatever his personal reasons may be.'

'It's *not* our fight.' Eli's raised his voice almost to the level of shouting. 'We will deal with him based on what he has done to us. Our people will want to see justice done. Free him now and you will show how weak you really are.'

Frida exhaled deeply. '*You* do not speak on behalf of our people,' she said, finally. 'I will decide what's right. This is not your decision. You do not get to decide whether Samuel lives or dies.'

Samuel pushed himself out of bed, his limbs still aching and raw. A cool air drifted in from under the closed door, where a small shaft of yellow light cast shadows into the room. He moved his ear closer to the wall as the conversation continued.

'Maybe it should be my decision,' spat Eli. 'Unless you've forgotten about my brother already? Don't you want justice?' His voice quietened again. 'I should go in there and kill him now. Should I just do that?'

Samuel, scared, backed away from the wall and looked around the dim light of the room. The window was high and too small to get through. Remembering what Frida had said, he tried to remain calm and moved towards the bed slowly but his heavy gait banged loudly on the uneven wooden floor. Within moments the door opened and Eli was in the room.

'Where do you think you're going?' he said, pushing Samuel back onto the bed. 'Trying to escape? You're lucky I didn't kill you and the woman on sight.'

'I wasn't. And we don't want any trouble,' protested Samuel. 'I needed help for Elvira – when she is well, we will leave. If you can't help her then we will leave as soon as the morning comes.' He held his hands up in defence. His guilt about what he'd done stopped any thoughts of anger or retaliation. The memories of that morning in the Deadlands haunted him – and as much as he wished he could make amends for what he had done, he could not take back those terrible actions.

Eli stood for a moment before pulling back his arm and punching Samuel clean in the face with his hard, knuckled fist. It took everything within Samuel not to launch himself off the bed and attack the man; instead he breathed deeply and raised his hand to stem the blood that flowed from his nose.

'Eli, what do you think you're doing?' yelled Frida, pushing him to the corner of the room. 'Get out and let me handle this!'

The man stamped from the room, slamming the front door behind him, shaking a vibration through the walls of the house. Frida left the room quickly and returned with a cloth, tossing it to Samuel.

'You need to do exactly as I say,' she scowled. 'And that does not include listening to my private conversations or trying to escape. I thought we had a deal?'

'I wasn't…' began Samuel before Frida silenced him.

'You don't appear to realise that we have real problems here.' She shook her head. 'You have done the right thing, bringing the woman here but you must have realised that your actions would not come without complications? Things here in the Township are not as simple as you may think.'

'I'm sorry,' said Samuel with a sigh, nursing his nose. 'But Eli wants to see me dead. I can't just stand by and…'

Frida bit her lip. 'It's the middle of the night, Samuel,' she said. 'Eli is still angry and you have travelled a long, difficult journey. We all need to rest.' She closed the bedroom door tightly as she left the room and Samuel heard a clicking sound as the mechanism locked.

A pale stream of yellow sun filtered through the thin covering on the window when Samuel opened his eyes the next morning. While his muscles still ached, it was the pain in his face that first caught his attention. Blood had caked around his nose and mouth, but at least the bleeding had stopped. A full cup of water and a chipped bowl of what looked like some sort of paddled grain stood on the table next to him. He spat on the dirty cloth and cleaned away the excess blood then poured the grain into his mouth and washed it down with the water in one gulp.

He got out of bed and tried the door but it was still locked. Pushing his full weight against it, he knew that even if he'd kicked it with the strongest force he had, it would never open. The window was barred but outside he could hear children playing. The melodic, carefree sound reminded him of his own home in the Village.

'Open the door!' he yelled. 'Where's Frida?'

Over the next few minutes he continued to call for Frida, determined to get her attention – until the lock clicked and she appeared in the doorway. 'Samuel,' she said, sternly. 'You're frightening the children. There's no reason for you to shout.'

'Why have you got me locked in here?' said Samuel, irritated. 'I told you I wouldn't cause any trouble.'

'It's for your own safety,' said Frida, pushing the soft curls of her hair behind her ears. 'I've told you I'll do what I can to protect you.

You have to believe I am doing what I can with Eli but you mustn't antagonise the situation.'

Samuel looked into the depth of her eyes. There was warmth and genuine care there.

'Let me manage Eli,' she said. 'And I'll do what I can to resolve this situation peacefully for you.' She patted Samuel awkwardly on the shoulder. 'For your brother's sake and for the safety of us all, I want him to succeed in his fight against the Industry. But Eli has other ideas about how this place should be governed. I know he wants to lead our people instead of me. But I can't let him.' Her eyes looked tired and her face worn, the spiralled lines hiding dark, wrinkled skin clouded with worry.

Samuel nodded, feeling helpless. There was little he could do with his friend in the Infirmary and having at least one person on his side was better than none. 'I want to see Elvira,' he said, finally. 'I want to know how she is.'

'She's not in a good way,' said Frida, rubbing her eyes before picking up the dirty bowl and glass, 'but I can take you to her now.'

Elvira opened her eyes when they entered the room and smiled when she saw Samuel. Her legs were bound tightly to long splints of oak and one of her arms still looked painfully twisted. The gash on her head had been cleaned but was dark with bruises and one eye was thick and bloodshot.

Samuel knelt down by the edge of the bed and touched her forehead gently.

'How are you?' he said, quietly.

Her voice came back gruff and tired. 'I'm alive,' she said with a weak smile. 'I suppose that's a start.' She groaned and motioned towards the jug of water that sat beside her bed. Samuel filled a glass and placed it close to her lips.

'She's taken a terrible battering.' Leanor, who stood with an armful of bloody bandages in one hand and a bottle of pills in the other, motioned to Frida and all three of them walked towards the other side of the room.

'Thank you,' said Samuel. 'It looks like you've done a great job.'

'It's going to take a long time for her to recover from this,' said Leanor, dropping the bandages into a waste bin. 'And she may never be able to fully walk again. Her legs have been badly broken. I've done what I can to reset them into the proper alignment but—' her voice quietened '—I've not worked on anyone this injured before. We knocked her out so that we could reset and stitch the wounds but, given the scale of them, I'm worried about infection.'

'I want to take her back to the Village soon,' said Samuel in a low voice. 'We have a medic there who may be able to help her. And more advanced medication than you have here.'

Frida shot him a look and he backtracked a little.

'I mean, you've done the best you can do but we need to get back to the Village. I need to get people to come with me to help my brother. He and Angel are down there in the Catacombs alone.'

'Absolutely out of the question,' said Leanor. 'Firstly, you can't move her. If you want her to live, she stays with us.'

'And secondly,' said Frida, 'given the circumstances, as I've already explained, you need to stay here. There may be consequences for all of us if I allow you to leave right now.'

Samuel bit his lip. 'I know,' he said quietly, 'but look at her.'

Leanor shook her head and went back to Elvira's bedside. She whispered something to her and the woman nodded sadly, taking the glass of water she was being offered in her good hand. She drank slowly and then rested her head back on the pillow.

'I think your friend wishes to speak to you,' called Leanor from across the ward. Samuel raised his eyes at Frida.

She took his arm and guided him over to her bed. 'We'll give you two a moment,' she said, glancing at Elvira. 'And then I will take you back to your accommodation for the duration of your stay – which will be as long as we decide.'

Samuel bit his lip. He knew his choices were extremely limited.

'Leanor will ensure that your friend is well taken care of.' Leanor nodded and headed towards the end of the room where she stood folding some bedding, moving it from one storage cupboard to another.

Frida headed out the door as Eli appeared in the doorway. He smiled falsely, first at Elvira and then at Samuel. 'You have five minutes,' he said as Frida stepped outside and he pulled the door closed.

Elvira breathed in heavily and then exhaled loudly, struggling to speak and breathe.

'What is it?' said Samuel. 'What do you want to tell me?'

'You need to leave here,' she said eventually, in a stuttering whisper. 'The man, Eli, was in here last night. He told me to tell you that I want you to stay with me while I recover and that we shouldn't go back to the Village.' She paused for a second regaining her breath. 'I don't know what they are planning but you *must* leave here. Don't argue with them or beg them as they won't let you go. You have to pretend to stay and then you must find a way to escape.'

Samuel leant closer towards her. 'I won't leave without you,' he hissed frantically. 'I will take you with me. And besides, Frida is going to help us.'

'No,' said Elvira in a firm whisper. 'There is a reason that they are keeping you here – their own politics are creating tension between Eli and Frida. He wants you dead.' Her chest heaved and her eyes rolled towards the back of her head.

'Elvira, I—' began Samuel but she grabbed his hand firmly.

'Get out of here. As soon as you get the chance. And whatever you do, don't come back. You and Carter are both in serious danger.'

The door opened and Eli came back into the room. 'Time to go,' he said gruffly and led Samuel out into the bright sunshine of the morning.

He breathed in the fresh air deeply, trying to hide his confusion and fear from Eli but determined that, whatever it took, he would get himself out of the Township alive and on to the Village to warn his mother.

Chapter Four

The Lab

Finally, when she was sure they were gone, Alice opened her eyes and sat up, pulling the sleep suit open. Looking up at the grate, she could see Carter pushing the grid away from the wall and pulling his body out and through into the room.

'Did you hear that?' Alice asked furiously. 'It sounded like she was threatening the people outside the Community – the Township and the Villagers. All those people…'

Carter nodded. 'And she plans to involve you, somehow. We need to get out of here,' he said. 'The next time they come back I don't think it's going to end well for you.'

Alice shook her head and pulled off the sleep suit, dragging the trousers from underneath her and putting them on. 'I told you that *thing* was evil,' she said, still shaking. 'Does your son know what he's dealing with?'

Angel dropped through the grate and landed next to Alice. 'From what I heard, I don't think he does,' she said. 'But he's not an extremist like her, that's clear.'

The cold grey walls felt to Alice like they were sloping inwards and a tightness in her chest forced her to breathe deeply. Her mouth formed a tight, defiant line. 'Either way, we need to find out exactly what she's intending to do and stop her,' she said. 'That girl has a vendetta against anyone and everything. Especially me.' She pulled the T-shirt over her head. 'We need to get to the Control Room or to the Labs – somewhere we can access a computer.'

'I vote the Control Room,' said Angel. 'That's where all the information is supposed to be.'

'The Labs would be less risky,' said Alice, watching Carter peer through the slot in the door. 'We already know that Ariel and Elizabet are on their way to the Control Room so we need to see what information we can find in the place where Izzy always felt most comfortable. She spent so much time down there with Barnes it makes sense that whatever else she's been planning, she'd be doing it from there. We might even be able to get hold of some sort of broadcast equipment.'

'You're right,' said Carter. 'If we can get there safely, we can decide what to do next.'

'Hang on,' said Alice, moving next to him and peering into the corridor. 'Don't you already have a plan? You've come down here, to unfreeze me and take down the Industry but you haven't told me anything about how you intend to do it.' She turned around to face him. 'How did you even get here?'

Carter thought back over his own journey – how he'd spent most of his life away from his own parents when they'd escaped from the Community when he was just a child and, following his own escape, how he'd found his mother again as the leader of the Village in the Deadlands. There was so much he had to tell her, and so little time.

'Let's get to the Lab,' said Carter, 'and then I'll explain everything.'

The door clicked quietly behind them as they crept along the corridor. Every cell they passed looked identical, row upon row of equally proportioned, grey-walled sleeping compartments each housing a silent, unmoving occupant. Most of them, Alice noticed, contained bunks from floor to ceiling on both sides. She cupped her hands over her eyes at each door opening they passed, stopping for only a second to scan the faces of the Sleepers.

She ran a rough calculation in her mind. There were six corridors that ran the length of the Catacombs under the Ship. They were at the far end, and they had passed twenty rooms, or so, on each side – less than half way to the central point of the structure. So that would make around one hundred and sixty rooms in each tunnel – and at six people per room, more than five and a half thousand on this level alone. Alice shivered deep in her bones. There had been at least eighteen floors in the lower part of the Ship just like this one – maybe more. That would mean possibly a hundred thousand people could be frozen down here.

She stopped at the next doorway and peered inside. Only those on the bottom bunk were really visible from where she was standing but she could just make out a small shape – probably a girl from the long, auburn hair. She looked young, about six or seven years old. Alice wondered how long the girl had been down there – and whether, like Alice herself, she was living in a body that had long outlived the era in which she'd been born. In the next room, there was a man – probably in his late thirties – with short cropped hair and a slightly crooked nose, his chest gently rising and falling silently.

'I think I know this woman,' whispered Carter, who was two or three doors ahead. Alice quickened her pace, glancing briefly at the Sleepers on either side. Carter was stood, open-mouthed at the doorway, his body rigid and stiff. His eyes were unblinking,

'Who is she?' mouthed Alice. 'How do you know her?'

'She was my teacher,' said Carter, his lip trembling. 'It's Professor Mendoza.'

He looked closely at the outline of her face and the thick, curly hair strewn across the pillow within her sleep suit. He remembered how much she'd taught him in the Academy. How she had saved him from the Industry's suspicions by encouraging him to have children with the strange girl with the red hair.

'We need to keep going,' said Alice. 'We need to get into the vents on this side of the building so we can move around without being seen.'

'Wait,' said Angel. 'Maybe this teacher can help us. Carter, you told me that she tried to support you, and your mother always said that if she had been Controller General, she would have led the rebellion.' She turned to Alice. 'Carter's mother is the leader of our Village. She knew this woman when she lived here in the Community. We need to unfreeze her, just like we did with Alice, and she can help us.'

'No,' said Alice, 'No more people yet.'

'But what about…?' started Angel.

Alice shook her head.

'She's right,' said Carter, thoughtfully, his words slow and deliberate. 'If we start building an army down here, it would take too much time to explain everything to everyone. We need to find a way to get ourselves more information about what's happening and work out what the weakest points of the Industry are before we amass a group. Then we tell the people the truth about what's happening.'

'But we can't do this alone,' said Angel, shaking her head. 'We need help from the inside, someone who knows the inner workings of this place.' She pulled Carter away from the door. 'If Mendoza can't help us, then there's only one other person who I think can.'

Carter thought for a moment, biting lip hard. 'I know who you mean and I don't know if we can trust her. The last time I saw her she stabbed me in the shoulder and told me she'd killed my daughter – but I've since been told that it was all an act, and that she's on our side.'

'Who?' said Alice, turning to Angel. 'Who do you think might be able to help us?'

Carter turned around to face Alice. 'Her name is Lily,' he said slowly. 'And she works for the Industry.'

When they reached the central atrium, Carter ran his hands across the panels of the corridor wall and pushed the third one aside. It came away easily, revealing a small, dark alcove. In the distance came the sound of footsteps.

'Inside,' he said. 'There are some things I need to tell you.'

Even after all these years, the inside of the panelled walls smelled the same to Alice: a dark, woody fragrance, spiced with the scent of artificial foods and a slight damp, earthy aroma. It transported her back to her childhood within the Ship immediately – of the nights where she and her friend Jonah would hide in the darkness and listen to Kunstein and the others talking about their plans for when the waters subsided and they could be above the ground again. The memories felt bittersweet; her life below ground had given her so much purpose and so much more to believe in, yet when the opportunities had come and the rains had stopped, her life had been pretty much the same as it had before the Storms – disappointment, sadness and betrayal by the people she cared about the most.

She listened intently as Carter explained briefly how he'd been unfrozen in order to become a contender for the position of Controller General and how he'd found the Community a different place from when he'd left it. She barely recognised what he described – the Descendants and First Gens who ruled, Second Gens who obeyed and the Lab Mades who served the Community.

'It's what we were born to believe,' he said, his voice full of regret. 'But then I met Isabella.'

*

As the last of the students drifted out of the Academy, Carter headed west, out towards the shallow, rocky caves hidden deep in a clump of trees at the top of the highest hillock in the Community. It wasn't high enough to see very far across the Barricades but there was enough tree cover at the summit that made it the best hiding place in their world. He didn't look back until he made it to the top – and then he watched as Isabella flitted from tree to tree, carefully checking that no one was following her.

'You made it.' Carter smiled as she pulled herself up onto a rock next to him. 'Where do they think you are?'

Isabella smiled. 'I hid my card near the Academy,' she said, her green-blue eyes sparkling bright. 'I have a little time.'

They'd sat there in the cool, late evening, watching night birds circling over the Black River and the sounds of the Community quietening into darkness. Carter had pushed his hand into his pocket and pulled out the hard, sparkling ring of trophene and held it to the moon. As it had caught the light, it had glittered a hundred shades of blue, green and yellow, swirling inside the hardened material like the surface of a FreeScreen. He'd held it out to Isabella.

'Trophene,' he'd said finally. 'It's indestructible. And multi-dimensional. And forever.'

Isabella had taken the ring from him and slipped it onto her finger. 'It's beautiful,' she'd said, a tight knot forming in her throat. 'Thank you.'

They'd sat in silence for a while, Carter inhaling the scent of Isabella's hair.

'When you come back, things will be different, won't they?'

'Yes,' he'd said. 'In a good way. And when they are different for everyone, they will be different for us.'

'Will you kiss me? Just once?'

Carter had looked deep into Isabella's eyes. 'You know I can't, it's against the rules. They'll freeze both of us forever if...'

Before he'd finished his sentence, her lips were on his, soft, delicate and warm. For the briefest of seconds, he'd felt her tongue touch his and the sky had exploded into a thousand fragments of light.

'Come back for me, Carter,' he'd heard her say as she got up to leave, heading down the slopes with a smile. 'In eight years' time, come and find me.'

'I promise,' he'd whispered, his eyes half-closed. 'I promise.'

*

Alice listened to Carter explain about how, when he'd returned many years later from being frozen in the Catacombs, Isabella had become an outcast from the Community. Although Carter had only been supposed to be frozen for eight years as part of the Industry's standard population cryonics programme, over fifteen years had passed, and Isabella had been in her late twenties when he'd woken up, still aged fifteen. Carter had promised Isabella that he would change the Community so they could finally be together – him, a Descendant and her, a Lab Made – but it had been too late.

While the information he gave her about Isabella was brief, he knew the tone of his voice told Alice all she needed to know about his feelings for her. He talked about how he'd gone to find out about the world outside and how Lily, his Industry mentor, had thrown the scissors into his arm.

'She stabbed you?' said Alice, a black frown covering her face.

'It was to break the tracking device,' interjected Angel. 'She wanted to make sure he couldn't be hunted down by the Industry.'

Alice felt sick. She remembered talking with Filip, not long after her best, childhood friend Jonah had disappeared across the Black River about how an identity chip or card would help them to find and save people who went missing – children or the elderly – but she had dismissed it.

'These people are not animals,' she'd said to Filip when they'd returned to the safety of the Ship. 'We may decide to build protection around us but we are not going to chip them.' She remembered how Filip had shrugged. 'It would be for their own safety,' he'd said – and they'd never discussed it again.

'What about Isabella?' she said. 'What happened to her after you left?' She watched as a veil of sadness clouded Carter's eyes.

'I don't know,' he replied, his voice breaking a little. 'The FreeScreens said she had been killed – but they said the same thing about me, so...' He scratched the back of his head. 'I can only assume she is dead – or has been frozen – so she could be anywhere. Or nowhere. But I need to know what happened to her.'

Alice nodded in the near darkness. 'I've not been above ground for eighty years or so, you've not really been part of the Community for the last fifteen years and you—' she looked at Angel '—you've never really been there, or in the Catacombs before?'

Both Carter and Angel nodded.

'Then we need to find this Lily,' said Alice decisively. 'She's our only hope of getting out of here alive and exposing the Industry for what it is.'

'She's quite a good liar,' said Carter. 'I'm not sure we can trust her.'

'If she's that good a liar and she's been deceiving the Industry for years then she's someone I'd like to meet,' said Alice, sliding across the panelling and peering out into the main atrium.

The room was silent; the great empty pod-shell with its six long tunnels, each branching off leg-like reminded her of a giant insect. A faint orange light glimmered at the end of each of the corridors. She pulled the panel back across and turned to Carter.

'If everyone in this facility has a tracker, then I assume Lily has one too?' she said. 'If we can get to a connected terminal, we can work out where exactly in this facility she is and how we can get to her.' She turned to Carter. 'I'm guessing there are still computers in this place?'

'There are,' he said slowly. 'But you need an access card to get into them.' He paused. 'My mother placed great faith in Lily,' he said. 'But I'm still not completely convinced.'

'We can't do this alone,' said Alice, stretching out her arms and legs and feeling the muscles tighten. 'And I don't fully trust anyone. Not even you, yet. But we need to find her.' She pulled aside the panelling again and listened intently. 'You said that you passed some labs – I know there used to be some on the higher levels so we go there, get into the systems and find this Lily character. And we do it quickly.'

'You don't trust us?' said Angel, disappointed. 'What would we be doing down here if we weren't attempting to do something about what the Industry have done to our people – and yours!'

'I don't trust anyone,' Alice said, a little roughly. 'Everyone I have ever cared about has either betrayed me, abandoned me or died. The only person left in my life is my daughter and I haven't even met her. The world I helped create has been built on a foundation of lies and deceit, and I've only known you for a few hours.' Her voice broke a little as she finished. 'So, no, I don't trust you.' She gestured towards Carter. 'The fact that we share a common enemy is the one thing that's giving me any hope that we can work together on this.' She paused for a moment and turned to Carter. 'Look, I don't mean to seem ungrateful but I don't know who you are – even if you think you know me. And you don't – whatever you learned about me at school is wrong. I'm not that person.' She felt a lump harden in her throat. 'I don't even know who I am any more.'

Carter shrugged and put his hand on Alice's shoulder. 'None of this can be easy for you,' he said, sympathetically. 'I feel like I've known you all my life and even that must be strange to you. But we need you and you need us if we're going to get out of here and put an end to what the Industry have been doing.'

Alice nodded, her face flushed red. 'Let's get moving,' she said, composing herself. 'This place doesn't seem to have changed much since I was here last and I think I can get us to the Lab.'

She beckoned Carter to the entrance and pointed to the tunnel on the far left-hand side. 'The back stairs at the end of that passageway lead upwards to the maintenance shafts that run along past the old labs. Most specifically, the private lab that used to belong to Barnes.'

Alice shivered as she thought about the mysterious experiments that the doctor used to conduct in the labs and the overbearing, insidious way she became involved in Alice's own pregnancy. She hesitated, then said, 'It's where they kept your great-grandfather, Richard Warren, when we brought him in from the Deadlands,' she said finally, 'after the waters subsided.' She paused again, not wanting to think about what might have happened to him.

'Then let's start there,' said Carter, helping Angel through the small gap in the panelling, then closing it quietly behind her. He watched as Alice bit her lip hard and wondered what confusion and chaos could be going on inside her mind. Whatever it was, she kept moving forwards, and he admired the strength and tenacity of someone who had woken into a world they no longer knew.

They crept along the side of the tunnel slowly, passing row upon row of small cells, stacked high with sleeping bodies, frozen in time. Just like the first set of rooms they had encountered, each individual was naked and nameless, wrapped in a plastic sleep suit laying still, except for the shallow rise and fall of their breathing. There were hundreds of them, and as much as she wanted to move quickly, Alice couldn't help but glance through at each room, her heart aching for every life that had, just like her own, been paused indiscriminately with no guarantee of when they would be restarted,

'What did we do, Filip?' she whispered to herself, her heart feeling like it would break. 'What did we do?'

The stairwell, hidden in the depths of the darkened passage of the rear of the Ship, smelled damp and musty. The stench of fermented chicker and whiteloaf breezed through from the ventilation shafts. Alice bent down, running her hands through the dust.

'This is where I would come to be alone when I wanted to get away from everyone in the Ship,' she said. 'Even though I was only eleven when I came to live down here, I knew things had changed forever.

That *we* had changed things forever. I never expected that those terrible promises we made to each other would shape the course of what Filip would do when I was gone. We didn't understand – well, at least some of us didn't.'

Her mind went to Kelly – the sweet, gentle girl who had become pregnant at the same time as her. At fourteen, Kelly had seemed so much younger than the others but they had all felt so grown up, so adult.

Angel touched her arm gently. 'You were a child,' she said. 'None of this was your fault.'

Alice shifted away from her, instinctively. 'Yes, I was a child,' she said, firmly. 'But much of this was my fault. I could have stopped Barnes and Filip but I didn't.' She pushed her fingernails into the grooves of the panels that lined the inside of the stairwell. 'I am partly responsible for what's happened here, and I need to make it right.' She set her mouth in the same determined line that used to stop her from crying.

They inched up the next couple of flights carefully, and when they reached the fourth or fifth set of stairs, Alice ran her hands up and down the wall again.

'It's here somewhere,' she said. 'Look closely.'

'But what are we looking for?' Angel asked, confused.

'A switch. You'll know when we find it.'

Carter looked up and down flexing his fingers into the grooves, copying Alice. He followed each line in the panelling methodically, feeling for anything inconsistent, anything different. He moved quickly, scanning by touch, his hands moving over the grainy wood carefully.

'Is this it?' He flicked a small lever, hidden in a crevice in the wall. He waited for a moment but nothing happened.

Alice checked the switch and nodded, looking relieved.

'That'll stop any alarms,' she said. 'While no one in the Control Centre will know we're here, it would be better if we could draw as little attention to ourselves as possible.' She pulled open a side panel in the wall, facing away from the main stairwell and reached her arm inside. A cool breeze blew past the three of them and Alice nodded. 'It's this way,' she said, opening the panel fully and stepping into the maintenance shaft.

'How did you know these air ducts would still be here?' said Angel. 'What if they'd modernised them?'

'This structure is what holds the whole thing together,' replied Alice. 'Most people don't know they even exist. This part of the facility is underground – if they took these out, the whole ventilation system would collapse.'

The shaft wound around itself and backwards along the very outside of the main body of the Catacombs. Alice still couldn't think of it as anything other than a Ship – in the early days it had been the sanctuary that had kept them safe as the Storms raged around them. But now it was a more like a ghost vessel, full of transient souls with no time or place that belonged to them. She shivered as the tunnel narrowed and they crawled on hands and knees past the first set of rooms that were all crammed full of Sleepers. As they travelled along in the inside wall at height, Alice could see the faces of those on the top bunks – nameless, empty faces that seemed almost featureless and devoid of character as they slept. Their stillness haunted her, the closed, unseeing eyes boring deep inside her conscience.

'We should be almost at the Lab,' she whispered back to Carter, behind her. 'If it still exists then we should be able to find a terminal here and access the basic elements of the Model.'

'What makes you think that the Lab will still be here?' said Angel, from the back. 'Surely they would have moved everything above ground or to another location?'

'Barnes and Elizabet built that Lab from scratch,' said Alice quietly. 'It's the place Izzy feels most comfortable – whatever she's planning, the Lab will be the place that she executes it – and where any information will be.'

'Isn't she more likely to do everything from the Control Centre?' continued Angel. 'She'll have access to more information, more people...'

'That's not how she works,' said Alice. 'Whatever she's doing, it will be done in secret, without people knowing. And whatever it is she's telling people – I would imagine it's ten times worse.'

The Lab was smaller and less intimidating than Alice remembered, but the chemical aroma and thick double bench that ran the length of the room, strewn with instruments of all kinds, still remained. They took it in turns to peer through the large ventilation grate and into the room. A layer of silky dust covered most of the higher surfaces but the bench had been cleaned down recently. Alice scanned the room.

'There's a tablet built into the wood on the far side of the bench,' said Carter, registering the disappointment in Alice's face. 'It's a newer version that projects onto the wall – we should be able to use that.'

They climbed down into the Lab, Angel moving quickly towards the door. She examined it closely – a whole range of locking mechanisms running the length of the door end to end: thick metal bolts on the inside, unlocked; an electronic locking pad at the top and bottom; and no viewing slot in the door.

'Someone wants to keep what they're doing in this room a secret,' she said, pulling across the heavy bolts so that the heavy lines of metal locked the door tight. 'Especially when they're inside.' She pushed her body against the door and felt the soft humming of the electric lock vibrating through the solid metal.

'I can't hear anything outside,' she whispered. 'No voices, no footsteps, nothing.'

'You'll hear her if she comes down here,' called Alice. 'Izzy can't do anything quietly.'

'Will you stay there and listen while we look around?' asked Carter, glancing over at Alice. 'If you hear anyone or anything, we should get the chance to jump back up into the vent, okay?'

Angel nodded and placed her ear to the door, listening intently.

Carter made his way straight to the back corner of the room, where he fired a small tablet into life. Immediately, it started to project an image on the plain end wall – first a lightning bolt logo, which quickly disintegrated, and then a series of twenty or thirty charts that took up the whole wall and moved a fraction of a millimetre upwards and outwards, backwards and forwards.

Angel stood, mesmerised, first watching Carter as he deftly moved elements of the screen into unintelligible shapes and then at the wall where those shapes were projected on screen; numbers and colours and shapes that were bewildering and confusing to Angel. She moved away from the door and focused directly on the wall.

'This is incredible,' she said, stunned.

'This tablet is configured for design mode,' Carter called softly to Alice. 'I will be able to get through to the personnel locator if I can just…' The image on the walls dissolved and when Alice glanced back, there was a map of the Community with thousands of tiny pinprick dots scattered across the wall. Like a sky full of stars, some were clustered in constellations across the screen. Carter flashed an indicator over a central area. 'This is Unity Square,' he said. 'You see how many people are there – it's some sort of gathering.'

'Can you see where Izzy… Elizabet is?' said Alice, nervously. 'And Ariel. And Lily.'

The boy moved back to the tablet and started tapping on the screen. 'This is all outside the Catacombs, not down here. There must be separate screens that I can log into to show who's in the Catacombs for work, those who are frozen, those who are on the various levels…' He scratched his head and breathed deeply.

'Find Elizabet and Ariel first,' said Alice, watching him closely. 'I know you want to look for Isabella but we need to work out where the danger is. Then find Lily.' She opened each of the drawers in a tall metal cabinet and looked through their contents. The bottom drawer seemed stuck and however hard she pulled, it wouldn't open. She slipped her skinny fingers under the catch underneath and removed a small bolt that had been keeping the drawer in place.

'Have you always been this good at breaking into things?' said Angel, watching her.

Alice grinned a little. 'I always was before,' she said. 'It's how I survived before the Storms.'

She pulled open the drawer and lifted up a large folder of papers onto the bench, flicking through them quickly. 'It doesn't look like this is a place that's open to the general Industry population – so unless they are making their way back down here immediately then I think we have a little while to look around.'

Carter continued to tap at the screen. 'I think I've almost got it,' he said, fervently. 'They've changed some of the codes here, but there's a pattern… and…' The map on the wall changed to a search screen and he typed in the names they were looking for.

'Look, there,' he said as the screen zoomed in on a flat, square building. 'That's the main entrance to the Industry, the part that sits above ground.' They watched as two of the small dots moved slowly away from them and towards the roads leading to the Community.

'They're heading west,' said Carter, tracing his finger across the screen. 'They're going towards the main centre – and they're on foot, you can tell by the speed.'

'How else would they be travelling?' said Alice, pushing the binder of papers back onto the bench. 'Car? Train?'

'We have Transporters now,' said Carter, back at the search screen, moving his fingers deftly across a number of alpha-numeric rows, flicking between different displays until a blueprint of the Industry building appeared on the wall. 'Lily's not outside which means she must be in here somewhere. I'll keep looking.'

Alice walked across the room towards the side door that led into the annexe that had once housed Richard Warren. The door, bolted on the outside, had no window and was much different to the one Alice remembered. She pulled back the bolts and took a sharp intake of breath.

The room had been expanded and was much, much larger than when she'd last been here. A section had been carved back to form a long, tunnel-like room. The walls still held the same pictures of Alice and Filip exploring the Deadlands for the first time, but the paint was dirty and faded, and traced with messy stains and other pieces of paper. Alice closed her eyes tightly and opened them again. There was no longer a single bed but a row of three on each side of the wall. And in each of the beds was a Sleeper.

Alice stepped closer. The first thing that struck her was the noise. There was a very low-pitched humming noise, followed by a series of regular high beeps that came from a boxed machine at the side of each bed. They looked different to those they had seen earlier – somehow more alive. Thin plastic tubes ran into and out of the bodies that twitched in unusual and irregular motions in their sleep. She moved to the side of the bed that was closest to her. The figure was a man, covered by a sheet and not inside a sleep suit. A light fuzz of hair covered his face. Above his bed there was a chart, etched with clear writing, observations, medications. He moved an arm, making her jump.

She walked along the length of the room, her footsteps echoing against the machine beeps ringing in her ears. The occupants of each bed were all the same, bodies covered by a single sheet and attached to a machine. She read the notes alongside each one carefully. When she reached the last bed, she stopped. Even through her sleep, the girl in the bed looked tired and world-worn; thin lines of sadness etched into her face.

'You should come here,' said Alice loudly, her words stilted and feeling heavy as they left her mouth. 'You need to see this.'

Carter and Angel stopped in the doorway, their faces confused.

'What is it?' said Angel. 'I thought it was important. It's just another room with more Sleepers?'

Alice pulled the papers from the wall above the girl and marched towards them, her throat dry and parched.

'Look closer, they're not just Sleepers,' she said, angrily. 'Well, not cryonically frozen Sleepers. They're sedated.' She thrust the paper chart into Carter's hands. 'Read this,' she said, her voice shaking. 'They're Elizabet's patients – she's experimenting on them.'

Carter turned the paper over, his face pale grey as he read the name scrawled in ink at the top of the page.

Isabella Delaney.

Chapter Five

The Message

Samuel paced the length of the room, his heart pounding hard in his chest like a drum. His head buzzed with confusion. Hadn't Frida assured him that she would manage the situation?

Since they had left the hospital that morning, neither Eli nor Frida had been in to see him. What Elvira had said had unnerved him. No arguing or begging to leave. He cursed himself. The deal he had made with Saul to capture Carter when they had first left the Community had seriously backfired.

*

He had left early and, even with all the shortcuts through the bushy forest that he knew, it had still taken him almost all day to find the tunnel, hidden near to the old, withered city. He had found Saul there, as he said he would be, at the entrance to the tunnel. Over the years he and Saul had traded the occasional piece of information but, in the main, had kept a respectful distance between their people.

'Do you have the drugs?' Saul sat on a crate, blocking the entrance to the low archway.

Samuel fished into his pocket and held the tablets out in front of him. 'You'll get them when the job's done. You're clear of the plan?' he said. 'Take him to your Township and hold him there – just for a couple of weeks until I have been into the Community.'

Saul shrugged. 'So, this guy is your brother? And you want me to kidnap him?' He rummaged around in a bag near his feet and pulled out a knife. 'With this?'

I want to be the one to take them on,' Samuel had said. 'He's too soft – not reliable and he won't be good in a conflict. We'll fail if he's there.'

'Do you want me to kill him?' Saul held his knife out in front of him. 'Or maybe I should use a gun?'

'No!' said Samuel, irritated. 'I don't want you to kill him. Like I told you, you just need to keep him out of my way so I can get on with it.'

'Will you be alone?'

Samuel shook his head. 'No. There will be two women with us but if you come at night, they will be asleep. Create a disturbance and my brother will come. Tell him you need him to go back to the Community because his son is in trouble or something.'

Saul nodded. 'Right. Take him at gunpoint back to the Township and hold him until you come to get him? Questions will be asked.'

'Not the Township. Take him somewhere else. Feed him but keep him locked up. Give him some time to think. He's had it too easy since he's been out here.' Samuel felt a sliver of guilt streak through him but pushed it away. 'It won't be for long,' he added.

When the thin cloud drifted across the crisp night moon, the sound of an owl alerted Samuel. He had been awake all night waiting for Saul to arrive so he could warn him that there were others. The crack of a twig in the darkness made him sure that Saul had arrived. He hauled himself off the balcony and onto the roof, peering out into the shadows. Now that *the brothers Aaron and Lisa had joined him them on their journey there was no way that Saul could overpower them all. He needed to tell Saul to leave – now. He couldn't afford for the brothers to capture him and start to question him.*

'Saul,' he whispered, but there was no response. 'Saul!'

He crept across the roof, his heart pounding with regret. As he reached the side of the house where he could climb down on the flat roof, he heard two gunshots and then the sound of Saul's voice shouting across the lawn.

'Carter Warren, if you are here you should identify yourself. We have a directive calling for your arrest.'

By the time Samuel had made his way to the back of the house, the brothers were already dead and Carter had Saul pinned to the floor. A sickening dread coursed through him as he watched them, frozen in his position behind a tree. Lisa and Aaron were gone and now Saul – who had deviated so far from the agreed plan – could tell Carter everything. Or worse, kill him. His gut hurt but he knew what he had to do. He reached in his pocket for his gun. Aimed. Fired.

*

Every time Samuel relived the moment he felt sick to his stomach. Guilt at his own stupidity and jealousy and each thought made him angrier with every snapshot memory of the event. He examined the windows of the room again and rattled the bars vigorously, but they were stuck hard. There was no way out.

He sat down with his back to the bed and picked at the dirt underneath his fingernails. He could rush at the door the next time they came in with food, but how far would he get? Probably not even as far as the edge of the Township. But what if Frida was telling the truth and she had everything under control? He thought again about

Elvira's words and her insistence that he should leave. And he thought about Frida – she had seemed so genuine. Was she just keeping him alive to trade with Eli? It couldn't be true. But while the people of the Township didn't trust him, there would be no opportunities afforded to him to escape. He looked around for anything that might help – anything he could use as a weapon, but there was nothing.

He sat and waited. More than anything, he wished Carter were there.

Late morning turned to afternoon, but it was early evening before Frida returned to see him –alone. She shut the door behind her and handed Samuel a cup of water.

'Where have you been?' he said. 'I've been here alone all day.'

Frida's face looked concerned; the spirals around her face tightened as she spoke.

'Elvira's doing a little better today,' she said, ignoring his question. 'We can't do much more than we're already doing but her leg does seem to be healing.' She shook her head. 'We can't guarantee she'll be able to walk any time soon – or ever.'

Samuel glanced at the door and then back at Frida who was watching him carefully.

'Eli is on his way here,' she said. 'So don't try to run. I know she warned you about this place.'

'I wasn't going to run,' said Samuel. 'I just wanted some air – I'm not used to being inside. I live in the trees, in the forest. Not in a brick building.' He shrugged. 'My people are different to yours.'

'Yes, you Villagers have your dwellings in the trees, swim in the rivers and risk your lives trying to save others.' She shook her head.

'While at the same time, you betray each other because of jealousy?' Her lips formed a tight line. 'Your brother is brave, but he is naïve if he thinks he can take on those people in the south single-handedly. They have more people and resources than you or I could ever imagine. He is one man.' Her words were short and pointed. 'A remarkable young man, but still just one man.' She smiled. 'There is something about his spirit and his honesty though that makes me think he can do this.' Her face clouded again. 'But they are a force to be reckoned with.'

'Then let me leave so I can try to help him.'

From outside the house came the sound of heavy boots on gravel, and the door opened wide. Eli lowered a plate of food onto the bed loaded with fruits and berries. Samuel assessed the distance between the bed and the door.

'Eat,' said Eli. 'It's the only meal you're going to get today.'

Samuel glanced at the plate and then at Frida. 'Thank you,' he said, watching Eli step away from the door. 'I want to help,' he added. 'If Elvira is going to be here for a few days recovering then I'd better get used to this place.' He ate some berries and gave a tentative smile.

Eli grunted back at him. 'Shut up and sit tight,' he said. 'Just consider yourself lucky that Frida is looking out for you.' He beckoned the woman from the room and shut the door tight. Samuel waited for the click of the lock but there was none. Outside he could hear the sound of children playing again and the stamp of boots against the shale around the edge of the brick building. He got up from the bed and put his ear to the door, listening intently for any sounds of Eli or Frida but apart from the occasional call or laugh from the younger members of the Township, there was nothing.

Samuel held his breath and put his palm onto the handle of the door.

Before he turned it, he stopped and stepped backwards quietly, and sat on the bed. After about fifteen minutes, there was the sound of Eli's boots again, this time moving away from the building, after he had turned the key in the lock.

The night was long and Samuel was awake for most of it. He lay on his back replaying everything he had seen since they had arrived at the Township – Frida's conflict with Eli and his aggressive determination that Samuel stay with them; Elvira's warning and the conversation he had overheard on his first night. While Frida was still the leader of the Township now, what if something happened to her? What if Eli's anger overtook him? Questions filled his mind and unease flooded through him.

Although he had only been there for two nights and one full day, it seemed like weeks, staring at the four walls of the room and waiting for the appearance of Frida. One door adjoined the rest of the house and another led to the outside – both were kept locked. He could try to break them but he feared that any action would precipitate Eli's anger and bring him bounding into the room, fists flying.

When he finally got to sleep, Samuel's dreams were ugly. He tossed and turned on the thin mattress, the sounds of early morning movement infiltrating his nightmares of deep, thick forests that swarmed with desperate men and women with guns instead of hands, shooting his mother over and over until the fabric of her face was obliterated. He woke up drenched in sweat and shivering, his mouth dry and parched.

When he opened his eyes the next morning, Frida was stood at the foot of his bed, a jug of water in her hand. 'You're finally awake,' she said, pouring some into a glass and handing it to Samuel. He sat up and took it.

'I need to see Elvira,' he said, pulling his legs over the side of the bed. Frida recoiled when she saw his filthy, six-toed feet, and attempted to hide her disgust. Samuel pulled on his trousers and boots and gulped down the remainder of his glass of water. 'Do you think I could do that this morning? We've been here for two nights now – when do you think you might be able to let me leave?'

'I'll check with Leanor if she's awake,' said Frida, taking the glass from him and glancing through the window. 'If she's not receiving treatment and it's a suitable time then I will come and collect you.'

'Any chance of some breakfast?' he called after her but she had already shut the door, locking it firmly behind her.

The hospital was clean and smelled strongly of disinfectant. Flanked by Eli on one side and Frida on the other, he walked through the main foyer into the ward. Leanor came towards them and greeted them coolly.

'She's in and out of sleep but you're welcome to come and sit with her for a while,' she said, briskly. 'It would be better if it wasn't a crowd.' She pointed at Samuel. 'Just him. And only for a few moments.'

Eli nodded in her direction and walked back towards the door. 'He gets five minutes,' he said as he walked away.

Frida put her hand on Leanor's shoulder. 'I'll stay with you,' she said. 'Just in case.' She tucked a dark curl of hair behind her ear and smiled at the girl.

'You said I could run this hospital,' said Leanor in a calm, quiet voice. 'Which means I manage my patients. If you're worried about this one leaving or bothering my patient, then you can wait in the foyer. Or at the bottom of the ward. But I don't want a crowd around her bedside. I can take care of myself.'

Frida glanced across at Samuel and smiled gracefully. 'The hospital is yours,' she said. 'Eli and I will be waiting by the door. No more than five minutes.' She touched Leanor gently on the cheek and followed Eli out into the foyer.

Samuel pulled up a chair next to Elvira's bed as Leanor glanced out towards the foyer.

'We're keeping her sedated for as much of the time as possible,' she said, 'her eyes shifting back and forth. 'But we're going to run out of painkillers soon.'

Samuel nodded. 'Thank you for getting rid of them.' He nodded towards the door.

Leanor smiled. 'I'm trying to help you,' she whispered. 'But this situation is more difficult than you know.'

'I need to find a way out of here,' said Samuel desperately. The words seemed to tumble out of him as he felt a warmth from Leanor. 'Frida seems trustworthy,' he added, 'but I know Eli wants trouble. What can I do?'

The girl shrugged and smoothed down the bed sheet evenly, raising a glass to Elvira's lips. She took a small gulp and groaned. From the foyer came the sound of raised voices.

Leanor tucked her hair back behind her ears nervously, her dark-brown eyes looked scared and uneasy. 'I already told Elvira to tell you to get out of here. You're in danger.'

'She said that – but I can't leave,' said Samuel, irritated. 'It's not like I can walk out of here; they keep me locked in a room.'

'You *have* to leave.' Leanor sounded desperate. 'You need to stay away from here. I want you to be safe.' She looked up as Eli's voice sounded through the Infirmary.

'Leanor,' he shouted. 'Almost time for Samuel to leave.'

Leanor pretended to attend to Elvira's dressings. 'Yes,' she said loudly, 'let me explain the bone fracture to you.' She held a small bottle of pills up high and ran her finger over the label, as she spoke again in a quickened whisper. 'In the early days, right at the beginning after the Storms, there was a group who lived out here – not in this location but further away, in a place called Woodford Hatch.'

'Yes,' said Samuel, hurrying her, 'the old Township. I know that.'

Leanor nodded. 'One of the residents, Joe, had a brother who was taken captive by those people within the Barricades and made to live there for months before he was able to escape.' She bit her lip nervously. 'They did very bad things to him. When he went back there, after his escape, he brought a girl with him, someone who was very important to the Industry.'

Samuel shrugged. 'Okay, go on,' he said. 'What has this got to do with me?'

'Listen,' said Leanor. 'Years ago, the girl, Alice, wanted to stay there at the Township but she decided to go back to the Community – she wanted to make things right there with them but something went wrong. Richard and Joe always thought she'd come back to us and bring her baby but our people never saw her again.' She rubbed her hand across her forehead. '*They* came instead.'

'The Industry?'

*

They came as night began to fall; the first stars had just begun to pin-prick their way through the dusky blackness when the low bass of a noise that sounded like distant thunder grew loud enough to become the march of hundreds of feet pounding their way across worn and tired tarmac.

But it wasn't the sound that alerted Richard to the arrival of the Industry guards. It was the smell of burning as they torched the first few houses on the outskirts of the Township. A dense, thick smoke floated in a dark veil across the landscape.

'They're here,' he called to his brother, panicked. 'They've come for Alice.'

'They'll leave when they don't find her,' Joe replied. 'We need to hide.'

As they ran out into the street, the first of them had arrived – guns held military-style out in front of them, all clad in black bio-suits, like assassins. Richard pulled Joe into one of the old houses and they climbed high into the attic, jamming the door closed tightly. They peered out of the skylight, watching, terrified as the Industry guards gathered in the streets, weapons aimed at the people of the Township who had been forced out into the square. As they were rounded into a group, the leader of the military raised a loudhailer and shouted through it.

'We're looking for Richard Warren,' said the voice. 'Richard, wherever you are, you need to make yourself known.'

Joe looked at his brother. 'Don't go,' he whispered, scared. 'Please don't leave me again.'

Through the window they watched as the guards lined up the people. 'I will kill them,' said the guard loudly, moving closer to the house. 'You know I will, Richard.'

'FILIP,' said Richard, angrily, his teeth gritted. 'It's Filip.'

'You know him? Is he the one that Alice talked about? The one she was afraid of?'

'Yes. He is the most dangerous man I have ever had the misfortune to meet.'

The clipped, angry voice came though the loudhailer again. 'I'll give you ten more seconds, Richard,' shouted Filip. 'And I will start to kill them.'

'What are we going to do?' wailed Joe. 'You can't go, they'll murder you.'

One woman, her hair in braids, ran out into the street to retrieve her dog who sat cowering behind a tree.

'It's Claudia,' whispered Joe, terrified. 'NO!'

They watched as Filip moved behind her and aimed his gun. The sound of children crying rained through the air.

She looked up and bent down again, shielding the tan and white terrier beneath her. Within seconds, the dog was bleached red in her blood as the guard fired a bullet into her shoulder. A man in the crowd threw himself at Filip and was immediately shot in the leg by the surrounding guards.

'I'm not joking, you see?' Filip looked up and scanned the houses. 'Wherever you are, I will find you.'

'Please don't go,' said Joe, beginning to cry. Richard felt his mind racing. A gunshot rang out loudly. A woman screamed and Richard heard the wailing of the children grow louder.

'I have to go,' he said, wrenching himself from his brother who held onto him tightly. 'Let me go, Joe.'

'Hurry, Richard,' shouted Filip. 'There'll be none left soon. If you give yourself up now you may be able to save lives. You have my word that no more will die if you come down now.'

'Joe,' said Richard, himself shaking. 'I can't let them do this.' He struggled desperately from his brother who had both arms around his waist, anchoring him to the ground. 'You have to let me go.'

'You're not going to come?' Filip turned to the crowd. 'This coward would rather let you all die than face his punishment. Guards, kill them all!' proclaimed Filip.

Next in line was a young girl, about eight years old.

Richard desperately wrangled with his brother who was sobbing, his grip so tight that Richard could barely breathe.

'NO! WAIT!' Richard screamed. 'Filip,' he called, his voice shaking. 'I'll come down. Just don't hurt anybody else.'

He shoved the sobbing boy away from him and hoisted himself down from the attic. 'I love you, brother,' he said, tears burning his eyes. 'Stay safe.'

'No. Please, Richard, please.'

'Maybe they'll let me see Alice,' he said, bravely. 'She'll tell them I didn't do anything wrong and maybe we can smooth this whole mess out.'

He knew he was less than convincing but he threw himself down the stairs and out of the house. In the main street, the lines of people had moved back from the bodies of their friends and stood, shivering, some spattered with still-warm blood. Most were crying or stood in a stunned silence. The dog whined pitifully and pawed at Claudine who lay cradling her shoulder.

'I'll come with you,' said Richard, trying to keep his voice steady. 'Just don't hurt any more of the people here.' Inside, he felt his bones turn to dust.

'It's you I want,' said Filip, an evil scowl on his face. 'And you're in no position to bargain with me, Warren.' The guards held Richard while Filip punched him square in the face. As Richard fell to his knees and some of the crowd moved closer, Filip drew his gun. 'Stand back!' he shouted. 'This man is a traitor to you – and a traitor to us. He committed several crimes while he was a guest in our Community and then led us here to you.'

'Take him and leave us alone,' shouted a woman from the back. 'We won't trouble you.' The crowd murmured nervously, some crying and others in heated debate.

Filip waved his gun amongst the people 'Would anyone like to stop me taking him?' he said, menacingly. 'You?' He pointed his weapon at a woman with a baby in her arms. 'Do you want to stop me?'

She looked at Richard, his face smashed into the concrete.

'No,' he stuttered through broken teeth. 'She doesn't want to stop you. Take me.'

The woman looked away, tears in her eyes. 'No,' she whispered and held her baby tight.

'I thought that would be the case,' said Filip and smiled broadly. 'We have much business to attend to now, so we will be leaving.' He nodded to one of the guards. 'Take him,' he said. 'His people have agreed that he can come with us and for that, their lives will be spared.'

A line of guards stood, their weapons raised as Filip and the others marched out of the Township. As the last of them left, Joe stumbled out of the house, tears streaming down his face. 'Why didn't you stop them?' he howled. 'Why?' before collapsing in the street sobbing, his heart broken.

And the little girl who had watched the whole event from behind a cupboard in the attic wept silently.

*

Samuel looked at Leanor in confusion. 'How do you know all this?' he said. 'This happened over eighty years ago.'

'My grandmother had been hiding there,' said the girl. 'This story became part of my childhood growing up. She always said to me that I should help people. She wishes she had helped Richard Warren but instead our whole village stood by while he got taken away.'

'I still don't get it,' he said. 'Why has this got anything to do with me?'

Leanor stood up as Eli finished his conversation in the foyer and started walking up the ward towards them.

'Tell me,' hissed Samuel, through a smile, watching Eli.

'Richard and Joe were Warrens, just like you,' Leanor whispered. 'And now I have a chance to do what my grandmother wished all her life she had done. The Industry are monsters who need to be stopped. I know what you and your brother are trying to do. I will help you get out of here.'

'Time's up,' said Eli, grabbing Samuel's arm as he came towards Elvira's bed. 'Back to your accommodation.'

Samuel stood up compliantly, his head spinning. He looked at Leanor but she looked away from him, rearranging some medication on the side table. 'But…' he started and then thought better of it. 'Thank you for letting me see her,' he said to Leanor as Eli led him out towards the foyer.

Leanor smiled weakly and turned away.

'I'll be back tomorrow,' Samuel yelled down the ward.

'If *I* say so,' said Eli, pushing him down the steps and out into the pathway that led back to the main part of the Township. Samuel looked around for a sharp stick or anything he might be able to use to attack him but the path was clear of rocks, foliage and people. There was no way of distracting him. He cursed Eli under his breath.

'Keep moving,' Eli spat at him. 'I've got work to do.'

In the early hours of his third night of broken sleep at the Township, Samuel was awoken by a sound. At first, he thought it was an animal scratching around by the door but as he listened closely, he realised it was someone tip-toeing on the gravel outside. He got out of bed and pulled on his clothes silently. The sound came again, this time closer, and right against the door. He pushed his body tight against the wall behind the door and waited while the familiar clicking sound of the lock came and the door opened. Before he could move, he heard her voice, whispering through the darkness.

'Samuel.' The figure came through into the room and closed the door. 'I'm here, just like I promised.'

Leanor went to the window and pulled back the covering. A thin stream of light from the moon filtered into the room and Samuel could just make the outline of her body through the dim light.

'You came,' he whispered in grateful surprise. 'Thank you.' He moved past her towards the door.

'Wait.' Leanor grabbed him by the arm. 'Listen to me first. You need to go around the back of this building and then down through the alley behind these houses. There's another gate on the east side of the Township that is only guarded by one person at night.' She pressed something cold and metallic into his hand. 'This is the closest I have to a weapon,' she said quietly. 'Don't use it unless you absolutely have to.'

Samuel took the metal bar and pressed it into his palm. 'Thank you,' he said. 'But what about Frida? And aren't you afraid of what Eli might do to you?'

'I'm more afraid of what he'll do to you,' Leanor replied. 'He and his men are planning an uprising against Frida and will kill you soon. And whatever happened between you and Saul, you did the right thing in bringing your friend all the way back here for help. That was a very courageous thing to do.'

'Who was Richard Warren?'

Leanor fell silent for a moment before speaking again. 'He was an ancestor of our people – of your people – and one of the first who helped to establish our Township. It broke my grandmother's heart that we didn't fight for one of our own.' Her voice quivered. 'I will not let Eli kill you just to prove to the Township that Frida is too weak to punish you for what you did to Saul.'

Samuel grabbed the door handle and opened it gently. The relief of the cool breeze of the night, infused with the scents of meat cooking, filled him with gratitude. He turned back to look at Leanor, so thankful to have someone on his side.

Her face looked strained. 'If your brother does start a rebellion within the Community and fails, and they send their military out here in revenge – none of us will survive.' A chink of light on her face showed Samuel how afraid she looked.

'But we all deserve a chance,' she added. 'So get as far away from here as you can. I will take care of Elvira and keep her as comfortable as possible but you need to do whatever you are able to in order to help your brother.'

'What will happen to you and Frida?'

'We will be fine. But you must go now. Wait for me to leave, until I'm past the central building and then go around the back. Do not hurt anybody unless you absolutely have to.' She touched his shoulder gently. 'Good luck, Samuel,' she said and slipped through the door into the night.

'Thank you,' he whispered and watched her leave through the main street. He held the bar tight in one hand, pushing the door open with the other. Leanor walked slowly, without turning back. Samuel snuck through the door and pushed his ample body right against the side of the brick building, checking in each direction for light or movement. Then, as Leanor made her way towards the outside of the main gathering hall of the Township, he saw something. There was a light, bright and red in the sky. It came towards her quickly, hovering low and making the quiet but unmistakable sound of a small engine. Immediately he thought of the attack on Company Five and what Carter had said to him about what the Industry used those types of machines for.

*

The mission of Company Five had been to explore the lands to the east in search of animals they could tame and keep with them in the Village. Samuel had hand-picked the best hunters and they'd set off early one morning, trekking through the thick woodland and into the lowlands to the north east. The company had been in good spirits as they'd settled into camp for the evening, joking with Samuel as he climbed into the foliage of a tall tree.

'Can't sleep at ground level,' he called down to them, cheerily. 'My life is in the trees.' He curled himself onto the small platform he'd constructed and tied himself to one of the flat branches. He sat there, sharpening a spear until the last of the light left the leafy canopy before he settled down to sleep. As his eyes closed, a strange buzzing, chirping sound came from below him.

'Hey, what's that?' he called.

'There's some sort of bird,' shouted one of the men tending the fire. 'It's not like any I've seen before. A strange thing.'

'Let it be and get some sleep,' said Samuel. 'See you all in the morning. Don't stay up too late, we've got a lot of ground to cover tomorrow.'

In the morning when he woke, it was unusually silent. He jumped from the branch with a heavy thump and landed near the still-smouldering embers of the fire.

'Hello,' he called loudly. 'Where are you?'

But the men and women of Company Five had disappeared. Along with their goods and belongings.

Carter had told him that it wasn't a bird at all. He'd called it a drone and the Industry used them to locate people, and for surveillance. They had used one to attack Company Five.

*

As realisation dawned over Samuel, he ran towards Leanor, shouting.

'Get out of the way, move, now!'

She turned around in surprise as Samuel darted towards her across the courtyard and through the grassy lawn, jumping over the path as he went. The buzzing sound above her startled her and she glanced upwards, scared.

'What is it?' she screamed. 'Why is it here?' She ducked down against the side of the brick wall and covered her face with her hands.

Samuel ran faster, his chest heaving and his muscles aching in the short sprint. As he reached the centre of the Township, the machine had drifted to just above head height and he leapt in the air, grabbing it between his hands. The machine whirred and buzzed as he pulled it down to the floor, forcing the full weight of his body on top of it until it stopped pushing upwards. Samuel felt around on the floor for the metal bar he'd dropped and found it inches away from his fingertips.

'Pass me the bar,' he grunted to Leanor, his body pressed against the machine, aware of the strong metal groaning sound coming from underneath him. She kicked it hard and to within reach of Samuel, just enough so he could grab it with one hand. Carefully, he raised his body off the floor and, keeping one arm and leg on the device beneath him, he pulled back the metal bar and smashed the thing into tiny, black plastic and metal pieces, stamping hard on the remains until there was nothing left but a scattering of debris mashed into the grassy turf.

Breathless, he bent over and examined the remnants. 'I think you're safe,' he said to Leanor, who sat on her knees next to him.

But she didn't look relieved; in fact to Samuel, she looked even more terrified than before. He turned around and then saw why. A small crowd of the Township were stood behind watching him and, at the front, was Eli, his eyes burning with anger.

'You have a lot of explaining to do,' he said to Leanor and grabbed her by the arm, pushing her into Frida's custody. He turned to Samuel. 'And you, come with me,' he growled, nodding to a group of men who hauled Samuel backwards, dragging him shouting back into the building from which he'd only just escaped.

Chapter Six

The Experiment

One day earlier

'She can't come with us,' said Alice firmly. 'We need to find Lily and get out of here.' The constant noise of the machines became an irritating backdrop of whirring and bleeping. Carter sat by Isabella's bed and stroked her face gently, tears glistening in his eyes.

'I'm not leaving her. Not again.' He shifted back the sheets a little to reveal her pale, milky collarbones, marked with incisions. Alice pulled the sheet back over Isabella and turned to Carter. Angel stood silent and motionless, behind them.

'We have to leave her,' she said, stepping forward and putting her hand on his shoulder. 'You need to get back to finding Lily – it's the only way of helping Isabella.'

'I can't leave her,' said Carter, raising his voice. 'She's part of the reason I came back here, I told you.'

'The most important thing we have to do is take down the Industry,' said Alice, trying not to get irritated. 'That's the only way we can save them all. We're all agreed on that, aren't we?'

'Yes, but…'

When Carter turned around, Alice could see that he had tears in his eyes.

'Carter,' she said, thinking of how badly she wanted to see her own daughter. 'Right now, our focus needs to be on how we help all these people. They all need us – not just Isabella and Jescha. Stay with us,' she added. 'We need you.'

Carter nodded wordlessly, his hands shaking a little. He thrust them into his pockets and squared his jaw. 'I know,' he said. 'I know.'

'We'll give you a moment with her,' said Alice, carefully, taking Angel by the hand and leading her into the other room, leaving Carter alone.

She directed her over to the pile of papers on the bench and opened them at a marked page, smudged with dirty fingerprints. As she scanned the text and diagrams, her stomach turned to lead and her hands felt numb. She took a deep breath, her head pounding.

'Read this,' she said, her voice catching in her throat. 'I feel sick just looking at it. She can't be serious.'

Angel took the pages from her and sat down on the floor. 'I don't understand,' she whispered, confused. 'What does it mean?'

'It's disgusting,' said Alice. 'Look at what she's written here.' She pointed to a section in the notes, deep wrinkles appearing in her forehead.

Angel repeated the words out loud to herself. 'Who would even think of something like this?' she said, bewildered.

'Izzy would,' replied Alice, shaking her head. 'She has no concept of right and wrong. No respect for human life.' She slumped down on the floor next to Angel and stared at the scrawls in disbelief. They sat there for a moment, scouring page after page.

'Explain it to me,' said Angel, finally. 'I'm not sure I really understand what I'm reading – can it possibly be true?'

'She's trying to create a new group of people. Her new followers.' Alice's voice was filled with dread as she spoke.

Angel looked pained as she tried to make sense of the papers. 'What?' she said. 'What does that mean?'

'Look, here.' Alice pointed at page of biological formulae written in Izzy's delicate script. 'She's using these people's DNA to create... clones, almost. Like a cult, with members that she can control.'

'That's sick.' Angel got up and paced across the room. 'How *could* she?'

Alice closed her eyes tightly, wishing it was a bad dream that would go away. 'She's doing it because she can,' she said quietly, pulling herself off the floor too. 'She's always been interested in what happens down here in the Labs and now she can use it to her advantage – to help her take control of the Community.'

'Just like when they created the Lab Mades,' said Angel, her voice filled with sadness. 'It's just another version of playing God.'

Alice felt a cold chill inside her grow. 'The Lab Mades,' she repeated, remembering what she'd overhead Ariel and Elizabet talking about.

Angel shrugged. 'Like Carter said before, when the news was broadcast that you had been injured in an attack at the Barricades and then died in childbirth, it was agreed that something had to be done. The Industry decided that the waiting period for new life was too long, and so they worked out a way to create embryos in the Lab.' She looked around the room. 'Probably this one,' she added.

'Who did this?' said Alice. 'Who in the Industry did this?'

'I don't know exactly – I believe it was a doctor called—'

'Barnes,' interrupted Alice. 'I'll bet it was Barnes. And that Izzy – Elizabet – was involved.' Alice remembered how Barnes had been instrumental in expediting the inseminations of the younger girls.

She'd insisted on administering her experimental drugs and controlling almost every step of the process. She shivered.

'A lot of the babies that were born were different,' Angel ran her fingertips across the soft, empty socket of her eye. 'The Industry cast them out of the Community – most of us were thrown in the waste, still alive.'

'So how did you…?'

'When Carter's parents escaped from the Community, they were able to set up a communications system with people who were still inside – Mendoza, Lily McDermott and others who were sympathetic rebels themselves. The system wasn't very sophisticated, just lights and signals – and often not very accurate. As many of the babies that could be rescued, were. But not all of us survived.'

Alice sat down on a cheap plastic chair that had been wedged under the bench. Each time she attempted to speak, the shock stopped her from uttering a word.

Filip and Barnes had used her to create a mythology about the world outside and about how they would repopulate the world, while all the time she had lain frozen underneath the very ground her daughter had been walking upon. And now, Izzy planned to take the idea even further. She felt sick to her stomach. Had this been what Barnes had been planning all along? Had they always been looking for a scapegoat? A reason to implement their plans? Her head felt cloudy. Was that the reason she had been chosen to lead the Scouts? She shook her head, unable to utter a word.

'How… how long had this been happening for?' she said eventually, hoping she was wrong. 'Did this start recently?'

'Since the very beginning.'

'And you're one of those who was made in the Lab?'

Angel smiled, but looked sad. 'Technically, yes. I was born here, in the Industry headquarters, but I wasn't deemed perfect enough to keep alive. A team of rescuers from the Village found me at the sluice gates where the waste flows out into the river. They took me home to the Village where I grew up. They call them Lab Mades in here – they're treated very… differently. But back home, we're part of a family.'

Alice shook her head. 'This is what Barnes and Izzy were really doing down here in the labs. And now, she plans to take these despicable plans to the next stage.' Her voice felt strained and her body ached as she flicked through the pages of the manuscript in front of her. 'It gets worse,' she muttered. 'She wants to build an army of workers with a *reduced mental capacity* to expand the borders out into the Deadlands.'

Angel shuddered. 'That would mean they're less likely to rebel, wouldn't it?'

'Yes,' said Alice grimly, with a look of disgust on her face. 'I'm guessing she's using genetic matter from those who were against the system, the rebels themselves, so that she could somehow change what's inside of them. With an army of people who believe in her, she would never be stopped.' She leafed through the pages despondently then stopped on one particular page. 'Oh,' she said, feeling her stomach drop deep inside of her. 'There's more.'

'What?' Carter stood in the doorway, his face lined with worry. 'What is it?'

Alice let the pile of papers flutter to the floor. Her pale brown face had turned an uneven shade of grey.

She picked up the papers and scanned through them. The pages were written in a thin childish script but contained hand-drawn maps and sketches of the landscape outside the Community. Plotted on the surveys were large circles indicating the positions of both the Village and the Township with scrawled estimates of resident numbers, strengths and weaknesses, potential weaponry and attack strategies. The heading *KILL OR CAPTURE?* had been written in block capitals. CAPTURE had been scored through. At the bottom the page, a few lines had been carefully added in red ink.

Stage 1, if successful, would gain additional land for resources and remove any threat of attack. Removing any threat of rebellion would secure the future of the Community as the only area of human habitation in the south of England. Then move to Stage 2 – using the additional power of the New Wave Army, full takeover of any other areas of population UK wide.

'We need to find Lily urgently and get her to use whatever communication system she has to warn people,' said Alice. 'Izzy plans to attack the Village – and the Township and destroy whoever and whatever she finds along the way.'

'But what about…' Carter looked back into the room at the six prisoners hooked to the machines.

'We have to leave them,' said Alice, urgently. 'Finding Lily is our only hope for stopping all this. Now where is she and how do we get hold of her?'

Reluctantly, Carter returned to the tablet and started moving coloured shapes and text across the screen. 'She's in here somewhere,' he said as the picture zoomed and focused back in on a map of the Industry building. One solitary dot flashed in a cluster of about a hundred or so.

'Looks like the second floor below ground,' said Alice, joining him at the tablet. 'And it seems like she's not alone.'

'It's the Synthetic Food Plant,' said Carter, grimly. 'We'll never get to her in there.'

'We have no choice,' said Alice. 'Describe her in detail so I know who I'm looking for.'

'If we can get a view of the people on the floor, I will point her out to you,' said Carter. 'But what if someone recognises you?' He shook his head.

'I'm about to take care of that. But I need something sharp,' said Alice, suddenly getting up and scouring the room. 'A knife – anything with a blade.'

'What about these?' said Carter, pulling the scissors from his bag. 'I've had them since Lily tried to stab me with them.' Alice froze, staring at the scissors, a strange expression on her face.

'Where did you get those?' she said in a ghostly tone. 'Give them to me.' She snatched them from Carter and held them close to her, staring at their blackened and orange surface.

'I found them,' he said, not wanting to think about how they'd been lying next to his daughter Lucia's lifeless body when he and Lily had discovered her in the tunnel.

Alice ran her fingertip along the clean blade. Although it had been more than eighty years and she knew it was impossible, she felt she could almost see traces of Hutchinson's blood – the man who had tried to attack her when she was just eleven years old and alone in the world. The man she had killed. Her fingers found the blunt, black, metal scissors that her mother had used for making clothes for her when she was a little girl; scissors that had belonged to her grandmother, and had been carefully carried from house to house, holding a legacy of history in their dull metal blades. The last time she had seen the scissors, she had hidden them in the tunnels when she and Filip had returned with Richard Warren to the Community. Her blood ran cold. How could it even be possible? She glared at the blades for a moment, anger building like a volcano inside her. Thoughts of Hutchinson attacking her, the desperate struggle to build the Community – only to wake up to a world filled with hate – made her burn with fury.

'We need to leave soon,' she said finally, when her anger had subsided a little. 'I need to sort this out once and for all. But this isn't going to be pretty.' She took a deep breath and raised the scissors towards her own head.

'Don't!' shouted Carter but, before he could stop her, Alice had begun hacking at her long, brown hair. She tore at it with the scissors, thick tresses falling to the floor in clumps around them. Angel stared at her in horror as Alice pulled and sliced her fringe at each side, then handed the scissors to her.

'Finish it,' she said, calmly, turning around. 'I can't do the back myself.'

The close clipping sound of the scissors echoed in the small room.

'You look... so... different,' said Carter, watching Angel cut the last of Alice's hair until her head was a fuzz of short stubble.

'I needed a disguise.' Alice smiled wryly. 'Now search the cupboards for something I can wear,' she said. 'Something that the workers might wear in the Food Plant. And get me an image of Lily so I know who I'm looking for.'

Wearing an old set of Industry issue overalls they'd found folded in one of cupboards in the annexe, Alice squeezed back through the vent and into the shaft first. Everything in the room looked exactly as it had when they'd first arrived. Carter had fashioned a mouth mask from a spare suit so that the majority of her face was covered.

'It'll take us around forty-five minutes or so to climb up and when we get to the factory, I'll get out and speak to her,' said Alice, pulling the mask down around her neck so she could breathe properly. 'You said it was the second floor below ground, right?' Carter nodded and the three of them crawled back to the maintenance stairs.

As they climbed higher, the smells and sounds that wound their way into the stairwell changed. The scent of artificial food became stronger making Alice retch and ache for a time when everything she ate was fresh – or at least had been real at some point in its existence. The silence that had surrounded them on the lower floors became a dull buzz of activity punctuated with long bangs and sounds of muted conversation as they left the sad darkness of the Catacombs and into the main body of the Industry building. They climbed quickly, pausing only briefly to catch a breath or to stop the harsh muscle burn. Alice felt thankful that they were in the enclosed stairway, rather than having to crawl past hundreds more Sleepers frozen in time.

'Are we almost there?' whispered Angel from the back, her hair matted with perspiration. 'I'm so thirsty.'

'Two more floors,' breathed Carter. 'And then comes the hard bit.'

When they reached the Synthetic Food Production plant, the stench of artificial food was overwhelming. Alice pushed open the panel silently, her stomach lurching, and they moved from the stairwell into the corridor that ran parallel with the length of the factory. Shards of light from the plant slanted through the grates that were housed at periodic intervals in the wall of the shaft. Loud clanking sounds of machinery and the steady throb of conversation filled the air. They moved along the shaft until each of them took a position at one of the small grated windows. Alice scanned the face of each individual, desperately trying to align the features Carter had showed her on the screen, but with the face masks, it was almost impossible.

'She'll be in that corner,' hissed Carter, beckoning Alice. 'This is where her station is.' The three of them moved quietly to the furthest grate and peered out onto the factory floor, watching as lumps of raw chicker and boeuf were dumped into machines and the workers formed them into steady blocks of productionised consumables. The whole process made Alice feel physically sick.

'There she is,' said Carter, his voice filled with urgency. 'I can see her, look there.' He pointed across the floor to a woman with long blonde hair, tied back in a ponytail. Alice instinctively put her hand to her own head and felt the scruffy fuzz, strewn with bald patches.

This is not a beauty pageant, she said to herself. *Pull yourself together.*

'How am I going to get out of here without being noticed?' she whispered, looking along the length of the room. 'There are people everywhere.'

'Not right at the far end,' said Angel. 'There's a vent that leads to a separate area and there's no one there.'

'Yes,' said Carter. 'I remember. They have a toilet area and a separate water dispenser with a divider between that and the factory. If you're quick, you can get through the grate while no one's using the facilities and come out of the cubicle and onto the main floor of the food plant.'

Alice rubbed her hand across her scalp. Until this point, it had all felt unreal, like some sort of crazy idea, but the thought of going back out into a world so far from her own, terrified her. She crept along the shaft to the grate. An older woman walked past, within inches of her, and filled a small paper cup from the water dispenser, looking up towards the passageway as she did. Alice pulled herself back sharply and pressed her body tight against the side of the wall, facing away from the plant. She closed her eyes tightly but above the noise of the machinery, she thought she could feel the woman breathing into the grate. She opened her eyes and glanced at Carter. He placed a finger to his lips and Angel's eyes were wide, scared. Alice swallowed and waited until she heard the woman's footsteps walk away. Slowly, she craned her neck around and moved her body back until she could just about see inside the plant. As she crossed the floor the woman stopped and turned back to look at the grate. She stared for a second and then turned around and went back to her work area.

Alice felt a thin bead of cold sweat run down her forehead. Her hands were clammy and warm.

'Go now,' said Carter. 'The stall is empty and there's no one approaching from this side. But be quick.'

Carefully, Alice removed the metal grate and pulled it aside. Angel came quickly behind her, ready to put it back into place. She twisted her legs downwards and lightly dropped her body through the hole and onto the floor of the cubicle. With a swift twist, she locked the door. From inside the stall, she peered back up at the grate opening in the wall. At the edge, on either side, she could just make out Carter and Angel in the darkness of the maintenance shaft. She breathed deeply and opened the door.

Behind the screen, she poured herself a cup of water from the dispenser and walked with her head high and confident across the floor of the synthetic food plant towards the area where Lily's control desk stood.

As she approached, Lily looked up, dark lines of confusion across her forehead.

Alice cleared her throat, her legs shaking. 'Hello, McDermott,' she said clearly, but quietly. 'My name is Alice and I'm new here. I understand you might be able to help me.'

Lily's bright eyes widened, in a combination of shock and excitement. 'I know *exactly* who you are,' she whispered, and pretended to smile nervously while looking across at a group of Industry guards who stood talking on the north side of the plant. 'What on earth are you doing here? How did you know to come and find me?'

Alice kept her eyes firmly on Lily and held onto the sides of her trousers to keep her hands from shaking. 'I have a friend who worked here for a while, a couple of months ago. He suggested you might be the right person,' she said, quietly. 'He's here with me now.'

Lily's face turned ashen. 'Carter? Where?' She turned as an older man approached them, hovering in the background.

'Lily,' he said, his voice booming in Alice's ears. 'We need a refill on the flavouring on machine four.'

'There's a canister on minus three,' she said. 'You have my authorisation to collect.'

'Thank you,' said the man in a deferent tone, but didn't move. He eyed Alice suspiciously. 'New girl?' he said. 'You a Lab Made? Are you supposed—'

'She's working with me. You can go now,' Lily interrupted. 'My shift finishes in twenty minutes and Stefano will take over as supervisor.' The man nodded and disappeared through a side door, looking over his shoulder as he went. Lily waited a few seconds before speaking again to Alice in a low voice.

'Where is he? Where is Carter?'

'He's close by,' said Alice, her voice remaining firm. 'We need your help. But not here – you need to tell us a secure location in this building that has a maintenance or air vent large enough that we can access the room.'

Lily thought for a moment, keeping her gaze on Alice. 'There's a storage room on minus five, on the north-east corridor, seventeen units across. I use it as a private office. How are you planning…?' But before she could finish her sentence, Alice was striding across the floor back towards the bathroom.

In the pale darkness of the stairwell, they climbed downwards in silence. At the fifth floor below ground, Alice pulled away the panel and they crawled through above the north-east tunnel. When they arrived at unit seventeen, Carter spoke first.

'I hope my mother was right to trust her,' he said, loosening the grate. 'I still don't know whether she killed my daughter.'

'I think it's a bit late for that,' said Alice wryly. 'We have no option right now other than to believe she's going to help us. And I think we should wait up here until she arrives.'

Half an hour or so later, the door to the storage room opened and Lily walked in carrying a bag. She looked upwards, directly eyeing the grate.

'You can come down,' she said, nervously. 'It's safe here.'

After Alice and Angel, Carter dropped into the room last. He looked at Lily suspiciously, his muscles twitching. Now that he was face to face with her, he felt uncertain, unsure of her loyalty. Despite what his mother had said, Carter's stomach burned with anger towards her. 'Before we start this, I need to know one thing,' he said, his voice sounding calmer than her felt. 'What happened to my daughter? Who killed her? Was it—' he swallowed '—was it you?'

Lily exhaled upwards, blowing her fringe from her face. 'Of course I didn't kill her,' she said, firmly. 'We believe that her movements had been under surveillance by the Industry for some time, from before you were even released.'

'And?'

'When Chess refused to dole out significant punishment for rebellious activities, the Industry teams started to get nervous. When they were brought in for questioning about their activities, some of the rebels had their trackers replaced with small devices. Some to the stomach, like Isabella, and others, like Lucia, to the wrists. Those with the wrist implants were warned that if they were ever to leave the security of the Barricades, the implants would tear holes in their skin and they would bleed to death. I think Lucia started trying to cut her trackers out herself when she realised she'd gone under the Barricades. And in the dark, the process was just too difficult – she cut herself too deep and knew that she couldn't save herself.' She looked him straight in the eye. 'I'm sorry we couldn't save her,' she said.

Carter felt a sadness overwhelm him, thinking of his daughter dying alone in the darkness. A hard lump formed in his throat.

Lily put her arm on his shoulder. 'I am genuinely sorry, Carter. I'm sorry I had to lie to you and I'm sorry you've had to suffer this way. But you've proved yourself to be the leader we all knew you could be. You found your mother, didn't you? And you made it back here – and quicker than any of us imagined you would. You're a credit to us all.' She paused for a moment, overtaken by a brief show of emotion.

Carter nodded, the enormity of the sacrifice so many people had made to make him successful sinking in deeper than it ever had before.

'But *you*...' Lily broke the silence and reached out to touch Alice's cheek affectionately, as though she'd known her for years.

Alice instinctively pulled away from her, the intimacy from a stranger a little too much.

'None of us knew you were still here,' continued Lily, looking quickly away. 'And no one guessed.' She shook her head. 'Were you the secret that was hiding in Chamber One?' Her genuine shock was apparent. 'We had heard it was something highly confidential but we never imagined if could be you. This is game-changing.'

She stopped for a moment to catch her breath. 'When I saw you on in the food plant I thought I was losing my mind. Your hair...' She looked at Alice carefully. 'Between you and Carter, things will change. This Community will change forever.'

'Good. Because this place disgusts me,' said Alice, moving away from Lily. 'The things that evil creature Elizabet is planning are horrific. You need to get us out of here so we can tell everyone the truth about the Industry and what Elizabet is planning.'

'It's not going to be as easy as...'

'We need clothes, food, water and weaponry,' Alice snapped. 'And quickly.'

Lily reached into her bag and pulled out a box of chicker and whiteloaf and a large bottle of water. She pushed it towards Alice who shared it amongst the three of them.

'We need to get a message to the Village,' said Carter, forcing down a mouthful of whiteloaf and lickerspread. 'Elizabet is planning to attack them – we need to let them know that we need more people here.'

Lily frowned and sank down into a chair. 'She's planning to attack them? How do you know this?'

'We found her workshop underground,' said Alice. 'We've seen her filthy experiments and I've read what she intends to do to the Lab Mades.'

'She has Isabella,' said Carter, angrily. 'She's doing terrible things down there to them.'

'To who? What things? I know she's planning something radical but she's incredibly secretive and nobody inside has been able to find out exactly what.' Concern lined Lily's face. 'You need to slow down. And tell me everything you know, from the beginning.'

When Carter had finished recounting the journey through the Deadlands and Alice had explained what they had discovered in the Lab, Lily's face had paled and there was a darkness in her eyes that was part anger and part sadness. She looked deeply distressed.

'You are right,' she said, finally after much thought. 'We need to let the people of the Township and the Village know they are in danger. And we will need more resources, more people to help us. There are many rebels within the Community but the Industry outnumbers them considerably. When the people of the Township know of their plans, they will come here to help us – they cannot avoid this conflict any longer, they will need to join with us and the Village.'

She paused. 'There's only one way we can reach them with a message this complex that will get there in time.'

'Then do it,' said Carter. 'Whatever it takes – we have to stop this and save the lives of the people we care about.'

'It's not that simple,' said Lily. 'Until now, my role here inside the Barricades has been about the children – about the ones we can secretly save and take to the outside. Since I went with you out into the Deadlands, my locations are being monitored and I can't leave this building – and the communications systems we've always used have simply been a system of lights and signals.' She tapped her fingers on the table, distractedly. 'Unless…'

'Unless, what? How can we get a message to them?' Carter's voice was raised in urgency and he stood up and paced around the small room.

'There's only one way I can think of that could work,' said Lily, quietly nodding to herself. 'It's dangerous and we risk getting caught. We will have to send an Industry drone.'

Chapter Seven

The Warning

Carter stood behind Lily, watching her programme the drone – tapping co-ordinates from a multi-coloured map on her tablet into the screen and then adjusting small levers within the mechanical device. Alice and Angel sorted through the spare clothes in a chest on the floor, and snacked on the remainder of the food from the bag.

'You could have just told me the truth,' Carter said as Lily paired the device directly to the tablet. Her fingers worked quickly, removing the camera and attaching a small metal container in its place.

'You wouldn't have believed me back then,' she said, distractedly. 'You needed to see for yourself that everything you knew about the Industry to be true was a lie.'

'I already *knew* something was wrong,' he said. 'Before I was even sent to the Catacombs I had a plan to revolutionise everything. I wanted to be Controller General to make a difference in the Community, to change the way Lab Mades were treated.'

'Which may have worked, if you hadn't listened to Isabella and gone out into the Deadlands,' said Lily. 'If I'd let you back in, you'd have been killed immediately. You'd never have made Controller General breaking the rules in that way.' She gritted her teeth in annoyance.

'Everyone had worked so hard to keep you from becoming a rebel yourself and to make you as Industry as possible, just so we had a chance at you becoming successful.'

'I know you were trying to help but what if you'd hit an artery or a vein?'

'I'm very skilled.' Lily looked over at Angel. 'Didn't you explain to him about the tracker?'

'Of course I did,' said Angel, breaking apart some fauclate, and making a face, 'but he's had a lot of lies and betrayal to unpick in the last few months.'

'If I had wanted to kill you, I had plenty of chances,' said Lily, turning to Carter. 'But I knew that once we were in the tunnels, there was no going back to the Community – at least not for you. The only thing I could do was to let you – no, force you to – escape and find your mother at the Village. She has always been a wise woman and I knew she would know what to do.' She paused. 'While I knew it would be a shock, finding out that she was alive after all this time, I know you'd understand eventually and become the leader we needed you to be. The time has passed for a Controller General who wants to make things more liberal – the selection of Elizabet has proved that. There would be no tolerating someone who had broken the rules before the promotion to the position – however senior.'

'You knew I would fail?'

Lily shrugged. '*They* knew you would fail,' she said. 'The warnings should have been enough, when Mendoza explained why you were being frozen, but when your daughter got to you the moment you were released, I knew it was going to be hard to keep you focused.'

Carter closed his eyes tightly as Lily finished the last modifications to the drone. He let his mind wander to Isabella, drugged and alone in the Lab and dreaded to think what would happen if Elizabet got back there before he could rescue her. Then came the scenes of the people of the Village, sat around their campfires and busying themselves in their carefully crafted houses in the trees, building simple and kind lives for themselves. Everything seemed a lifetime away and so different from the cruel, cut-throat world he had grown up in. If he'd ever had any nostalgic sympathy or affiliation left inside him towards the Industry, or any concern that their mission had been a mistake, it had disappeared completely, leaving only a sadness and regret that he'd not been able to stop everything by becoming Controller General himself. Inside him his resolve to destroy the Industry, whatever the cost, strengthened.

'Concentrate,' said Lily, loudly. 'I need you to confirm what message you want to send to the Township and the Village.'

'How will it work?' said Angel, running her fingers over the smooth metallic surface of the drone. 'I always thought these were dangerous. They send information back to the Industry – that's what you said,' she whispered, looking at Carter.

'They do,' said Lily, moving the body of the drone towards her. 'But this one has been modified to create outgoing communications only.' She opened the capsule body and showed them the intricate system of wires and plates inside. 'Speak,' she said to Carter, moving towards the tablet attached the drone, 'tell me the message you want to send.'

He began speaking clearly, his voice determined. 'To the residents of the Township and the Village,' he started, Lily typing as he spoke. 'This is a message from Carter Warren. I am inside the boundaries of the Community and I have discovered a plot to destroy anyone who lives outside the Barricades. This is no longer simply a threat, but a reality. The leader here intends to invade the land you currently call your own and claim it in the name of the Paradigm Industries. To help us defeat these people you should amass all those who are prepared to fight and provide support to us and meet us at the south side of the Barricades in three days' time at sunset.'

As Carter came to the end of the message, there was a moment of silence as the magnitude of what they were asking of the people of the Village and the Township, and what they were about to do, hit them all. They looked at one another in disbelief, yet with a sense of undeniable purpose.

'How will it work?' said Angel. 'The drone, I mean.'

'It will send a message to a pre-programmed area in the Deadlands. I'll release it into the Barricades, late this evening,' said Lily. 'There's an area near where Isabella's tunnel was that's been cleared and securitised.'

'Doesn't that make it more dangerous?' said Alice, circling the drone.

'The rebels won't go anywhere near that area now,' said Lily, pushing the machine towards Alice. 'And as a result, the Industry doesn't bother with it either. It's sort of a no-go zone for anyone. They never actually knew exactly how you escaped, just that it was a place where Isabella used to hang out.' She paused. 'I told them I shot you – and wounded you so badly that I knew you'd bleed out.'

Carter raised his eyes. 'So, I'm dead and Alice is frozen but nobody really knows about it? Neither of us exist?'

'Technically, yes.'

Alice nodded and tapped the side of the drone with her fingertip.

'You've seen one of these before?' said Carter. 'Even in your time?'

'Of course,' said Alice, a little indignant. 'We used them as toys. And military weapons, I suppose.' She rocked it back and forth and then turned it upside down.

'Well, this one isn't a toy,' said Lily, taking the drone from her. 'You asked how it worked. It's programmed to release two copies of your message, electronically printed on one of these.' She pulled out a thin piece of metal from inside the guts of the machine and held it out in front of Carter and Alice. It was engraved with the words Carter had spoken and Lily had typed.

'We've never used this method before,' said Lily. 'And we've never communicated directly with the Township.' She hesitated. 'There's a risk that it won't even make it past the Barricades if the Industry catch me.'

'How will it get a message to both the Township and the Village?' said Angel, in awe. 'That's impressive.'

'It flies,' said Lily. 'I've pre-programmed the co-ordinates to simulate two drops. Each at the locations where we approximate the locations of the Village and the Township to be.' She held the drone on one side so they could clearly see the underneath. 'This,' she said, pointing to a small red light, 'this seeks out heat. Individuals and groups – the more people, the greater the signal. It will circle the two co-ordinated areas until it focuses on a point where it determines where the maximum number of people are. And then it deploys the message at a low altitude.'

'So it has the maximum chance of being retrieved?' said Angel. 'That's amazing.'

'How long does it take?' Alice picked at her fingernails.

'It will be there by morning,' said Lily, replacing the slice of metal containing the message. 'If I can send it this afternoon, then it will be there by tonight – early morning at the latest. And it will send a signal directly back to my card to confirm it's been delivered.' She smiled. 'Now we have to find a way to get the three of you out of here and back to my dwelling in the Community. It's too risky to stay down here.'

*

When Lily returned a few hours later, Carter took her to one side. She put a bag down on the table and opened it.

'Did you send the drone?'

Lily piled some clothes on the table and nodded slowly. 'Yes, it's made it over the Barricades but now we have to wait. And in the meantime, I need to get you all out of here.'

'If we leave the Catacombs then we're still going to need direct access to the Model and a way of exposing what Elizabet is planning,' he said. 'And I want Isabella out of that Lab.'

'One thing at a time,' said Lily, handing him a set of workwear. 'You can't stay here in this room and if you're going to start this rebellion for real, then you're going to need some allies on the outside. A lot of them. There's no pausing this rebellion to save your girlfriend, Carter, not now the movement has started.'

He looked at her almost sheepishly. 'We save everyone or we save no one. I get it.'

Alice pushed herself off the table and grabbed a set of clothes from Lily who handed Angel a set of dark glasses and a military-style uniform. Angel looked at her and put on the glasses.

'This was the only one I could get at short notice,' said Lily, smiling. 'And therefore, you are going to be one of the Industry élite.'

As they stepped out into the main corridor, Carter felt a rush of cool air and the same fleeting, fresh scent of the freedom he had first experienced after waking from the Catacombs. The tunnels were much brighter here and cleanly paved, regularly trodden by Industry employees. He looked back at Alice, who was wearing a tightly fitted net hair covering, her skin having been lightened slightly by the chalk dust on the inside of the walls. His hair was now dark, soaked by Lily in plant juices then dried a red clay-like mud to disguise the soft blondness.

'You have to remember that you are all distinctive and recognisable,' said Lily as she had applied their disguises. 'While Alice may have massacred her long hair, her face has been in most school FreeScreens for years as part of the history curriculum, Carter was publicised as a candidate for Controller General and Angel has physical features not seen before in the Community.' She had paused. 'If just one of you gets recognised, it will be the end of us all.'

'We can't be seen together,' Carter had said, agreeing. 'When we are outside, we will need to split up.'

As they neared the turn at end of the corridor, the sound of clipped footsteps and lowered voices got louder. Carter felt his muscles stiffen and he looked across at Angel, smartly dressed in the Industry uniform of black and gold with a thick lightning strike logo on each lapel.

'Remember what I told you,' Lily hissed to her. 'All of you – look ahead, keep walking and don't say a word.'

Two guards appeared around the corner, flanking a man dressed in the same workwear as Alice and Carter, but his suit was smeared with traces of wet blood. A large cut on his forehead leaked blood down the side of his face and onto the floor. He was struggling desperately to get away but each time he loosened an arm, one of the officers would cuff him across the face. Carter felt a surge of anger rising inside him, but he calmed himself.

As they came closer, one of the guards looked suspiciously at them and addressed Angel directly.

'Officer,' he said, nodding in her direction. 'A bit dark in here for those, isn't it?' Angel touched the glasses that hid the hollow of her left eye and swallowed hard.

'Stops me having to look at the filth down there,' she said quickly, gesturing with her head towards the end of the corridor. The guard nodded while the man they were holding spat blood onto the floor.

'You're all evil,' he said, angrily. 'You'll never get away with this. It was the kid's birthday. She's only a child!'

'Shut up, Lab Made,' said the other guard roughly, and then turned back to Angel. 'This one thought he could address our new Controller Generals directly with his issues – ran right up to them and started shouting. So, he's off for a time in the Catacombs. We're taking him the long way down so he can think about his actions.'

Then they both pulled the man upright while Angel nodded politely.

One of the men grabbed Carter by the arm.

'Want us to take yours with us? Your supervisor there looks like she's in a hurry and if you need these two putting away, we can manage them.'

The other looked at them, stony faced. 'They become a lot more compliant when you give them a shot of this.' He held up a syringe, a dark smile on his face.

'No. We're on our way back to the food plant,' said Lily briskly. 'These two have been helping with supplies.'

'I don't see any supplies,' said the guard who still had hold of Carter's arm. He turned back to Angel. 'Leave them with me and I'll claim the extra credit on my service record if you're not interested. Did you know Elizabet's doubling rations this week for anyone who puts a rebel away?' A further note of suspicion had entered his voice.

'I have other orders,' said Angel, the firmness in her voice tinged with nerves. 'We need to get back.'

'Have it your own way,' said the guard, releasing Carter and shoving him into the side of the tunnel. He fell to the floor and, when he got up, he came face to face with the bloody man sandwiched between the guards.

'I know you,' said the man, slowly. 'I know you.'

'No, you don't,' said Carter under his breath. 'I've never seen you before.'

'You're Carter Warren,' cried the man loudly, turning to the guards. 'He's Carter Warren.' He pulled his arms away from the guards and poked Carter in the chest. 'I'd know you anywhere,' he continued, before one of the guards punched him square in the face and he slumped awkwardly between them.

'Carter Warren is dead,' said Angel, her voice beginning to break. 'Now, we really must go. I have to get these two back to work.' She pulled roughly at Alice's arm and they moved away from the guards who stared at them as they walked off down the tunnel. The man continued to call after them as the guards beat him and dragged him away.

When they reached the lift and the doors had closed, Angel put her head in her hands. 'That poor man,' she said sadly. 'We could have helped him.'

'Not without drawing even more attention to ourselves,' said Alice, looking at Carter. 'I feel for him, but that could have been the end of us. And he isn't the only one who might recognise Carter.'

'We have to keep moving. You did brilliantly,' said Carter to Angel, putting his arm around her shoulder. 'And we're not just going to help that man – we're going to help everyone.'

The lift doors clicked open at ground level and the four of them stepped out into a wide foyer, humming with people moving in and out of the long corridors. Most kept their heads down, marching towards their chosen direction with purpose. Lily guided them carefully through a large group watching a FreeScreen that covered the upper part of one wall. Alice glanced up and, to her horror, saw old footage of Filip being streamed – his voice muted by the conversations and movement around her, but unmistakeable.

'We will defeat and destroy anyone or anything that threatens our way of life,' came his voice. 'Our brave new Scouts have already razed to the ground one group of militants in the Deadlands who were planning significant action against us.'

Carter pulled her away from the screen. 'This is very old film,' he whispered. 'Don't worry, he's not here now.' He watched her face change as they moved away from the foyer and into one of the long tunnels.

'Everything he did to you happened a long time ago,' he said. 'And he's gone.'

Alice's eyes burned dark and angry.

'For me, it happened yesterday. If anyone can understand that, Carter, it should be you.'

They walked through the rest of the tunnel in silence, walking separately rather than in a group and always with their heads down, with the exception of Lily, who adopted the same level of confidence Carter had witnessed in the genuine Industry guards. The tunnel spurred off into different directions as they followed her, and she occasionally nodded in salutation to individuals as they passed through towards where the Transporters were.

As they came to the end of the last tunnel, it widened out into a large station area where people were piling onto the three carriages that lined the edge of the platform. He took a place at the back, followed by Alice and then Lily. Angel stood across the carriage, sweat beading on her forehead, her face unreadable underneath the dark glasses. Alice stared out through the window as the Transporter pulled away and the dark-red bricked wall melted into a haze of darkness.

When the carriage stopped, they each stepped out onto the platform and Lily led them west, through a small tunnel and out, into the darkness of the night. They each took a moment to breathe the fresh, cool air into their lungs, and, above them, Carter watched as black, smoky clouds drifted past the pale moon.

'We need to keep walking separately,' said Lily as they gathered together. 'We're heading east, away from Unity Square. I have a place in the south where we can base ourselves. It's in the wood – not far from where I took you training, Carter.'

As they passed through the main centre of the Community and out into the darkness, Carter felt the familiar smells and sounds flood back to him: the dark hum of the underground Transporters, the gentle aroma of lavender and crushed ferns of the forest as they trampled through the undergrowth. While the Village had become a place where he felt comfortable and accepted, there was something about the Community, however corrupt it had become, that would always feel like home.

The house Lily took them to was deep in the woods, in an older, less developed part of the Community, a long way from the town. By the time they arrived, exhaustion had almost taken over and as soon as they were shown their room, they were close to sleep. Angel lay down immediately, but Carter watched from his bed as Alice sat at the window, running her finger up and down the glass, humming quietly to herself.

'Want to talk?' he asked, sitting upright. An owl hooted a deep, throaty call from outside.

'No,' said Alice, her finger moving in a circular motion, tracing patterns on the window. 'Not now.'

She moved to her bed without looking at him and laid down, her eyes open. Carter blew out the candle. As he drifted off to sleep, all he could hear was the heavy sound of Alice breathing.

When light streamed through the window the next morning, Carter found the room cold and empty. The thin plastic covers that had clothed them through the night were folded on a chair in the corner alongside the Industry guard uniform that Angel had been wearing.

He rubbed the sleep from his eyes and looked out of the window. Apart from one other house, they were surrounded by a small copse of trees; in the distance he could just make out the metallic glint of the Barricades that sliced through the sun and cast a shimmer across the Black River. He shivered.

'Carter, are you awake?' The shout from downstairs roused him.

He pulled on the work trousers and ran his fingers though his hair then climbed stiffly down the stairs. At a small wooden table sat Angel and Alice, while Lily moved between the room and a small kitchen where she unpacked boxes of synthetic food and brought them to the table. The sour look on her face neutralised any appetite Carter may have had.

'What's wrong?'

Lily bit her lip. 'The drone didn't work,' blurted Angel. 'The signal has gone.'

Carter took a seat at the table and screwed up his forehead. 'What happened?' he said to Lily. 'How do you know?'

Lily came in from the kitchen, sighing loudly. 'It made it as far as the Township,' she started. 'But then the signal stopped. Completely.'

'Do you know if the Township received the message at least?'

Lily shook her head. 'It never deployed,' she said. 'Either it malfunctioned. Or…'

'Or what?'

'Or maybe someone got there before us.'

The four of them sat around the table in silence. 'We can't just leave them to die,' said Angel. 'And we also can't do this on our own. We still need to get a message to the people outside.'

'Well, I can't get hold of another drone,' said Lily. 'It's only a matter of time before the Industry realise that one is missing.'

Alice sat in silence, pushing a piece of chicker around her plate. 'One of us needs to go out there,' she said, in a matter of fact tone. She turned to Lily. 'You said we needed to separate. Well, that's one way of dividing the task.'

Lily shook her head. 'It's too dangerous,' she said. 'Even if one of us makes it into the Deadlands, there's no guarantee we'd make it to the Township and the Village and back.'

'I'll go,' said Carter. The three others looked at him. 'I'm the one person that both the Village and the Township will listen to and I'm too much of a liability here anyway at the moment. He looked at Alice. 'I'll co-ordinate our resources on the other side of the Barricades and you work on the rebels in here.'

He paused. 'But you have to promise to help me save Isabella. We're going to need to bring in as many people as possible into our plans in order to defeat the Industry. We need to find people we can trust and let them know what's really happening both in here and out in the Deadlands.'

Alice laughed dryly. '*Veritas liberabit vos,*' she said softly.

Lily looked at her quizzically.

'The truth will set you free,' replied Angel and Carter in unison.

'It's the motto of the Township,' explained Alice. 'And that's what we have to do for everyone living in the Community. They've been living under the reign of the Industry for so long that they've become trapped. We have to fight to tell them the truth.'

Carter exhaled deeply, the depth of expectation weighing on him greatly, and he moved to the other wide of the room, glancing nervously out of the window and across towards the Barricades.

'I can do this,' he said to himself. '*We* can do this.'

As the sun reached the highest point in the sky, they set off for the Delaney house. Carter's bag was packed with as much food as Lily could sneak out of the plant.

'In six days' time, Elizabet and Ariel are presenting a live broadcast from Unity Square,' said Lily. Everyone will be there to hear the new Controller Generals speak in person for the first time. If you can get back here by then, we may have a chance of getting people into the Community – but Alice, Angel and myself will need to do a great deal of work before then to make it happen.'

Carter looked at her seriously. 'Do you think we can break into the Control Room?' he asked.

Alice, who had been gazing out into the Deadlands, turned back to face them, an excited look on her face. 'If we can, we can take over that broadcast and show everyone that what they thought the Industry is all about is a lie. We can use their broadcast against them.'

Carter nodded eagerly. 'If I can convince enough support from the Township and the Village and get back here in time, we can show the people of the Community that life outside the Barricades exists and that the Industry hasn't been telling them the truth since the Storms.'

'Yes,' said Angel. 'We can prove to them that everything they have ever known isn't true!'

'The broadcast will be around sunset,' said Lily. 'Come to the western side of the Barricades. There's a blue gate that's largely unmanned because the terrain is so difficult. The Black River stands between you and the gate; it opens out onto a small floodplain and you'll be able to see the gate.'

Carter nodded and held up the master key. 'I assume this will let me in?'

'It should do,' said Lily, 'but I will aim to make it there to meet you at the gate and ensure you have a clear path back to Unity Square. You need to leave now.' Lily handed Carter his things. 'The roof fall was relatively minor – take the tools I've put in your bag and dig your way through. There are torches and a knife too.'

Carter nodded as they headed down towards the entrance to the tunnel out into the Deadlands. 'And the map?' he added.

'I've made some amendments to it,' Lily said, hurriedly, 'and marked out a route that should take you to the Township in the shortest amount of time.'

'Okay. Then I guess I'll see you in six days.' He smiled. 'Make sure you get as many people on side here as you can.' There was a slight wavering in his voice as he made his way closer to the opening of the tunnel.

'Take care, Carter.' Alice looked at him anxiously, her face pained. So much of their plan and the safety of so many people rested on him. She tried hard, for his sake, to look confident. 'It'll be okay,' she added with more certainty.

'See you soon.'

Carter carefully edged his body inside the hole in the ground and the others watched as he disappeared into the darkness while the sun shone down brightly in the pale-blue early afternoon sky.

Chapter Eight

The Control Room

Alice poured herself a glass of water and hunkered over Lily's tablet, scanning the map of the Community. Her thoughts turned to Carter and his journey into the Deadlands. She hoped he would make it to the people he had talked to her about – the Township and the Village where life, in some ways, seemed to be so much easier. Part of her wished so desperately that it could have been her pushing her way through the tunnel and out in the world, away from the Community that made her skin crawl like an infection.

Many things seemed very, very different from when she had left – not far off a century before. She traced her fingers over the lines of the Transporter tracks that criss-crossed the terrain and looped underneath the Barricades to the world outside. The map reminded her of the old London she had left before the Storms, with its tall iconic buildings and the underground network that she had known so well. She knew from her own time in the Deadlands that some of them were still half-there, broken and forlorn, eerie spires reaching desperately up in the cold sky and the bricked-up tunnels that were sunk deep underground housed dark secrets and the remnants of people from a time that was now so very long ago. She scanned the map further out into the Deadlands to where Prospect House stood. It, like the other areas that Lily had mentioned that had been marked with large red blocks, had been identified as inhabited by outsiders – areas for 'development'.

She shivered.

'So, what are you thinking?' said Lily, coming up behind her. 'If you're planning to release everyone from the Catacombs, they're going to need food, somewhere to live, medical and psychological care…'

'I know,' said Alice, switching off the tablet. 'And we need to find a way of understanding exactly how many people are underground to be able to do that.' She slumped down into the chair. 'My estimate was around one hundred thousand – maybe more. I could study this thing for hours but without all the information, and the right way to interpret it, there's just no way we're going to make any progress. It's too confusing.'

She remembered the conversation she'd had with Quinn, standing at the edge of the stage in Unity Square, about the numbers, the projections and how brilliant the whole plan had sounded at the time. She sighed heavily. 'We only have a few days until Carter plans to return with reinforcements from the Village and the Township. In that time, we need to work out exactly how we can release these people safely as well as exposing Elizabet's plans and getting the Community on our side.'

'Surely once they know what has been happening in here, they'll turn against the Industry?' called Angel from the back of the room. Alice sat curled on a small bed, trying to make sense of everything. She hadn't taken off her guards' uniform since she had first put it on.

'Some will,' said Lily, slowly. 'But maybe not all. As terrible as things are in here, most of our people have only ever believed in the Industry. When something is your whole life, and you've never known anything else, it's difficult to imagine that it's all been a lie – or that there is any other way to live.'

'She's right, Angel,' said Alice. 'You're taught in here to believe that the Industry is the only way of thinking. Even when deep inside I knew some of what we were doing was wrong, I really believed it was for the right reasons.'

'How can there be any right reason for leaving children to die in the waste pipes? Or having one part of society become better and more powerful than another, just because of what they were born into?'

Alice looked at her sadly. 'That's exactly the opposite of what we were trying to achieve – what we wanted to achieve,' she said. 'We always talked about a world that worked for everyone – an equal world where money, race, beliefs, who you loved, wouldn't matter. That if we started everything from scratch, from absolutely nothing, we could create something new.' She sighed heavily. 'It started to go wrong with little things that took away people's independence and increased their reliance upon the Industry. And then, when my best friend Kelly became pregnant, it started to all become clear – we were too young, too inexperienced, to do all of this. But the force of the Industry and the plans we had made got out of control. And this—' she looked around the room and outside to the Barricades '—this is what happens when you give people the power to change anything. They – we – warp the circumstances to our own advantage.'

Angel walked around the room picking up objects and putting them down carefully. The tablet, a box of chicker, Lily's electronic card, the cup of water. She held each one for a moment, ran her fingers around the edges and sniffed them. 'Your rooms are so… sparse,' she said finally. 'No books, no paintings, no things – nothing. Everything is so empty, so soulless.'

'It's not allowed,' said Lily. 'Remember, the fires the First Scouts set destroyed most things.'

Alice shook her head. 'I feel ashamed,' she said. 'Ashamed that I was a part of it.'

'But how could you all continue to live like this?' sighed Angel, raising her voice. 'Without song and dance and reading, games? It's incredibly sad. Beyond the fact that there are thousands of innocent people locked away down there, waiting to become lobotomised servants to that evil girl, the *lack* of everything – including humanity – is just terrifying.'

Alice watched the girl as her face darkened with anger.

'It's just not fair,' she continued bitterly. 'The way they have destroyed everything that was good and – not content with that – the disgusting way they've controlled everyone else. They poisoned our water, set fires to destroy our crops and now their leader has decided to send an army to kill our people and those of the Township.' She stopped, breathless, her hands shaking and her voice a broken echo.

Alice closed her eyes tightly, a dirty wave of guilt and regret washing over her. 'I could have changed things,' she whispered. 'Deep down, I knew what we were doing was wrong but we were so convinced that everything had to be different. So completely different to what happened before that we created this.'

Lily pulled them both close to her. 'We have a chance here,' she said, softly. 'A chance to change the future of all these people – but we need to understand the numbers and how we can do this safely. We need someone who knows cryonics and the Model better than we do.'

Alice thought for a moment. 'In my day, I used to have a friend called Quinn. Although she wasn't much of a friend towards the end.'

'Quinn Fordham,' said Lily confidently. 'Everyone knows Quinn Fordham. She was one of the original Scouts and, along with Dr Barnes, they changed the way we live today.' The last part of the sentence Lily said in a strange parodied voice that sounded very much like a television commercial to Alice – understandable, as she'd learned the history of the Community by heart in school. Alice shuddered.

'Yes,' she said, pushing thoughts of the past as far away as she could. 'Quinn developed the Model and all of the statistical analysis that went along with it – we need someone with her level of skill to be able to undo all of that and work out how many people we can unfreeze and how often so that we can create something sustainable. Unless we have a plan, none of this will work and we'll end up in a more chaotic situation than we already are.'

Lily smiled. 'Cryonics and Censomics are traits that are encouraged to run in the family,' she said. 'Anyone with the Fordham gene has been trained to follow in that line of mathematical brilliance – take Carter, for example. He's fourth generation Fordham and, although he's got Warren genetics in him and a whole load of others, he's still imminently more skilled at manipulating the Model than most. He learned from a very early age that he would be expected to be an expert in that area and had access to the Model since he was young. He's had the gift, and has been in training, ever since he was a child.'

'Well, Carter's not here,' said Alice, bluntly. 'So who do you suggest?'

Lily shrugged. 'There's a woman who runs all the Model interactions currently – Catherine – she's a Fordham and an Industry high ranker,' she said. 'She won't help us willingly but she's stuck to her genetic specialism of cryonic modelling and she's probably the most skilled person we have currently.' She laughed sardonically. 'It's what

Fordhams are famous for. Lots of the Descendants are schooled in their original disciplines.'

'Willingly or not, we get her – I don't care how,' said Alice, determined. Although as she spoke, something nagged away inside of her; something that she didn't want to ask. But did anyway. 'Just out of interest, Lily,' she said offhandedly. 'What is it that Davenports are famous for?'

'Bearing live children,' said Lily, immediately feeling the scratch of disappointment in Alice's face. 'Unfortunately, it's what your ancestors have always done best.'

The Industry guard uniform was tightly fitted and the shoes rubbed Alice's feet as she walked alongside Lily into the Industry building.

'It was the best I could get,' Lily had said when they had agreed that Angel should keep her uniform and stay at home while they investigated. Her second time in the building was infinitely less terrifying than the first, but there was nothing about the stench of synthetic food nor the stares from the other guards that made her feel in any way relaxed. She was thankful for the dark glasses on her face and the gun in her pocket. She held onto the barrel and felt some security in the hard, cold metal that she had been instructed by Lily not to use unless the circumstances were absolutely necessary.

The upper corridors were a new part of the building to Alice that hadn't been there before. They wound around the inside of the upper part of the building in spirals and had been built with reinforced trophene that Lily said had been declared indestructible.

'Just like the Titanic,' Alice had mumbled ironically but like so many of the phrases in her head, the words were lost on everyone around her. She found herself almost desperately clinging to the memories she held before the Storm. Travelling on the Transporters made her feel a thrill of excitement. When she closed her eyes, she was charging like a thunderbolt along the Underground into central London: Elephant and Castle, Lambeth North, Waterloo, Embankment… When she was a little girl, the closer to the city she got, the more excited she had always become. But as she had travelled into the Industry headquarters with Lily that morning, the excitement had soon dissipated and transformed itself to fear at the thought of stepping inside the building again. She held on tightly to the gun.

When they reached the outer section of the Control Room, Alice shivered. It was the same place that she had visited on so many occasions when she'd been a part of the Industry, dreaming up big plans for the future with the people she thought she could trust. Now, the additional sections that had been built up around the outside gave no indication that it would be somewhere that was familiar to her.

Guards milled around the corridors, politely nodding their heads to them both as they stood waiting for the corridor to clear.

'There will be others working in there, under Catherine Fordham's direction,' whispered Lily, nervously. 'This is incredibly risky.'

'But we can't execute the whole plan without her knowledge,' said Alice, shaking her head. 'We have no idea what we're doing here otherwise. Even if we were to take down the Industry we can't leave all those people there indefinitely.'

'But if we're caught, we'll be joining them. No one stands in our way, Alice – we may have no choice but to defend ourselves.'

Alice shuddered at the thought of being forced to use violence against the guards – but if they were caught, she doubted Elizabet would freeze her again. A bullet to her head would likely be Elizabet's choice.

'I know,' she said, firmly. 'So let's make this work.'

As they reached the final ante-chamber, Lily paused in front of a small, nondescript metal door with a large keypad. She punched a long series of numbers and letters into it before the plate slid open just enough for the two of them to squeeze inside.

'This is a highly restricted area,' whispered Lily. 'The code is only available to the highest-ranking officials within the Industry.' She smiled. 'But as Carter may have told you, this is my third tenure here and I've managed to charm some of the most granite-like Controller Generals into sharing information.'

Alice bit her lip nervously and narrowed her eyes, hidden by the dark glasses she wore as part of her uniform. 'Here goes nothing,' she said quietly and they stepped inside as the metal plate door closed behind them.

The first thing that struck Alice was the low-level buzz and hum of the machines at work. She trailed two steps behind Lily, the mass of screens, dials and switches that covered the walls making her gaze flit from one section to the next, both exhilarating and confusing her simultaneously. A huge map projected onto one wall displayed what Alice recognised as London with the borders of the Community overlaid in a thick green line, circling the loop inside the river and then the areas beyond scattered with red blotches that she imagined could only have been what Angel and Carter referred to as the Village and the Township.

While the layout of the room was different, and there had been several extensions of the space within it, Alice felt a deathly sickness as she remembered being tied to the chair and interrogated in the middle of the Control Room in the moments before Kunstein had led her down the stairs to the Catacombs to her eighty-year sleep. Instinctively, she rubbed her hand over the empty space of her stomach where her baby Jescha had been and felt a gnarling sadness deep within her core.

In the corner of the room, where she had always seen William Wilson crouched over his computer, playing with various dials, sat a small girl in her mid to late teens deftly dancing her fingers over a screen that replicated the action onto the large projection in front of her. Light orange-coloured ringlets poured down her back and the shock of the similarity between the girl and her old friend Quinn forced a sharp intake of breath. Her stomach churned as images of the betrayal flashed in front of her.

Barnes.

The chair.

Filip towering over her.

The lights flickering red and green in front of her.

Her baby.

Alice swallowed hard. The pale-skinned girl at the desk tapped at a keyboard and then cleared her throat as they approached.

'You were quick, Elizabet,' she said quietly. 'I wasn't expecting you to be back so soon.'

Alice's heart thumped in her chest. Izzy? Coming here?

'It's just me, Catherine,' she heard Lily say above the pounding in her ears. 'I need to talk to you urgently.'

The girl span around in her chair and came to a sharp stop in front of Lily. Her milk-white skin, dotted with light-brown freckles framed with dark auburn hair, perfectly curled, looked so much like Quinn that Alice felt her jaw drop open. She closed it quickly and tightened her lips into a neutral smile. The girl nodded in their direction.

'Well, you'll need to make it quick; I have a briefing with the new Controller General in about thirty minutes,' she said efficiently, and turned back toward her screen for a moment before locking it so that the projection on the wall in front of her turned black. 'And you needed to bring a guard with you, because…?'

'It's a confidential matter,' said Lily, calmly. 'And one which needs your attention immediately.' She looked across at Alice. 'Elizabet sent me to brief you directly as she has been unavoidably detained with an incident in the Food Plant.'

'An incident?' Fordham looked at her, concerned, and moved her hands away from the keyboard, all the time watching Alice.

'Nothing you need to worry about,' said Lily carefully. 'But she sent us to consult with you on her behalf regarding any modifications to the Model.'

Catherine Fordham eyed her suspiciously. 'I am under strict instructions not to discuss changes with anyone but Elizabet. Not even the other Controller General, Ariel Warren-Davenport.' She glanced at the door. 'And how did you get in here, anyway? This is a classified area not available to anyone other than the Controller Generals, under Elizabet's instructions.'

Alice shuffled uncomfortably as Catherine stared at them directly, her hand moving to a button under the desk. As Alice looked at the button, she took a deep breath. She knew she had to stick to the plan they'd agreed on – whatever the cost. Refusing to allow the regret and hesitation she felt show, she drew her gun and pointed it at the girl, her hands shaking.

'Don't you dare touch that,' she said, her voice stern. 'Move away from the desk now.'

Catherine froze, looking first at Lily and then at Alice, eyes wide with fear and shock. She backed slowly away from the desk in her wheeled chair, her eyes flitting from the gun to Alice and then to Lily.

'It's an alarm,' said Alice, nervously. 'She was about to press it.'

Lily nodded and pulled out her gun too, moving around so that it was pointing directly at the girl's head. Alice felt sick inside as she watched the terror on Catherine's face.

'What the hell do you think you're doing?' said Catherine, loudly. 'I'm just doing my job. Are you rebels? Lily? You're working with the rebels?'

Alice looked at the girl who reminded her so much of the young, innocent Quinn, executing orders but understanding very little of the detail and motivation that underpinned them. She felt sorry for her and at the same time hated what she was doing, but held her gun firmly and reminded herself that, like Quinn, the girl presented a real threat to what they needed to do.

'Listen to me,' said Lily, her voice stern and clear. 'What you're about to do for Elizabet is going to destroy whatever humanity it is that we have left. So, instead, you're going to help us to work out how exactly we are going to save the lives of thousands of people and—' she cocked her gun and placed it against Catherine's temple '—you're not going to indicate that anything is amiss should Elizabet enter the room. Do you understand me?' She swallowed hard.

The girl nodded. 'I'm just an engineer,' she said. 'I'm a censomics expert, that's all. I don't know anything about destroying humanity. I'm not a bad person, I'm a Descendant – you know that.'

Alice felt herself becoming angry – less with the girl but more at the manifestation she represented. 'As if that means anything,' she said with a disgusted tone.

'What do you want from me?' The girl seemed genuinely terrified and yet there was something about her that Alice did not trust. 'I'm under strict instructions from Elizab—'

'You're now under strict instructions from us,' interrupted Alice, trying to make her voice sound authoritative but less threatening.

Lily turned to her. 'We're going to need Catherine to speak to Izzy before we leave here otherwise she'll come looking for her.' She exhaled deeply. 'We can't risk Izzy suspecting anything before the others arrive.'

'Others arrive?' This time Catherine looked shocked to the point of terror. 'What do you mean others? Where from? Not from the North? They're not coming here? Tell me they're not coming here.'

Alice screwed her forehead. 'You know about the others? You know that there are other people out there?'

'Yes,' said Catherine, her voice trembling. 'I don't know much but I know she speaks to them.'

'You're in communication with the Village and the Township?' This time it was Alice's turn to voice her disbelief.

Catherine looked confused. 'The Village? You mean those wild animals that run around outside building fires and living like Neanderthals? Of course I don't mean them. I mean the *others*.'

Alice moved closer and grabbed hold of her workwear jacket. 'Tell me what you're talking about,' she whispered, her gun dangerously close to Catherine's skull. 'What others?'

'I can't,' trembled the girl. 'Elizabet would kill me if I did.'

'And I will kill you if you don't,' said Alice, pushing the barrel of the gun between her eyes, frightening herself with her own anger. She paused for a moment, disgusted by her own vehemence and anger towards the girl. She bit her tongue. 'You need to help us,' she said, less unkindly.

From one of the control panels there came a clicking sound and Lily nudged her sharply as a red light blinked on the dashboard near Catherine.

'There's someone coming,' she hissed. 'We need to do something.'

Alice looked around, her eyes scanning every wall, her gun still fixed on their captive. 'You need to do everything we tell you to, otherwise I will kill both you and your Controller General,' she said, her voice wavering. 'I will have my weapon pointed on you at all times. One movement toward that button or any indication to Elizabet that anything is wrong and I will shoot you. Do you understand me?'

The girl nodded silently, her lip quivering. Alice motioned to Lily to get behind a cabinet that stood in one corner of the room. She crouched underneath the long desk on the opposite side of the room, her body pushed against the desk edging where she couldn't be seen. The gun barrel remained pointed at Catherine, who watched her nervously. Within seconds there was the grating metal sound of the door opening and, for the second time in as many days, Alice found herself in the same room as the child she had taken in as her own. The child who had betrayed her in the cruellest way.

'Here are the instructions.' She threw a sheaf of handwritten papers down in front of Catherine without the pleasantries of a welcome or hello. 'Make sure you execute these exactly as I have written them, without exception. I would suggest you don't have any questions or concerns but, if you do, direct them to me only. Ariel has very little background in matters relating to the Model so I am managing these modifications myself.' She sighed heavily. 'As I am most things,' she added.

Catherine nodded and leafed through the papers wordlessly, her hands shaking wildly as she did so.

'A thank you would be a good start,' said Elizabet sharply. 'Or at least an acknowledgement that you fully understand my order.'

'Y-yes,' stammered Catherine, her gaze drifting to the cabinet where Lily sat crouched in the shadows, her gun pointing at Elizabet's head. The Controller General turned and looked around the room.

'What's the matter with you?' she said. 'You're not usually this pathetic. Has something happened with the Model that I need to know about?'

Alice held her breath underneath the desk and moved closer, controlling the desperate nervous beat of her heart until it stilled in the seconds between each breath. She watched as every thought and action that could possibly have entered and left Catherine's head did so in the matter of a millisecond.

'No,' said Catherine, preoccupying herself with shuffling the papers, scanning each sheet with trembling hands. 'Nothing wrong here.' Her eyes left the paper for a second and glanced across at Alice who held the gun at head height and shook her head slowly.

Elizabet took a seat on the desk and moved threateningly closer to Catherine until her body was almost touching the girl. 'Let me remind you that I am the most powerful person in the Community,' Alice heard her whisper. 'If there are any secrets around here, I will find them and I will ensure that those who are harbouring any sort of confidences or surprises – however small they think they are – will be punished under the most severe of terms.'

The girl visibly cowered at the threat and held tightly onto the papers that shook in her hand. 'There…' she began, nervously. 'There was one thing, Controller General.'

'Yes,' snapped Elizabet, her face edging closer to the girl.

Alice's heart sank as she watched Catherine stuttering her question. She held the gun in her hand, ready to shoot.

'I wanted to ask about this point here,' she said, pointing to one of the pages. 'When we wake up these people in the Catacombs after their surgery, you've said you want them to immediately be sent outside of the Barricades to attack the other villages.' She paused. 'Do you think we need to allow them some rehabilitation time? They may not be strong enough to—'

Elizabet stood up and spoke in a half-whisper. 'Your role is to execute, not to question,' she said in a dangerously gentle tone. 'These people have been frozen for too long to be much of an asset to us, except as our warrior force. They have slept long enough and need to earn the vast amount of resource poured into them. They have been a drain on us for far too long.' She pushed a piece of paper into Catherine's face. 'Except the ones on this page – I will deal with them myself. Do you understand me?' The last phrase was almost without any sound at all.

'Yes,' stuttered the girl and exhaled heavily. Visibly terrified of Elizabet, she looked through the papers carefully and methodically.

'Are you really going to do this to them?' she asked finally. 'They are real people with families and...' she paused for a moment. 'My sister is on this list.'

'Your sister was frozen because she was caught trying to make a musical instrument, wasn't she?' said Izzy. 'A rebellious act?'

'Yes, but I don't think she—' began Catherine, her hands shaking.

'There are no exceptions.' Elizabet moved her face uncomfortably close to Catherine's. 'Our world is changing and you either work with me or I add every other member of your friends and family to this list. Including that child of your sister. Now are you with me?'

'Yes,' stammered Catherine. 'Please don't hurt her.'

Alice held her gun tightly and glanced across at Lily, who too was poised to fire.

'I want you to start the thaw process so that they are ready to be released on the day of the broadcast,' said Elizabet, her temper subsiding. 'The results of the experiments I have been undertaking in the Lab will be completed soon. Now that I've identified the part of the frontal lobe that causes rebellion we can ensure that the new generation of Lab Mades we create are a simple breed. And those in the Catacombs, with some additional drugs in their wake-up serum, will come back into this world completely compliant.' She smiled proudly, looking incredibly pleased with herself.

'How will we manage those people who have friends and relatives amongst the Sleepers?' said Catherine timidly. 'Not that I disagree with you but there may be some reluctance among them to accept that we are reducing the mental capacity of their loved ones to something that's—' she hesitated whilst finding the word '—something that is less than the people they were before.'

'We won't be telling them,' said Elizabet. 'Once you have administered the medication and it has altered the part of the brain that is responsible for autonomous thought, the Sleepers will speak for themselves and their so-called loved ones will need to listen.' She smiled that sweet, sickly smile that Alice remembered so well. 'And, besides, anyone who has anything to say about this will need to deal directly with me and we have already discussed how the levels of punishment for misdemeanours in this Community will change now that I am Controller General. Haven't we, Catherine?'

The girl shuddered visibly. 'Yes, Controller General,' she responded, her head buried deep in the papers.

'So, if there's anything you need to tell me, you should do it now,' said Elizabet. 'You don't want me to inform *them*, do you?'

The silence felt icy cold and fell heavy and thick like the softest of snow into the room.

'There's nothing,' whispered the girl, her voice stilted and short. 'But if anything comes up, I will call you directly.' She gulped. 'Like we discussed.'

'Good,' said Elizabet brightly and jumped off the desk, gymnastically. 'I'll be in the Lab if you need me this afternoon, and then I'll be meeting and greeting some of the Lab Made underlings in the Community with Ariel. You can arrange to have someone contact me if it's urgent.'

Catherine smiled weakly and nodded. 'Of course,' she said quietly, and then Alice watched as Izzy skipped from the room, a nasty smirk winding its way across her face. She moved her gun hand, aching with cramp and started to move back into the room when the door reopened and Elizabet poked her head around the door.

'I almost forgot about Chamber One,' she told Catherine. 'Don't forget that the thing that resides in there is to be kept separate.' She laughed to herself. 'I want that cheap council estate half-breed to watch all of this.'

Alice's temper snapped and she raised the gun above the desk, her hand shaking but firmly poised.

But before she could pull the trigger, the door snapped shut with a metalling ping and Izzy had gone from her sight.

Chapter Nine

The Journey

Outside the Barricades, Carter held the torch high above his head and illuminated the length of the tunnel. About four or five metres in front of him was the roof fall. He inched towards it slowly, tapping the line of wood and impacted mud as he went. When he arrived at the pile of earth that reached from floor to ceiling, he pushed his fist through it until he could feel cool air the other side.

The wooden beams that reinforced the tunnel were still in place – it looked to him like Lily had simply removed two of the boards and scrabbled a large amount of dirt downwards until it had formed a steep mound blocking the walkway. He cursed himself for not looking closely when they had first come through, but at the same time, he thought, maybe Lily had done the right thing by forcing him out into the Deadlands. He shrugged to himself – maybe she did it the wrong way, but for the right reasons.

He dug through the dirt with the small trowel Lily had put in his bag and pulled it apart with his hands, just above head height. As he burrowed through it, very little extra earth fell through. The thin triangular-shaped mound narrowed right at the top and he estimated that by squeezing his body through the roof waste as high as he could, he would be able to make it through. Carter pulled the square of fabric and plastic goggles Lily had given him from his bag and fashioned a makeshift mask from the materials. The earth was dry – and thinner than he'd expected – but still he needed to find a foothold in the wall to get enough leverage to push his way through. One of the props that had been used to hold up the roof was bent out at an angle and he snapped it from its hold, helping him to ram the earth through and create enough of a hole to wedge himself past.

Halfway, with his head and arms through the dirt and his legs still squirming through on the other side of the tunnel, Carter almost started to laugh at the ridiculousness of the situation. Just a few months ago, he had been training to become the most powerful person in his world and now he was fighting his way through a mound of soil, his hair, ears and nose caked in dark-brown muddy dust. He wriggled his whole body and his legs, gaining more traction until he was able to tilt his body through and slump onto the ground on the other side of the roof fall.

He lay there for a moment, breathing in the dank air of the tunnel, gathering his thoughts. His first stop would be the Township to warn them of Elizabet's plans and then he would let the people of the Village know they needed support and he would lead them back to the Community. His thoughts wandered to Isabella lying helpless in the bed in the Lab, and he felt sick. Getting her out of there was one thing but destroying the Industry was a whole different game – and one with a very short timescale. He knew he had to do both.

He jumped to his feet and started to move along the tunnel, following it carefully, remembering to crouch down where it started to gradually slope upwards until he had to crouch down and crawl on all fours through the carefully constructed wood-lined passageway.

He got down low on his stomach under the smashed-brick part of the tunnel that led into the annexe to the old cellar under the old farmhouse where they had found Lucia. He bent down and sat in the space near where she had been. His heart ached as he read the words she had carved into the floor.

I AM SORRY.

He rubbed dust over the words with the edge of his shoe. A fresh, cool breeze drifted in from the hole in the wall that led to the main cellar, sweet and filled with the scent of the world outside. Carter took a deep breath and squeezed into the cellar, full of empty glass bottles, barrels and crates. The low, rectangular space with faded-white painted walls was filled with a dim light that came from the room above. Carter climbed up onto the table and then onto the chair he and Lily had placed there and hauled his body up into the pale darkness of the kitchen of the old farmhouse.

As he sat on the floor and looked around at the room, everything was just as they had left it. Outside, the sun had all but set; tiny ribbons of pink sky laced with dark clouds that drifted past the window and the air had cooled to an evening chill. It had taken all afternoon to get through the tunnels, and now there wasn't much ground Carter could make before nightfall.

He pulled out a box of chicker from his bag and picked at it thoughtfully, unfolding the map that Lily had printed for him. It was a combination of lines and swirls from the old world, overlaid with prints and sketches that Lily had downloaded from the Industry servers. On top of that, she had traced a route between the farmhouse, the Township and the Village.

Carter stood up and looked out across the garden wall and out towards the east, where the land flattened out into a thick forest.

He opened the bag again and pulled out a battered bronze compass, engraved with old writing and letters. The needle span around, the directions clear and sharp on the dial, and Carter turned his body until he could work out where north-east lay. He held it to the light. It would be dark in less than thirty minutes and there would be no guarantee of shelter in the forest. Already the shadow of evening was forming in the sky. He made up his mind. He would rest in the house and start out early in the morning.

Upstairs in one of the bedrooms, Carter lay down on an old mattress and pulled down a handful of books from the shelves. He loved books. Different books, new books. When he'd first arrived in his mother's Village, after leaving the Community, he'd found great comfort in reading and it had helped him to understand the old world and all its idiosyncrasies.

After spending his whole life in the Community, everything had seemed so unreal and alien, and devouring the words written in the books in his mother's home had helped him comprehend the outside world and everything that had been forbidden. He thought back to his mother's house, in the heart of the Village, built high in the trees, and could almost feel the comforting sway of the branches and swish of the leaves. Part of him ached to be back there, and he let his mind drift there until finally his eyes, heavy with sleep, closed, and he fell into a world of dreams.

The next morning he rose early, before the sun had started to throw golden rays across the land surrounding the farm. As he left the house, he walked past the grave he and Lily had dug for Lucia and cut down some lavender, placing it on the soil. Already, the earthy mound had started to become overgrown with young plants and creepers, some small flowers pushing through the earth. He paused for a moment and stood silently thinking of everything Isabella had told him about the young girl who'd wanted to make a difference in the world.

A halo of crows circled above him, cawing loudly, their wings whipped by the light wind that had accompanied the gentle rise of the orangey-tinged morning sun. Carter reached into his bag for a bottle of water and drank some, then dropped a little on the new flowers decorating Lucia's grave before he took the path that led up in to the forest that loomed ahead of him.

Although it was still before noon by the time he reached the centre of the forest, there was very little light ahead of him. The terrain was rough, and the path was so ragged with brambles and weeds that they tore at his clothes and ripped thin cuts into his arms and legs. He checked his direction with the compass and then reviewed the map; if he continued through the trackless forest he estimated that he could make it to the Township as it got dark if he picked up his pace.

Where he could, he ran – but most of the time Carter's journey was slow and difficult. He climbed deftly over mossy trunks of fallen trees and darted through grassy clearings until he came to the edge of the forest and a glassy blue lake. He took out the map again and measured the size of it against his thumb. The last of the afternoon sparkled off the surface of the water; deep-blue ripples extending outwards towards him like gentle waves. For a moment, Carter stood there and watched as a brightly coloured bird swooped down across the water and pulled out a fish, flying across back into the forest with it flapping in his beak. For a moment, he was lost in the beauty of the world outside the Barricades.

'Everyone deserves this,' he whispered to himself as he set off around the edge of the lake, thinking of the thousands locked deep in the Catacombs. 'Everyone.'

As the sun faded into darkness and the moon took its position in the sky, Carter reached the stockades of the Township. The entrance was heavily guarded; several men and women stood with sticks cut from large saplings and shaped into pointed spears. Flaming ochre torches were thrust into the ground in a semi-circle in front of the gate, spitting occasionally down into the dirt. He breathed a sigh of relief and held the compass tightly in his hand, grateful for his safe arrival but slightly nervous at the prospect of meeting with the people of the Township. He remembered how Frida has graciously let them leave, just days before, when he'd explained how they were planning to overthrow the Industry. He hoped she'd be welcoming and kind.

Carter stepped apprehensively out of the shadow of the trees and moved slowly to the front of the group led by Eli who immediately drew his spear. 'Hello, Eli,' he said, approaching cautiously. 'I have something very important to tell you. Let me speak with Frida.' The remainder of the group of men and women of the Township lifted their spears above their heads and aimed them at Carter. They inched closer to him as Eli eyed him suspiciously, scrutinising his tattered clothes and scratched skin.

'Look at the state of you,' he sneered. 'First one and then the other. Two Warrens within the space of a few days! We certainly weren't expecting a reunion so fast!' He leaned out and grabbed Carter by the shoulder, pulling him into the circle of spear holders. 'I knew you'd never made it into the Community. Useless coward.'

Carter jerked himself away from Eli and grabbed his bag tightly – rage and confusion rising inside of him. 'What do you mean two Warrens? Is Samuel here?' He shook his head as Eli advanced with his spear. 'I am here to warn you,' he said, angrily. 'You are in danger. You are *all* in danger. You don't need to attack me. I am not your enemy.'

Eli pulled Carter close to him. 'We have been in danger since the moment you and your useless brother decided to take on those that live behind the Barricades.' He nodded to two of the burlier men standing at the front. 'Take him inside,' he said. 'Put him the same hole as that loutish brother of his and tell two of the others inside the gate to take your place out here.' He took a knife and slashed the straps of Carter's rucksack, snatching it from him. 'And I'll keep hold of this,' he said, menacingly. The men stepped forward and they grabbed an arm each, dragging Carter through the gate and into the Township, with unnecessary force.

'There's no need for you to do this,' said Carter, struggling but attempting to remain calm. 'I just need to tell you about what the Industry has planned. Take me to Frida!' He tried to get his arms free from the guards. 'You are in danger,' he yelled back out to the stockades but Eli ignored him.

Small groups of people gathered, whispering as he was paraded through the centre of the Township and guided towards a small brick-built hut at the back from which came a series of thuds and then shouting. 'Where are you taking me?' demanded Carter. 'I want to see Frida!' The guards said nothing until they unbolted the door and shoved him headlong into another man who was banging on the other side. Both of them careered onto the bed and the guards grunted, slamming the door tight behind them.

'Samuel?' Carter got up off the man he could identify simply by smell.

'Carter?' Samuel, equally surprised, and – Carter noted – not as unpleasantly surprised to see him as he usually was. 'What the hell are you doing here?' His tone darkened. 'I thought you were supposed to be defeating the Industry?' His voice lowered to a whisper. 'Where is

Lily? What did you do with her? Did she get captured?' He leapt off the bed. 'Where is she?' he repeated, this time pulling at his clothes and pummelling Carter's chest. Then he hugged him tightly.

'I've never been so pleased to see you,' he said, finally, his voice a range of emotions.

'Samuel,' breathed Carter, heavily. 'Stop squashing me, you idiot, and I'll tell you.'

They sat on the floor in the darkness, sharing a small glass of water. Carter sipped intermittently then passed it to his brother, wishing he had the food from his rucksack. They shared their stories about what had happened in the days since they'd been apart.

'So Elvira's going to be okay?' he said

Samuel nodded dolefully. 'But Eli has kept me here. He's going to kill me to prove to the people of the Township that Frida is too weak to do it herself and therefore a bad leader for them and that he will exact the revenge she should have done when they found out I killed Saul.' He spat on the floor. 'Which means they'll probably kill you too now.'

'What about the girl who tried to help you? What happened to her?' said Carter.

'Leanor?' Samuel shrugged, grumpily. 'Eli took her off somewhere after I smashed up that flying drone thing you sent; I don't think she'll be back to help us any time soon.'

Carter shook his head, exasperated. 'If you hadn't smashed—'

'I thought it was a weapon of *theirs*,' said Samuel, sulkily. 'The last time I saw one of them was the last time I saw Company Five, I told you that.'

Carter exhaled loudly. 'Well, if she can't help us then we need to work out a way to get out of here ourselves and back to the Village.'

'But I thought we needed the help of the Township. You said it yourself – there are thousands of them. Even with them, your idea is never going to work. There isn't enough time. Even if we could get out of here and leave in the morning, we've got four days to get to the Village and back to the Community.' Samuel sat despondently, kicking his foot against the bed. 'We never should have come here in the first place.'

'Well, we did, and we're back here again,' said Carter, irritated. 'Now, tell me how often they come in here – who comes and what happens. We *have* to get out of there. We don't have an option and I don't think we can rely on Frida to help us – we have to warn the Village. Now help me get the legs off this bed.'

When the morning came, Carter's back ached from sleeping on the cold stone floor, while Samuel had taken the mattress. 'I've been here longer,' Samuel had chortled as they'd finally stopped planning their escape in the early hours of the morning. 'Night, brother.'

He rubbed the base of his sore spine as he crouched behind the door, one wooden leg of the bed firmly gripped in his other hand. The thin crunch of foot against gravel came close to the building and Carter tensed his body.

'When he comes in, smack him over the head and then we run,' hissed Samuel. 'We take the path around the back of this building and then down through the alley. We'll have to take our chances with the guards.'

Carter nodded and grabbed their makeshift wooden pole with both hands, ready to swing. When the door opened, he stepped back and raised his arms and, as he swung downwards, he noticed the soft curls of Frida, stopping just short of the back of her head as she entered the room.

'Do it!' shouted Samuel, annoyed. 'Just do it!'

Frida span around and saw Carter, shocked, the wood falling to the floor at his feet.

'You boys thought it was Eli coming?' she said, amused, picking the bed leg from the floor and holding it out in front of her. She shut the door and stood in front of it before Samuel could bolt through.

'Frida,' stuttered Carter. 'We… we were…'

'Yes, you were trying to escape. Eli guessed that, which is why he suggested that I come in to give you your breakfast.' She smiled. 'I should have warned you it was me.' She pulled her other hand from beneath her black velvet cloak and a showed the glint of the metal barrel of a gun. Her smile dropped. 'Now sit down, both of you.'

Carter held his hands out openly in front of him in surrender and moved carefully towards Samuel and sat next to him on the mattress. 'I didn't come here to cause any trouble – or to try to rescue my brother,' he said, slowly. 'I didn't even know Samuel was here.'

'I believe you,' said Frida, pointing the gun first at Carter and then at Samuel. 'But now you are here, what is important to me is what is happening behind the Barricades and how I can protect my people from them.'

'You can't protect them,' protested Samuel. 'We're all in danger unless we overcome them in some way. My brother here has a plan but while we're being kept prisoners by Eli here, you, the Villagers and Angel are in danger. You must let us go.'

Frida raised her eyebrows. 'A plan?' she said. 'Now that is interesting. But I have a separate problem. Unless I prove to my people that

I am a strong leader and exact your punishment, our people will be at war with each other. Eli is intent on deposing me as the leader of this Township – unless, of course, I kill you.'

Carter felt a cold chill run down his spine. 'You're a good woman,' he said. 'I helped your daughter when she was sick and I know you understand that we cannot stand back and let the Industry continue with what they have been doing.' He paused. 'They're planning to kill your people and mine. One of our party got injured, as you know, but myself and Angel carried on. We entered the underground Catacombs and discovered a laboratory where the leader is experimenting on some of their people to develop a subservient race that she can arm and send out here to destroy your people and mine.'

He shook his head. 'We need to unite in order to find a way to overcome them. What the new Controller General is capable of makes what has happened before pale into insignificance. Our only chance of staying alive is to expose them to their own people.'

Frida looked thoughtful. 'And how do you intend to do that?'

Carter motioned to Frida to put the gun down. 'There will be a live broadcast, on huge screens that will be played to the entire Community,' he started. 'We intend to intercept that broadcast and explain who we are and that the Industry have been lying to their people for years.'

'We?' Frida looked at him quizzically. 'You and your brother here?'

Carter paused. 'Not just us,' he said, looking from Samuel to Frida and lowering his voice. 'While we were in the Catacombs, we discovered something very important, which will prove to the people that they have been lied to.'

Frida shook her head. 'I can't imagine anything that would change the minds of those people,' she said. 'Even finding out about life outside those walls that surround them.'

'Have you ever heard of a girl called Alice Davenport?'

Frida's jaw dropped in shock. '*The* Alice Davenport?' she exclaimed. 'The same girl that came to our people almost one hundred years ago?'

Carter nodded. 'She's alive and well,' he said. 'And right now, she's waiting for me to return with support from our people and yours to help defeat the Industry.'

Frida rubbed her brow and shook her head. 'That's…' she began. 'That's… impossible.'

'Well, it's true,' said Carter. 'You know I am not a liar. I am giving you this chance to help us.' He looked Frida deep in the eyes. 'We need you,' he said, finally.

Frida shook her head and turned the gun to Samuel. 'If you had not made a deal with my husband, we would never be in this situation.'

'But you would – *we* would,' continued Carter, frustrated. 'These plans were already underway, regardless of any actions we took that got us to this point. The leader, a girl called Elizabet, has designs on capturing an area fifty miles in every direction of the Community as it stands today. She *will* come here and kill you all and all this—' he waved his arm outwards towards the Township '—all this will be gone.'

Frida looked pensive, considering what Carter was saying. 'I hear you,' she said, curtly, and lowered the gun a little, 'but we are afraid of what will happen next. If there is anything we can do to save ourselves, then we will. Eli is determined to make an example of you.'

'The best thing you can do to save yourselves is to fight with us,' said Carter. 'We are meeting with the rebels on the inside in four days' time at the blue south-west gate at the Community.' He rubbed his forehead thoughtfully. 'We can finally settle this and go back to living the lives we have always wanted to, safe in the knowledge that the people of the Community are free to choose the types of lives that they wish to too.'

Frida glanced at Samuel who was looking earnestly at Carter. 'You seem to have forgiven your brother very easily,' she said. 'Did you forget that he almost got you killed?'

'Forgiveness and acceptance are very different things,' said Carter. 'Samuel made an error of judgement and has already made an effort to try to make amends. He brought our friend here when she was in trouble and I believe he also tried to save a girl from your Township, Leanor, when he thought she was in danger.' He nodded slowly. 'Although, yes, Samuel betrayed his friends, and caused the death of Saul and two innocent people, he has also risked his own life to help others.'

Frida shook her head. 'If I let you go, I put myself and those loyal to me in danger,' she said. 'But if what you say is true and I keep you here, then we will all die anyway.'

'We must leave,' said Carter, edging towards the door. 'You know in your heart you are doing the right thing.' He held out his hand and handed Frida the warm bronze compass that he had wedged into his pocket. 'Take this,' he said, quickly. 'Either follow us south-west to the gate or north east until you are far enough away that they cannot find you. If you cannot be with us, please do not be against us.' He pushed Samuel ahead of him towards the door.

Frida stood, her mouth slightly open and her eyes bright, turning the compass over in her hands without looking at it. 'Move quickly,' she said, more quietly this time, gesturing towards to the door.

'Thank you,' said Carter, his eyes focusing directly on her as Samuel pulled open the door and stepped outside. 'Thank you, Frida.'

He followed Samuel out of the door, closed it quickly and bolted towards the back of the building. His brother was already making for the high stockade, taking large strides towards the gate. Behind them, Carter could hear the sound of shouting and the shaft and feather of an arrow passed his shoulder so close that he felt the wind-whirr of it on his skin.

'Run,' he shouted to Samuel. 'Faster!'

As they reached the gate, Carter had caught him up, but the group running behind them had grown to four- or five-strong. Samuel, breathing heavily, made a foothold with his hands.

'Get to the top,' he wheezed, 'and pull me over the top.'

Carter put his shoe into Samuel's interlocked fingers and hoisted himself to the top of the thick posts that surrounded the Township. Another arrow sped past him as he held out his hand to Samuel, who used it to propel himself to the top of the barricades. The bulk of Samuel's weight tore into his muscles as the darts whirred past them, sticking deep into the wooden posts. He pulled hard on Samuel's arm until his brother launched to the top, letting out an excruciating yell as he covered Carter's body and pushed him over the stockade to the other side. They slammed into the floor with a horrific thud, Carter feeling an electrifying pain in one shoulder. He grabbed Samuel by the arm, pulling him deep into the forest while some of the people of the Township struggled with climbing the stockade, others starting to pour through the gate.

'Keep running,' he panted to Samuel, who let out a periodic grunt of pain. 'Whatever you do, don't stop.'

They pelted through the forest at terrific pace for what seemed like hours, running up and over fallen branches and darting through clearings until eventually, the sounds behind them diminished into nothing and they were finally alone. They threw themselves into a deep hollow and waited. When the coolness of the forest turned silent and their breathing had almost returned to normal, Carter looked over at Samuel who lay on his stomach, the back of his chest moving in and out in a shallow beat, his eyes tightly closed.

A long, thin shard of wood stuck out from his back, a thick dark circle of blood soaking his clothes where it had pierced the skin.

'I've been hit, brother,' he wheezed, between deep breaths. 'They've shot me.'

Chapter Ten

The Community

In the Control Room, still trembling with rage, Alice pulled herself up from under the desk, the pistol in her hand shaking from side to side. The vicious words that Izzy had just spoken still pierced the room like uneven shards of glass, slicing into her with painful accuracy. Not since she was a small child at school had she felt more personally affronted. Every cell in her body blazed with fury.

Catherine sat at her desk, clutching the papers, her eyes fixed on the tablet in front of her. Alice snatched the pages from her and spun her around in the chair to face her and Lily who had stormed across the room behind her.

'You see what a cruel, vindictive, terrible person she is,' Alice raged, holding the papers in front of Catherine's face. 'And what a horrific plan she has constructed. She's desperate for the chance to wield her power over everyone at any cost.' Her voice burned as the words left her mouth. 'At *any* cost,' she whispered, her throat hoarse with a tight lump of pain. She removed the dark glasses to wipe hot tears of anger from her eyes.

It was a few moments before Catherine dared to lift her head and look at Alice. She gasped in shock and then backed her chair away from her slowly. 'You're… you're…' she began.

'Alice Davenport,' said Lily, gently taking the papers from Alice's hand and leafing through them. 'Yes, she is. And, before you ask, she is the previous and only resident of Chamber One. This is the secret that the Industry have been hiding since the very beginning.'

'You mean to tell us you didn't know? Who did you think she was talking about?' Alice wheeled on the girl.

Catherine shook her head, the spiralled auburn curls looking brighter than ever against her whitened complexion. 'No, I thought…'

'Alice did not die during the birth of her first child nor was she attacked by outsiders. Despite what you may have learned at school, none of it is true.' Lily licked her finger and snapped through the papers. 'She's been in the Catacombs the whole time and now, understandably, wants the good people of the Community to know the truth about the society we live in.'

Catherine looked stunned; her eyes were wide and her mouth gaped open in shock. 'But the Model is based on—'

Alice let out an impatient huffing noise and glared at Catherine. 'Don't you get it? It's all lies constructed by the Industry to control everything. To create a whole Community of people who are so blindsided by their lies that they believe anything and everything that they are told.' She felt the temper rage inside of her again. 'There were no attacks from outside – the Barricades are there to keep you people *in*, not to keep the others out.'

Lily put her hand on Alice's shoulder. 'We need to have this conversation elsewhere,' she said calmly. 'We're not safe in here and we need to get back to Angel.' She waved her gun at the girl still dumbfounded at the desk. 'Do I need to hold this against the back of your head or are you going to help us?'

'I... I... don't know,' stuttered the girl who looked so much like Quinn that she made Alice feel nauseous. She bit at her nails furiously and tapped one foot against the floor. 'I mean, I just run the Model; I don't know how I can help you. I need to do this work for Elizabet and it's going to take days, so I can't just—'

Alice took the gun and knocked Catherine's nervous fingers away from her face with the barrel, slamming it onto the arm of the chair, scratching a dent in it. 'We need you to help us stop this,' she said viciously and then immediately regretted it as scared tears welled up in the girl's eyes.

In that moment, Alice hated herself more than she ever had before. She took the gun and placed it on the desk next to the Catherine, who looked at it briefly and then looked away. Alice pulled a chair up next to her and put one hand gently over the girl's thumb, which was beginning to flower with a bruise from the gun barrel. Catherine flinched at her touch.

'I'm sorry,' she said quietly, forcing back her own rage at Izzy. 'I'm angry and frustrated at Elizabet, at the Industry – at everything – but it's not fair for me to take that out on you.' She bit her lip. 'I know that you understand what she's doing doesn't feel right – even under the skewed rules that you live by; you know that what she wants to do to those people underground is wrong, don't you?'

She waited until, finally, Catherine nodded her head. 'I'm just a censomist,' she said quietly. 'An engineer. I've never been frozen and I don't ever want to be. I liked my life here before Elizabet. I was top of my class at the Academy and I just want to make people happy and do my job well.' She started to breathe unevenly. 'I had two babies that the Industry took away from me because they weren't good enough. I only have my sister. I just want to do well at my job. But I don't like Elizabet; she's cruel to me.' The girl started to cry a little.

'You're smart, Fordham,' said Alice, with a brief smile. 'I know you're very clever and also, whatever you've been asked to do, I know you're *able* to do it.' The girl nodded again as Alice continued. 'So, the question is – do you want to do it?'

The girl swallowed as a fat tear rolled down her cheek and onto the desk. 'I have to do it,' she whispered. 'Or she'll tell them. Or she'll kill me. Or something worse.'

'Who will she tell?' said Lily, but Alice looked up at her and shook her head.

'Catherine,' she said carefully, keeping her words simple. 'When I was here last time, there were some very bad things happened. I knew that what we were doing wasn't right for a long time but I couldn't quite decide why they weren't right. We had talked about them – we'd planned for a very long time about what we would do and how we would do it but actually making something happen – something you know that is wrong and will hurt a lot of people, well—' Alice broke off and thought for a moment '—making something happen even when you know it's what's expected of you and because you said you would do it, doesn't make it right.'

Catherine nodded dolefully. 'It's my job,' she said, finally. 'Elizabet will make me do it.'

'It might be your job right now but what about the hundreds – no, thousands – of people whose lives will be destroyed by what you're about to do? What about their families and friends?' She paused for a second and gently stroked the bruise that was forming on Catherine's thumb. 'I heard what you said to Elizabet about them. I can tell that deep inside of you, there's so much doubt about what the right thing to do really is.'

The girl nodded again and sighed heavily. And then reached under the desk and pressed the red button.

*

Every morning, as she had since she was a little girl, Catherine unwrapped one square of chicker and a piece of whiteloaf for breakfast, eating it quickly so that she could be on the early Transporter and be at her desk in the Control Room before Elizabet came in to bark her orders at her. The only time Elizabet allowed her to take a break since she had started to take over her role as Controller General was to collect her niece Melody from the Academy, the day her sister was taken for an unscheduled freezing.

'An unauthorised attempt to create a musical instrument,' the Industry official had said to her. 'The child will be put out to a family who do not have the important role you do within the Headquarters. You have twenty minutes to say goodbye. If you are back in good time, I will ensure that the child stays above ground and is allowed to prove herself.'

Melody had wept uncontrollably when Catherine arrived to say goodbye and had then swiftly been renamed to something more appropriate and rehomed on the other side of the Community where she would undergo intensive therapy to ensure the rebellious tendencies of her mother would not resurface. Catherine had been forbidden from seeing her.

'Mention the kid's name once in my presence and she gets frozen,' Elizabet had said on her first day. 'You belong to me, Fordham. I am in control of you and of her. If you prove to me you do not have the dissident qualities of your sister, you will be allowed to live.' She had smiled. 'The child is doing well,' she added. 'She barely remembers who you are any more.'

Each afternoon, Catherine waited for Elizabet to provide her with her task lists that spanned on into the late evening until she was allowed to take the last Transporter back to the small house she had been placed in with two Industry officials. It had been exactly forty days since she had last seen her sister and Melody.

*

Alice watched as everything that happened next happened so quickly and yet it seemed like it was in some sort of special slow-motion movie. She dived for the gun that she has so carefully laid on the desk, but Catherine got to it first, snatching it away from her.

She initially covered her head with her hands and closed her eyes, but then realised that while her actions would not protect her from a bullet, she was not the intended target of Catherine's shot. It was only when the door opened and Elizabet walked into the room that the sound of the gun shattered the silence. She watched as Lily leapt back behind the cabinets out of sight and Alice swore she saw the slow trajectory of the bullet as it flew across the room, catching Elizabet somewhere in the upper part of her body, although the order of all of the individual things Alice saw was confusing. Terrifyingly, Izzy made no sound – not a call nor a cry out; there was just the dull slump of her body to the floor that followed the confused look on her face as she opened the door to a gun trained on her by the Industry's Chief Censomics Engineer.

When Alice opened her eyes again, there was a sound she couldn't quite place; a thin grating sound that repeated itself over and over. She looked up. The door bucked back and forth, automatically closing and opening itself on the body of Elizabet that was lying across the threshold, legs being clipped by the sliding piece of metal.

'Lily,' she mouthed, meaning to speak but no sound came out when she tried. 'Lily, we need to move her and lock the door.'

Whether Lily had understood her or perhaps had the same idea didn't matter; within seconds they were hauling Izzy's body from the doorway and the metal plate slammed shut. There was a further clunk of metal as Catherine dropped the gun to the desk and sat down, putting her head in her hands. She made a muted sound like an injured animal, a grumble that gestated into a low-level disconcerting wail of a sound.

'She's not dead,' said Lily, pulling the girl across the floor and feeling Izzy's neck for a pulse. 'Her heartbeat is weak – but she's not dead.' An ugly smear of blood wound its way across the floor from underneath her body. Catherine sat whimpering at the desk while, for a moment, Alice sat shell-shocked, biting at the half-moon cuticles of her fingers in absolute silence.

'We can't stay here,' she whispered, finally. 'She can't stay here – none of us can.'

A small wail came from Catherine's direction while Izzy's breathing was shallow and irregular.

'I agree,' said Lily, scanning the room. 'We need to get her back to the house. Angel said she knows something about medicine.'

'She needs a hospital,' said Alice, shaking her head 'And besides, how on earth are we supposed to get her out of here – there's no way she can walk and—'

'I can't believe you want to save her after everything you have said that she is going to do,' said Catherine, bitterly, lifting her head from the desk, her eyes red-rimmed and her cheeks blotchy.

'We need her alive to show the people of the Community who she really is and what she has planned,' said Alice, pulling herself off the floor and staring at Izzy who lay crumpled in front of her. 'Killing her is not the answer – not right now, at least.'

She scanned the room, her eyes ablaze within confusion. 'Now what can we use to get her out of here?'

*

As Alice started to scratch the blood from the floor, Lily disappeared out in the ante chambers of the Control Room and returned with a trolley and some dark sheets of plastic-type material.

'We can't get her out of this building and across the Community without arousing suspicion,' said Alice. 'We need to take her to the Laboratory and keep her there.'

Lily nodded. 'There will be some sedatives and supplies there, at least, and we can bring Angel here to work on her.' She lifted Izzy from the floor and located the wound on her shoulder, binding it with a thick piece of gauze that had an almost metallic sheen to it.

'This should stem the bleeding until we can get her into the Lab,' she said, working deftly as Alice poked around the Control Room. Catherine sat at the desk watching them, her eyes flitting back and forth between the two of them.

'What's going to happen to me?' she asked, nervously. 'Are you going to tell anyone?'

'You're going to help us,' replied Alice, 'that's what's going to happen.' She moved towards Lily, who was jabbing a small hypodermic into Elizabet's arm.

'We need to keep her sedated until we can secure her and work out if we can save her,' said Lily, pressing an extra film of gauze into the wound before checking the girl's breathing. Between them, they lifted Izzy carefully onto the trolley and covered her with the dark-coloured thin plastic sheeting, tucking in underneath her so that her body was fully covered. Catherine stood observing them from her desk, her hands shaking noticeably.

'Where are we going?' she said. 'Where are you taking her?'

She looked terrified – scared beyond belief. The more she looked at her, the more Alice could see the young outline of her old friend Quinn and she wondered how different things would have been had she been able to get through to Quinn and between them, stood up to Filip and Barnes. She smiled tightly at the girl, just enough to reassure her that she understood, but did not condone, the events of the last few minutes.

'We're going to take Izzy somewhere we can help her – and where she can't hurt anyone else,' she said, calmly. 'But we are going to need you to help us, okay? Can I trust you to do that? I don't need to use my gun?' Alice knew inside herself that the last thing she ever wanted to do was fire the weapon against anyone, least of all the spindly, studious girl who had, for once, stood up for herself against her oppressor.

Catherine nodded. 'You can trust me,' she muttered, sadly, clinging to the sheaf of papers that Elizabet had thrown at her. 'But I don't see how I can help you.'

'We'll talk about that once we've put Izzy down in the Lab,' said Alice. 'Make sure that you pre-programme anything that needs to happen with these machines for the next day or two. I don't know when we'll be coming back here.'

Catherine nodded and scanned her screen, pulling up some charts and adjusting dials on the master switchboard on the wall behind her. The deftness of her actions fascinated Alice, whose reverie was sharply broken by a concerned call from Lily.

'We need to leave,' she said, urgently. 'This place is making me nervous and I would prefer to make sure we get down to the Lab before Izzy wakes up.'

Catherine shook her head as she finished the last of her adjustments and cleared down her screen, tucking a small tablet under one arm. 'If she does ever wake up, never ever call her Izzy,' she muttered, looking up at Alice. 'She hates that name almost as much as she appears to hate you.

When Catherine tapped in the code to the keypad, the grating noise of the metal door sliding open made Alice shiver. They wheeled the trolley into the Lab as Lily checked Izzy's pulse.

'She's stable,' she said. 'But we're going to need to keep her medicated.' Alice bolted the door and glanced up at the metal grille, half-imagining she could see herself and Carter watching the scene from above. The room was pretty much how they had left it, except when Alice went into the side room that housed Elizabet's experimental subjects, she noticed one bed was empty.

She ran back into the room where Lily and Catherine huddled over a tablet. 'We need to find her,' she garbled. 'We need to find Isabella; she's gone and Carter's going to be devastated.'

Lily looked up from the tablet. 'What do you mean "gone"?'

'Not in her bed. Gone. Disappeared. Not in her bed.'

Alice rubbed her forehead and walked over to the trolley. She stood over the girl, her hands shaking as they hovered above the plastic sheeting that covered her. She bit her lip and willed Izzy to wake up.

'What happened to you?' she whispered. 'What made you so cruel?'

'Alice!' Lily pulled her away from the trolley and back to the bench where Catherine stood hunched over the small screen, her forehead crunched into tight lines as she looked up at another projection on the wall, her forefinger moving quickly back and forth.

'This room has its own network and data,' she sighed. 'There's information restricted to this room that I need to extract before we leave. Information that only Elizabet has had access to up to this point.' She scratched the side of her head nervously. 'Restricted,' she repeated.

'What information?' Alice looked up at the projection on the wall. 'This looks just like what we've seen before.'

'I need to decrypt the data,' said Catherine, filtering through text and numbers. 'I don't want to do that here.' She looked around the room, her glance falling on the trolley. 'Just in case,' she added.

Lily stood up and pushed the trolley into the annexe. 'Alice, come and help me move her to the bed,' she called, grabbing some ropes from her bag. 'I'm going to secure her and give her another shot before we bring Angel here.'

As they removed the plastic and lifted her into the bed, Alice felt her skin brush against Elizabet's and she shivered at her touch. Her mind flashed back to the nights in their old house in the Community when she would tuck the small girl into her bed and kiss her gently. The empty scar of her stomach ached as she remembered that when she had last put Izzy to sleep, she'd been just weeks from having her own child. A desperate feeling overwhelmed her. She doubled up as her stomach made her retch violently.

'I hate her,' she whispered. 'I hate what she's done.'

Lily eyed her critically. 'You need to get out of here,' said Lily, shaking away the memory from her. 'You're too emotional about her and might do something you regret. You should get away from her, from this place, just for a few hours.'

'We're leaving just as soon as Catherine has the data,' said Alice, swallowing back saliva. 'I need to stay and help.'

'We'll finish the analysis when we're back in the house,' said Lily. 'We'll have about three hours to get back there before Elizabet wakes up, which gives us plenty of time and Catherine can help me. I want you to get away from her. Go back and wait for us.'

Alice glanced across at Elizabet. The very sight of her made her insides feel queasy.

'I should stay,' she said, taking a deep breath. 'What about—'

'Go now,' insisted Lily, moving her out into the main room, sensing her discomfort. 'We can take it from here and we'll see you back at the house later. You need to rest.'

Alice finally nodded and pulled the dark glasses out of her pocket, pushing them down over her eyes. 'Okay,' she replied, exhaling deeply. 'Thank you.'

'Alice…?'

But the door had closed and Alice was already making her way down the corridor, her guard's hat firmly pushing down against the short straggle of her hair and her mind focused on where she needed to be.

As Alice stepped off the Transporter, she felt the coolness of the late evening air, and a small cluster of insects buzzed around her head. She remembered how much she used to hate the gnats and mosquitos that picked at her skin, leaving pockmarks in the heat of summer that itched and burned but somehow, now, their presence made her feel somewhat normal – if there were any such version of normal anymore.

She took the path to the south that had been stripped of weeds, a gravelly tarmac that was well worn from the traffic of the Community. The trees on either side of her bent slightly in the breeze, the branches barren of fruit of any kind, laden only with washed-out orange leaves – a poor, pale version of the lush greenness she had recollected of the world before. As she walked, she breathed in the air deeply exhaling big breaths laden with regret and anticipation.

At a fork in the road, without hesitation, she took the path to the left.

The forests that crowded the old housing estate that Alice vaguely remembered had spilled out across the path until they'd almost formed a dark tunnel of conifer above her head. Fractured buildings stood crumbling in the dimness of the tree line, many of the houses having been demolished in the eighty years or so since she had last been there. When they had first emerged above ground, this estate had been one of the places they'd considered expanding out into, before they'd taken the decision to expand westwards from Unity Square and Morristown Row. There had been an underground station near here and a market in the old days; and a café, Alice remembered, where the owner gave her a free biscuit when she visited as he was a friend – a client – of her mother's. Her mother had called them 'special friends' and it had taken Alice a few years to work out the truth but when she had, she took every free gift they offered her to keep her quiet, while they led her mother away to somewhere private. As the memories flooded back, the girl felt a knot of pain inside her that ached continually. Thoughts of the old world swirled around and around like tepid, dirty bathwater spiralling down a plughole.

She had been eleven when the Storms had drowned her world and taken with them everything she had ever known to be real. She glanced back into the old estate, the houses that she had once despised and held her breath to stop the inevitable tears from rolling in heavy rivulets down her cheeks. She bit her lip hard until the metallic taste of blood leaked onto her tongue and blinked her eyes dry. She pushed one foot in front of the other, her heart pounding in her chest.

The house was exactly where she had seen it on the map. It hadn't taken her long to work her way around the simple functions of the Model, watching Lily as she'd tracked Elizabet and Ariel's movements. Typing her name into the search box had been difficult, forcing her fingers to key in the letters and watch as a small red dot had appeared on the screen far to the south of the Community. She'd switched it off as soon as Lily had come up behind her. 'So, what are you thinking?' Lily had said.

I wish I could tell you, Alice had thought.

From behind a thick tree, Alice watched the silver line of a crescent moon illuminate the sturdy metal roof with its solid brick walls. The house was large, much bigger than those around Unity Square.

Taking a deep breath, she walked to the front door, removing her dark glasses and her guard's hat. She knocked and, when the door opened and an old woman answered, her eyes filled with tears and the line across her stomach burned with sadness.

'Hello, Mother,' said the old woman, wrinkles lining her face. 'I wondered if you'd come.'

Chapter Eleven

The Brothers

Carter ripped open the bloody shirt that soaked the back of Samuel's body. A thin arrow had wedged itself into the edge of his shoulder, stuck fast into his flesh. He moaned in pain when Carte touched the skin anywhere close to it.

'Don't pull it out,' he groaned. 'The shaft will remove itself from the head and then it'll be stuck in me.'

'I know that,' said Carter. 'I'm trying to see how embedded it is.' He looked around the forest. Tall pines towered above them, the spiny needles that had fallen forming a soft bed beneath them. It looked quite deep. 'How far is it to the nearest village? Do you know where we are?' he said.

Samuel lifted his head slowly, sweat pouring from his forehead. 'There's a place to the west of here, it's not on the main route, probably about two miles from here, I think... an abandoned town but nobody goes there any more.' His head slumped back to the forest floor.

'Why doesn't anyone go there?' said Carter. 'Is it dangerous, too far, what?' He shook his brother's leg. 'Stay awake, Samuel,' he said. 'You need to stay awake and I need to get you there.'

After they had rested for a while, Carter propped Samuel up against his own shoulder on the opposite side and they set off through the darkening wood. 'The wound isn't that deep,' he said, trying to reassure his brother. 'I just need to get us some supplies – a sharp tool so I can remove the arrow and something to clean the wound with.' Samuel grunted in pained response, as they stumbled their way through the verdant thickness of the wood.

'There.' Samuel pointed to a path through the trees, his breathing laboured and difficult as he dragged himself behind Carter, leaning hard on his shoulder. 'We need to head towards the western edge of the forest. There's a town.' He paused in between each word, sweat pouring from his brow. His bulky weight forced Carter's shoulder down and a dull ache moved through his body.

They half-staggered what looked like a drunken dance through the forest until the tree line thinned out and they crossed an old tarmac road where weeds struggled through the surface. Two rusted metal boxes with empty windows that Carter recognised as cars stood at either end of the strip. He heaved Samuel across the road and they slumped up against one of the cars.

'Thank you,' said his brother. 'You could have just left me there to die.'

'No, actually I couldn't have,' said Carter, sweat beading on his neck. 'I couldn't do that to you.'

By the time they reached the centre of town, the sun was a scorched ball of orange high overhead. Neat rows of desolate shops lined either side of an overgrown track and, unlike the other villages that Carter had walked through, this seemed less ravaged and empty. He couldn't imagine how many towns had been out here in the Deadlands before the Storms. And how many of them had been inhabited afterwards.

'Secret outpost,' explained Samuel, reading his mind. 'They reckon the main road into here was blockaded before the Storms so most people stayed away. And it's surrounded by the forest. This town is slightly higher than most in the area, that's why it stayed preserved for longer.'

A light breeze blew a gust of papers past them on the street. 'Do you know if there's a chemist or doctor's surgery on this street? Somewhere I can get supplies to sort out your injury?'

'Two streets away,' groaned Samuel. He pointed towards the east. 'There's a supermarket there. See the one with the orange sign? Do you know what you're looking for?'

'A scalpel – or a knife, something to suture the wound with, antiseptic and some painkillers,' said Carter, brightly. 'You know, I have been studying – and practising this for months now.'

Samuel closed his eyes tightly. 'Just go,' he said finally. 'This thing hurts and I need you to get it out.' He stopped for a moment. 'Please,' he said and then looked away.

Carter got to his feet. 'I'll be back soon,' he said, patting his brother on the shoulder gently. 'Sit here and wait for me.'

Except for the skittering of birds across the broken road, the town was empty. Carter picked his way down the street, avoiding the fallen tree branches and the damaged masonry littered with papers and empty cans that whistled as the wind caught them. He turned back and checked on Samuel, who still sat on the metal bench, his legs outstretched in the sun. The world seemed so different to the one he had woken up in just a few months ago. While the idea of the Deadlands had, at first, terrified him, it was now the Community that filled him with more terror than he ever thought imaginable. His world had been one where achievement had been everything and his personal survival had never been in question. He had been happy, in many ways.

Except for Isabella.

For a moment he let his mind think back to Isabella and how many sunsets they had watched together, staring out at the Deadlands and daring to dream what terrors lay outside the Barricades. His heart sank as he thought of her trapped deep within the Catacombs at the mercy of Elizabet and whatever plans she had for her. The image of her in the Lab made him feel physically sick and the guilt of having left her behind haunted his bones and gnawed at the sinews inside him.

'Come on, Alice,' he whispered to himself. 'Save her, please save her for me.'

Inside the supermarket, there were visible signs of looting but it had mostly been contained to the front of the store. Carter scanned the aisles – faded signs, still intact, hung from the ceiling.

FROZEN FOODS. TINNED VEGETABLES. BOOKS AND MAGAZINES.

He wandered around picking up the various items and putting them back down exactly where he had found them. The tin cans were a little rusted on the outside and most of the labels had faded or disappeared, but some of the plastic packets still held traces of what was inside them.

'Rice?' he said, opening one, which smelled foul, and he returned it to the shelf where an insistent fly began to buzz around its contents. An old clock on the wall, hands stationary, stared down at him. He walked to the end of the aisle in silence, stashing bottles of water in his bag, wondering what it might have been like before the Storms. Angel had explained to him some of how society had functioned – about shops and supermarkets, schools and churches and the books he had read had told him even more and filled in some of the details that Angel hadn't known. The complexity of it all bewildered him and now, in one of those actual buildings that hadn't been completely ravaged by the Storms, he found himself overwhelmed and in awe of all that had come before him and all that was outside of the walls of the Community.

In the back corner of the store was an area separated by a counter and a large green and white sign that said PHARMACY. Most of the drugs on the front counter were water damaged but a small door separated the frontage and another room that backed into the darkness of the staff area. The door was locked. Carter kicked it hard with his foot and the hinges smashed, shattering the warped wood into pieces and he climbed inside the small room.

Most of the goods were stacked high on shelves, wrapped in plastic and had been relatively well protected from the Storms but in the darkness, Carter could barely make out what they were. He filled two bags with everything that looked usable, including two bottles of disinfecting cream, then made his way back out into the main body of the supermarket, in search of the kitchenware.

Suddenly, towards the doors, Carter heard a scuffling noise.

'Samuel?' he said, cautiously. 'Is that you?' There was a silence and then the noise started again. Carter crept to the edge of the aisle and peered around the corner, his heart beating fast. At the entrance, he could just make out the shape of two wolves, their dark-grey coats shadowed in the sun.

He threw his body back around against a row of glass jars, sending them spinning to the floor with a deafening crash. The sound of padding came thundering up the aisle and Carter darted away from them, sprinting across the back of the supermarket, towards a ladder propped up against one of the sets of shelving.

'Not again,' he cursed to himself, remembering when he and Lily had first entered the Deadlands and had been chased by a pack of the same creatures. That time, their gnashing teeth had terrified him and he'd spent hours with Lily on the roof of a small building until the rains came, sending them away. But when he looked behind, they had simply congregated around the smashed jars licking at the festering contents tentatively before walking back out of the supermarket despondently.

Carter breathed a heavy sigh of relief and climbed down from the few rungs he had ascended, his hands still shaking a little. He made his way to HOMEWARE, passing a confusing array of items that looked incredibly useful even though he was unclear to what purpose he might put most of them. He grabbed a handful of items including a sewing kit and some large knives and stuffed them into one of the bags.

As he stepped out into the sunlight, he felt his eyes burn a little from the brightness. He blinked hard, looking left and right for any sign of the wolves but he saw nothing. He squinted in the direction of the bench where he had left his brother. And again, he saw nothing.

'SAMUEL!' he yelled, running down the street. 'Where the hell are you? SAMUEL!'

His chest heaving, he pelted down the road towards the bench but it was empty. A small trail of blood inked the ground away from the direction of the supermarket. Carter scanned the street but he was nowhere to be seen.

'Samuel!' he shouted. 'Samuel, where ARE you?' He listened but the only sound came from the cawing of crows overhead. He dumped the bags on the bench and ran, following the trail of blood until it stopped. What if Samuel were more badly injured than he thought? What if he had been taken by someone? The Industry maybe, or someone else? Then, a thread of doubt ran through him – his brother had betrayed him before. What if the entire idea of sending him to the supermarket had been a trick? He pushed that thought as far from his mind as he could and scoured the streets, shouting Samuel's name. However he had behaved, the thought of losing his brother now was more than he could bear.

'Sssh!'

The sound came from across the street. In the doorway of what would have once been a sports retailer Carter spotted Samuel, slumped in the shadows, his eyes barely open.

'Don't shout, you'll alert the animals and I can't run very fast at the moment, I'm easy prey.'

Carter felt relief wave over him. 'Why did you move?' he said, angrily. 'I was worried about you, I—'

'You wondered if I had left you, didn't you?' said Samuel. 'You still don't trust me – and I don't blame you for that but, Carter, look at me.' He lifted one arm weakly. 'I can't go very far. I just needed some shade. The sun was so hot.'

Carter shrugged. 'Maybe I don't trust you – not just yet – but you are my brother and I was worried about you. It did cross my mind that you might have left but what frightened me more wasn't being alone out here; it was the fact that you could be out here alone, injured.'

He knelt down beside Samuel and put his arm on his shoulder. 'What you did for Elvira was brave and I know that while you have your faults, I also have mine. We may not have been raised in the same way and our backgrounds are very different but we are brothers and, ultimately, we want the same thing – to take down the Industry.'

Samuel shrugged and winced in pain as Carter removed his shirt. 'I never considered that you could be a good person,' said Samuel, his head hung low. 'Mother always talked about you as the saviour of all people. She said that when you became Controller General, the troubles would all be over. But then you turned up and you weren't this great hero. You didn't do what they all said you were going to, and it made me—' he narrowed his eyes '—it made me so mad that you were the one who had been left behind to live this great life and I'd been the one dragged out here into the forest. And you hadn't even made the most of it, so I wanted to teach you a lesson.'

Carter bit his lip. 'That kind of makes sense,' he said, quietly, opening the bottle of disinfectant. 'Okay, this might hurt a bit so hold on tightly to something.'

Samuel yelled in pain as Carter dug the knife into his shoulder, making short, sharp incisions until the arrowhead popped out from underneath the skin. He placed a pad in some disinfecting alcohol he'd found in the pharmacy and pushed it down firmly onto the wound.

'It's clean,' said Carter as Samuel gritted his teeth. 'Now I'm going to sew it back together.' He handed Samuel a bottle of vodka from the bottom of the bag and some painkillers. 'I don't think these will work as they've been there for so long, but the alcohol should numb the pain – I read that this stuff can work wonders. As well as causing a great deal of societal problems and addiction, but I think we can overlook those in the circumstances today.'

Samuel gave a half-smile as Carter set to work on stitching his brother's wound.

'What was it like, growing up in the Community?' he said. 'Tell me something to take my mind off the pain.'

Carter thought for a moment. 'The truth is, I didn't know anything different,' he said, finally. 'My life was always about becoming Controller General. I was born a Descendent – do you know what that means?'

'Special,' said Samuel. 'You weren't like the others.'

'I suppose that's part of it,' said Carter. 'In the Community, it all depends on who your ancestors are. Mine, ours, were born from the first explorers and those people who set up the Community in the first place – so I guess, in some way, it's our ancestors who are to blame for what they created in there.'

'If you were supposed to help us when you became Controller General, why were you so hostile, so Industry, when you came out here?' said Samuel. 'That was why I hated you. Mother – Jacinta – said that you were one of us but you didn't act like that.'

'I didn't know about you, about the rebellion, about what the Industry were doing at all,' said Carter. 'I just knew that everyone wanted me to become Controller General and I...' He stopped for a moment. 'And I had my own personal reasons for wanting to change what was happening inside the Community.' He pulled the last stitch tight and pressed an antiseptic soaked pad onto the wound, fixing it tight with tape.

'It was a girl, wasn't it?'

Carter nodded. 'Her name is Isabella,' he said, his mouth quivering. 'We were at school together – she's what they call a Lab Made.'

Samuel looked thoughtful. 'I've heard of those,' he said. 'Made in a lab, kind of what it says on the tin, right?'

Carter nodded sadly. 'When I was sent underground, she stayed above. She's almost in in her thirties now and I'm still only a teenager. Even if I could get to her, our time together has gone.'

'Where is she now?'

'I thought she'd been killed when I left. She's damaged, Samuel. She's been hurt badly and now that girl, Elizabet, has her locked in a laboratory and she's doing experiments on her.'

He felt his chest rising and falling quickly.

'I have to get back to her, Samuel. I have to.' A pain speared Carter's chest hard, a pain that was only reserved for when he thought about Isabella. He looked up at Samuel.

'We will get her back,' said his brother, pressing his hand in a rare display of affection and smiled, his teeth a little fractured, but the sentiment so genuine. 'I promise you Carter, I will make sure of it.'

As they made their way towards the Village, Carter explained to Samuel how they had found Alice Davenport and who she was in the Community. He asked few questions but volunteered his opinion frequently, proclaiming his distaste for the Industry and his determination for revenge. Their talk then moved on to how Samuel had betrayed Carter, and caused the deaths of their friends and Saul from the Township.

'I don't know how I can ever make up for this. And Jacinta will kill me if I tell her the truth about what I've done,' said Samuel, despondently. 'Loyalty and family are what's most important in the Village. I don't know how I am going to face her.'

'I trust you and her to do what's right,' said Carter. 'What you did was wrong but, right now, there are bigger enemies than those inside our own camp.'

As the night drew to a close, he guided them towards an older outpost, built high in the trees where they were able to get some rest and they shared the remainder of the vodka and a packet of stale biscuits that Carter had brought from the supermarket. As the final rays of the sun cast their last light over the platform in the trees, Samuel reached across and put his hand once again in his brother's.

'We will do this, Carter,' he said, his words a little slurred from the alcohol and medication. 'We will do this for Isabella and for Mother. And we'll do it together. But first, we get help from our brothers and sisters in the Village.'

Carter watched as the dark shadow of his brother blackened into night as he held his hand tightly, waiting for the dawn to break and to bring with it the hope that his return to the Community would not end in sadness for Isabella and the heartbreak that he dreaded.

As the darkness descended, he steeled himself for the next stage of their plan – the return to their Village and, finally, the confrontation with the Industry. It was then that he remembered the master key, the one that Lily had given him to get back into the Community. With a shock that was almost painful, he realised it was firmly tucked into the pocket of the rucksack that had been taken from him by Eli, when he had entered the Township.

Chapter Twelve

The Daughter

Alice stood on the doorstep shivering while her daughter, Jescha, stared outwards at the moonlit sky, her eyes dark and unforgiving, glinting in the moonlight. A black shawl around her shoulders gave her a shadowed, sinister look that scared Alice a little.

'I've always wondered if you were still alive,' Jescha said, glancing across into the forest. 'I'm sure you've risked a lot to come here and find me, but I can assure you that there's very little I want to hear from you.'

She shook her head, grey-black curls hanging thin down the sides of her face and took a deep, laboured breath. 'You should come in before the Industry catches you out here – I'm shocked you've not been recognised yet.' She stepped aside to allow Alice to walk into the house. 'Although you look dreadful,' she added, coughing heavily, 'so maybe I shouldn't be that surprised.'

Inside the house, Alice felt a sickness well in her stomach. One wall was covered by a large FreeScreen, just like all the other houses in the Community but, on the opposite side, was a huge reproduction of Filip with the words OUR FIRST SCOUT, displayed resplendent across the bottom of the wall. In his arms, their baby Jescha, who sat across from Alice. His eyes, dark and piercing cut into her, but what hurt Alice most was the smile on his face as he looked down at their daughter.

Jescha gestured to her to sit. 'My father was a great man.' She smiled, looking up at the wall. '*He* was the founder of our Community; whatever the history books tell us, I know that he was the one who fought for what was proper and good in our world. And we have survived for this long only because of *his* commitment to what was and what is right.'

Alice studied her face: Jescha's skin held the same light-brown heritage as hers and her hair, although grey, would once have been dark like her own. But her eyes... although there were wrinkles that circled the outsides, they were the darkest green, and had the same intense depth of her father. She shivered.

'You don't seem very surprised to see me,' said Alice, finally. For the entire journey to the house she had thought about what the first words she might say to her daughter. These had not been the ones she'd anticipated. The woman before her was old, but she was sharp. Even though the welcome had been cold, indifferent almost, Alice felt her heart warm towards the daughter she had never known.

Jescha raised her eyebrows and shrugged a little. 'Before we lost her, my granddaughter Lucia was convinced you were alive and would come back. Her father, Carter, had recently been released from the Catacombs – a mistake, in my opinion – and she believed he would change the way we live here.' She smiled wryly. 'I am an old woman and I am sick. My time here is running out. Some days I don't remember what happened the day before and barely a week passes without some sort of interrogation from the Industry.'

She paused and exhaled deeply. 'I was never sure whether to believe Lucia when she told me she thought you were still alive. I had hoped you were dead. It is better for everyone that we forget about the old days.'

Alice felt the knot tighten in her stomach. 'How can you say that?' she said softly. 'I am your mother.'

'That's what Lucia kept telling me.' The woman pressed her hands tightly to her chest and sighed. 'That girl was always so optimistic,' she said, a sadness resonating in her voice.

Alice stretched out her hand to the woman who immediately withdrew it from her reach. 'They took you away from me,' she half-whispered. 'They forced me into the Catacombs and took you away from me – whatever Filip told you, I didn't ask to be separated from you.' She held her head firm and looked deep into Jescha's eyes. 'You are my daughter and I love you.'

Jescha snorted in disbelief. 'You are, what, sixteen years old?' she said. 'You have no idea what love is.' Her voice held the same clipped tones as her father's, striking a sharp pain inside Alice. 'You betrayed my father with that *traitor* Richard Warren and broke his heart.'

'I didn't betr—' Alice began but Jescha silenced her with a searing look.

Her withered hands shook as she spoke. 'Filip wouldn't let *me*, the first child born outside the Ship, born into the Community, grow up to be the daughter of a traitor. That stigma would never have left me so he made many, many personal sacrifices to allow people to believe that you were a victim and keep your honour – so I could keep mine. In those early years he rarely spoke of you, but when he did, he never told me what a terrible thing you had done.' Her words were angry, venomous and targeted.

'When I was four years old and I started school, the professor showed me, and some of the older children who had been brought up from the Ship, the footage of the Deadlands.' She cleared her throat and breathed heavily, coughing from deep within her body. 'I don't think I could have been prouder of my parents – both of them.'

Alice studied her daughter: her face was gnarled and wrinkled, although she didn't quite look the eighty or so years old that she must be. Her hands were well worn and there was a depth of sadness in her face that pained Alice terribly. She thought of her own mother and how much she had missed her since the Storms, how much she had missed the person she had been before her father had died.

'I watched you,' said Jescha between heavy breaths. 'I watched you on that screen over and over, trying to learn more about the mother I had never known and wanted so desperately to hug and kiss and be told that everything was going to be okay.' She looked bitterly at Alice. 'Instead I had a father who was heartbroken and a sister who despised my very existence.'

Alice was immediately taken aback.

'A sister?' she gulped, taken aback. 'Filip had another daughter?'

The old woman closed her eyes. 'My *sister* Elizabet Conrad, the new Controller General.' She was now hostile, angry to the point that the pale brownness of her skin had blushed to dark crimson and her bottom lip was shaking. 'Your adopted daughter. My *sister*,' she repeated, spitting the word out in the room. 'And now she's been released too.' Her face filled with dread.

'Izzy.' Alice, closing her eyes. 'What did she do to you?'

Jescha stood up slowly and awkwardly, the joints in her knees clicking loudly. Her face contorted briefly in pain as she made her way to the corner of the room and grabbed an old, gnarled stick. She winced in pain as she made her way to the large portrait of Filip and her on the wall. 'In the first few years, Filip made her responsible for me – she fed me and took care of me – and by all accounts made a fairly good job of it.' The old woman exhaled deeply and rubbed her hand against her chest again. She looked at the picture of Filip and pressed her palm against his face. 'Then, when I was almost five years old and Elizabet turned sixteen, she was old enough to qualify for the trials for Controller General, but Filip told her that she wasn't allowed to apply.' The woman took her stick and hobbled to the end of the room and sat down in a chair. 'She wasn't allowed to apply because my father told her that her responsibility was to take care of me and to try to start a family of her own. He...' She swallowed deeply. 'He told her because you had left us it was her responsibility to take care of the family. He was very traditional that way.'

Alice felt a flurry of recognition and nodded, no words coming to her. Flashbacks of Filip's controlling insistence, his anger and his determination to make her a mother came over her in waves and, for a brief moment, she felt sorry for Izzy – for the shattering of the small girl's hopes and dreams – before she remembered her cruelty. 'But how...' she began, before the old woman continued.

'I came home from school one day, just after my birthday. There had been an Industry event for the fifth-year inauguration of the new Community and everyone had been in Unity Square to celebrate our successes. There were speeches commemorating the Scouts achievements and I ran all the way back here afterwards to tell Izzy about my day. She was in the garden, practicing targets.' The old woman shuddered. 'I was so excited and so proud that both of my parents had been the first Scouts.'

Guilt ached through Alice as she sat there, unable to move, watching the sad figure of the old woman recall a memory that was clearly so painful. For all these years she had been only a few miles away in the deep underground Catacombs, unable to move, unable to help.

'I ran across the grass towards my sister, shouting about how proud and excited I was and as I got close, she turned her bow on me.' Jescha's voice trailed off again and her eyes turned dark. 'She told me that everything I had known about you wasn't true. That you were a traitor, that you left us to run off with another man but that you'd been caught and…' Tears welled up in her eyes. 'She said that because of you, her life had been ruined. That Filip was going to make her take care of me and then have her own babies with one of the Scouts, just like you had. She said that she was sick of everyone thinking that Alice Davenport was some sort of hero and that she would get her revenge on you as soon as she became Controller General.' Jescha's breathing quickened and her eyes welled with angry tears. 'She said it would be better if I had never been born and that she should have killed me and you when she had the chance.'

Alice felt her eyes widen and her mouth become dry. 'What… what did she do?' was all she could manage. She thought of Izzy's venom – her anger.

Jescha pursed her lips into thin lines. 'She raised the bow and released the arrow.' She pulled back her shawl to reveal the dark pink shadow of a scar on the lower part of her neck. 'The only reason she missed my head was because Papa Filip saw her and shouted at her. I think she was angrier that her aim was off target than the fact that she'd been caught.'

Alice reached out her hand again but Jescha was already heaving herself out of her chair with a deep sigh followed by a heavy, chesty cough. When she had finished, the room was silent, except for a soft pattering of rain on the tin roof that could be heard from the living room downstairs. The rhythmic, soft noise was in some way comforting in the depths of the terror that Alice was hearing. She desperately wanted to hold her daughter, to comfort the old woman but found herself glued to the chair, unable to move. She opened her mouth to speak and then closed it again. Everything suddenly made some sort of terrible sense.

'You survived. But what happened to her?' she stuttered. 'She can't be more than sixteen now, so...'

'She was sent directly to the Catacombs,' said Jescha. 'I was sent to the Infirmary to recover and I never saw my sister again.' She swallowed hard. 'That night Papa Filip came to visit me in the hospital and he said that Elizabet had to go away for a while. He said that I was never to repeat any of the things that she had said about you – that they were all lies and that she was just jealous because she wanted to be Controller General.' The old woman leaned heavily against the wall. 'It wasn't until Lucia started fraternising with the rebels that I found out that some of what Elizabet had said was true – that there was a rumour you were alive and in the Catacombs too.' As she spoke, she coughed again and her body crumpled against the wall, her shawl falling from her shoulders, her fragile frame exposed and delicate. Alice leapt from her chair and held her daughter, guiding her over to the chair. She kissed the top of her head, pushing her face gently into her hair and inhaling the smell of her, as if she were a newborn.

'Let me get you a drink or something,' she said, awkwardly, moving into the kitchen. Her head swirled with confusion as she left the room and stepped out into the hallway. She followed the passageway to the end and out into a small, plastic-roofed extension. Bottled water stood in lines on the countertop and boxes of chicker and boeuf were stacked next to them. She picked up a bottle and poured out two glasses. Every action felt mechanical and took her back to the flat in Prospect House where she would often take care of her own mother on the cold winter mornings when she staggered in from her work on the streets. She shook her head. Nothing and everything made sense.

Jescha sat rocking slowly in the chair when Alice handed her the glass of water. 'Drink this, it will make you feel better,' she said softly, gently rubbing the shoulders of the daughter who was old enough to be her grandmother.

'I'm sorry,' she added, slowly. 'I'm sorry for everything you've had to go through alone, Jescha. I wanted to be there for you, I honestly did.' She felt the tears start to roll down her cheeks in hot, thick, ticklish lines. Her first step, her first words, her first day at school, her toys, her first kiss. Alice watched the memories like an imaginary filmstrip flash past her; the content was all imaginary but the instances were real. Her tears gave way to heavy sobs of upset, followed by anger, followed by regret. Every tear she shed was encircled with hatred for Filip and a horrible, conflicted sadness and rage for Elizabet.

Alice felt the woman's shoulders heave as well and a heavy malaise passed between them for the lives they could have lived.

'You should not have betrayed Papa Filip,' breathed the woman. 'He was a good man who built everything we have today. Without him, we would have nothing.'

Alice stepped back and wiped her eyes. 'Jescha,' she said quietly, 'he was not as good a man as you think he was. We...' She paused for a second. 'All of us Scouts could have done things differently – we made some terrible promises down there in the Ship that we couldn't live up to. I never betrayed Filip in *that* way, but I had to know what the outside world was like. It wasn't like they told us it was – and it still isn't.' She paused for a second to catch her breath. 'There are other people out there, Jescha, people just like us who are living normal lives, trying to survive. What you have in here is some sort of weird, disturbed existence.' She looked up at the wall. 'Our First Scout,' she read out, a note of disdain her voice. 'Scouts, Descendants, First Gens, Lab Mades… do you even realise how awful that is?'

'It's the way things are,' said Jescha, turning to face the picture of Filip. 'It's the way they've always been.'

'It's *not* the way they've always been,' said Alice, suddenly wildly frustrated. 'Before the Storms there were millions of people desperately trying to create a world where there was equality for all because they believed that was right. And then when we came back above ground we developed – somebody developed – this horrific class system that was way worse than what we had before. People are not equal in this society – *no one* should be better than anybody else based on their gender, the colour of their skin or what they were born into.'

'But Descendants *are* better,' said Jescha, curtly. 'It's a matter of science. Genetically, they are the bravest and the best that society has to offer.' Her voice was old, gravelly and tired but Alice could see that deep inside her, it was what she actually believed.

'Lab Mades are something we constructed to prove our superiority,' she continued. 'Alongside her doctor friend, Elizabet put years of experimental work into the theory behind making a new type of human being. Except she never got to fully realise her dream of Version Two, the fully modified Lab Mades, because she was sent underground.' Jescha's lips formed a weird smile. 'She blames you for that, Alice.'

The room swirled with darkness, the regular pattering of rain on the window reminding Alice of what had brought her to this point in her life in the first place. A cold, heavy, devastating torrent of deadly weather that had flushed away the sins of the world and given them a blank canvas to start again. But when Alice watched the pellets of light hail tap against the window and part of her wanted – more than anything – that it would never stop. Never.

Jescha shook her head. 'Nothing good can come of you being here,' she said sadly. 'However you made your way out of those damned Catacombs, you need to make your way back there. Elizabet would never have released you so I can only assume that somehow you've had help – and whoever that person is, I can guarantee you they will be dead by dawn.' She coughed again, harder this time, and attempted to get up from her chair. Her spindly arms failed to hold her body weight and her shawl fell awkwardly to the floor. She sat, slumped, her hand covering her chest loosely.

Alice moved towards the chair, her arm around the old woman. 'I'm not going anywhere,' she said firmly. 'I am here to change things and to be the mother – the family – I always wanted to be to you.'

Jescha made a sound that sounded like an animal in distress.

'You're not fit to be a mother,' she groaned. 'You were all I ever wanted when I was a little girl, but it's too late.' Her voice became breathy. 'It's too late.'

Alice felt the void in her stomach ache like a deep, precious and unquenchable thirst. She watched the life of the old woman in front of her flash before her eyes – the child being ripped from her womb, the young girl shot by an arrow, the woman who had given birth – at least once that she knew of – and the grandmother who had taken care of the twin children who, in their own individual ways, had become Community prodigies. There was so much she wanted to say and even more that she wanted to ask but each time she opened her mouth, no words would come out. She moved to sit in front of the woman who was sat with her eyes closed, breathing deeply and wheezing in her exhalation. 'Jescha,' she whispered. 'Jescha, are you okay?'

Her daughter opened her green eyes. They were even darker than they were before but now appeared watery and seemed lost in another world. Her mottled skin was grey and pale.

'Go,' she growled, her throat crackly and dry. 'Get out of here and don't come back.'

'No,' said Alice, her heart breaking. 'I carried you inside me, I dreamed about you and I wanted a better life for you than I had. And now I've found you. I'm not going anywhere.' She let out a small sob. 'I love you,' she added. 'You're my daughter.'

'I am *Filip's* daughter, not yours.' The woman took another deep breath.

Alice fought back the tears as she thought about her own mother and how she'd had to go through her hardest years alone. 'B-but I can be with you now,' she stuttered. 'I want to be a part of your life, to find out more about you and—'

The woman held up one hand that started to shake uncontrollably. 'No,' she said, swallowing with difficulty. 'You must leave now and never come back. Because of you, Elizabet made my childhood hell – and tried to kill me.' A thin line of spittle covered her lips. 'Papa Filip never really recovered after your betrayal, and sending Elizabet to the Catacombs broke his soul.' Her breathing became faster and more erratic, her words tumbling from her mouth as she tried again to rise from the chair. 'You're not my mother, Alice; you're a traitor and nothing like the great leader that the Academies make you out to be. When I found out the truth I was never proud to be your daughter, I was ashamed. And I did everything I could to forget about you.' The thin curls around her face were drenched with sweat and her breathing quickened and Jescha's whole body started to shake.

'GO!' she spat, her final breath pushing all the air from her body. Alice felt a terrible pain wrack her body and, as she took her arm away from the woman, she felt her skin clammy and cold beneath her.

'I…' she began, but as Jescha brushed her away and tried to stand, her whole body crumpled onto the floor, a template of skin and bone. She shook and moaned for a moment before becoming completely still.

'NO!' screamed Alice, moving Jescha onto her back and desperately trying to feel for a pulse. She shook her and breathed into her mouth, clinging to Jescha and willing her back to life. She pressed her hands on her chest and counted like she'd seen television dramas in the days before the Storms. In that moment, she was reduced to that eleven-year-old girl who had so often had to revive her drunken, drug-fuelled mother in the early mornings before school. Alice tried once more to blow air into her lips, her stomach churning and her fingers shaking.

But this time, the woman – her daughter – was gone for good.

Chapter Thirteen

The Village

When the flickering sun cast bright shards through the leafy greenness, waking Carter the next morning, Samuel was already at the base of the tree tending to a fire.

'They've got the key card,' he said despondently. 'It was in my bag, back at the Township.'

Samuel groaned loudly. 'We can't go back for it,' he said quickly. 'They'll kill us.'

'I know.' Carter kicked the leaves at the base of the tree. 'We're just going to have to hope Lily or Alice are on the other side and can let us in somehow.'

'Can we get over the Barricades? Break the door down.'

'There's no way. They'll have alarms that will alert the Industry.'

'Then we'll have to find a way.' Samuel shrugged. 'We have to.'

Carter shook his head and exhaled deeply. 'I can't believe I forgot they took that from me.' He slammed his fist against the trunk of the tree in annoyance. 'This is so stupid! I might have lost my only chance at saving Isabella.'

'Calm down,' said Samuel. 'We'll find a way in. From what I know of McDermott, she won't take any chances with this – she'll be there.

And maybe Mother will be able to make some contact with her when we get to the Village.' He grimaced awkwardly. 'Will rabbit do you for breakfast?'

'Rabbit is great,' said Carter, dropping his body down from the branch onto the forest floor. He sat there while Samuel roasted the meat and wrapped it in dark brown textured leaves. He handed one to Carter.

'So, this Alice, she's what, nearly a hundred years old?'

'I suppose so – but she's only my age.'

'This freezing thing – it really works? But what's the benefit? You're the same age as that kid of yours and Alice, she's got great-grandchildren?' He shook his head. 'I woke up trying to work it all out. It's a mess, Carter. A real mess.' He exhaled deeply. 'I just don't get it – the whole thing, whatever it is they've got going on with the perfect babies and the freezing. I never understood it when Jacinta tried to explain it to me. I mean, who comes up with all that shit?'

Carter laughed. A deep, gut-wrenching belly laugh that echoed through the forest. Samuel's simple honesty and the way he spoke was so different to him and yet the more time they spent together he felt like a slightly warped mirror image of himself. He bit into the rabbit, so succulent and tender with the sweet edge of herb.

'I like this,' said Carter. 'You've cooked it well. I think this has to be my favourite dish.' He paused. 'How's your shoulder?'

'It's fine,' said Samuel, stamping out the fire. 'Eat quickly, we need to get back on the road if we're going to get to the Village today.'

While Samuel led the way, Carter stayed close to support him as the heat heat gathered pace towards midday and the darkness of the forest lightened through grassy clearings. Stone buildings littered the journey and Samuel pointed out the ones that held emergency supplies and those where they could stop and rest, close to the forest springs and vegetable patches where they could snack and gain some strength.

They followed a small stream that wound its way through the forest and peaked at the grassy headland that eventually opened out into the great waterfall that fed the river close to the Village. As they approached, exhausted and hungry, people from the Village – Samuel's friends – ran to greet them, helping them down the steep cliff that unfolded into the fields that surrounded the waterfall.

'What was it like?'

'Did you get inside?'

'Where is Angel? What about Elvira?'

They fired question after question until Carter's head span. Then, one voice stood out amongst the rest, clear and guiding – a voice that both he and Samuel were attuned to, a voice that made them feel like home.

'My sons,' said Jacinta. 'You've come back.' She pushed thin strands of silver hair behind her ears and looked at them both with pale-blue eyes. There were signs of relief at seeing her sons, but etched into her face were also lines of concern, knowing that they were back too early. She stood taller than Carter remembered, exuding authority over the others as she quietened them. She was calm and, even though he had lived without her for so long, she still had the qualities of his mother – someone who was able to reassure him that everything would be okay.

Jacinta guided them to the house in the trees, pushing back the crowds who were eager for news. 'Later,' she said firmly. 'The boys will provide you with an update this evening. But now, I will speak with them to understand the progress of our mission.'

Inside the house, both Samuel and Carter lay down on the wooden beds as Jacinta administered cold compresses to their limbs, asking questions that gently probed their journey and what had happened in the days since they had left the Village.

With his heart heavy, Carter explained what had happened from beginning, with Samuel nervously adding in the situation regarding the brothers, Aaron and Lisa, and he held his brother's hand tightly as he explained how he had tried to betray him by bribing Saul from the Township, in order to go to the Community alone and try to find Chamber One. Jacinta looked at Samuel with disgust.

'You have let me down,' she said sadly. 'Your pride and selfishness has resulted in the death of two of our finest hunters and two very capable and kind souls.' She shook her head slowly. 'I risked my life to bring you into this world to do good – not to jeopardise the lives of others.' Her eyes suddenly flashed with anger. 'And that you would use the sickness of a child to manipulate that man is simply not forgivable. You put the most important mission of our survival in danger because you—' she poked her finger deep into his chest '—because *you* believed that being better than your brother was more important than the safety of the people who have raised you and cared for you, your whole life.'

'I'm sorry. I am very, very sorry.' Samuel rubbed his face with a dirty hand and looked closely at Carter. 'I hated him,' he said finally. 'Ever since I was born, you and everyone else always talked about how he would save us. I wanted to be the one who did that. And I know now how wrong I was – Carter is a good person – even though he grew up as one of them, he's one of the most loyal and bravest people I've ever met.' He took a deep breath and paused for a moment.

Carter put his arm around him. 'Over the last few days, I've got to know my brother and who he is,' he said to Jacinta. 'When I first arrived, I hated him too – I was jealous of the fact that I believed you chose him over me and took him away from the Community to live with you and Father. I know now why you did that, but without the vision of hindsight, it's difficult to control the emotions that drive us.' He bit his lip thoughtfully. 'Two of our friends have already died and many more are in jeopardy,' he continued. 'Samuel showed great bravery when Elvira was injured and I know deep inside that he fully regrets his actions.'

Samuel nodded his head. 'I was stupid and thoughtless,' he said. 'I didn't want for the brothers to die though, I truly didn't.'

Jacinta looked from one son to the next, her eyes finally resting on Carter. 'What would you suggest his punishment should be?' she said. 'We will need to tell our Council, of course, but it is you and the brothers he has wronged, and I believe that you will make the best decision about what to do here.'

Carter looked his brother square in the eye. 'Samuel,' he said slowly. 'What you did was contemptuous – but I know you know that and I know you're deeply ashamed. I don't believe that you intended for it to turn out the way it did.'

Samuel tried to interrupt but Carter stopped him.

'I have not always been the person I want to be,' he continued, thinking of Isabella and how badly he had hurt her the night before he had been sent to the Catacombs. 'And many of the decisions I have made have been based on trying to control my situation and my emotions – sometimes without understanding exactly what was happening around me.' He paused for a moment, reflecting on how much he had learned in the months since he had been expelled from the Community. 'The world as you and I know it is different – there is so much we still have to learn but one of the greatest qualities is being able to understand and learn from your mistakes.'

Jacinta nodded, her head bowed.

'I believe you have learned from the terrible thing you have done and the guilt of that will haunt you for the rest of your life – if you are the person I truly believe you are, brother, you will continue to try to make amends for that and that will shape you as a person.' He turned to Jacinta. 'I need Samuel to complete this mission,' he concluded. 'My brother will stand by my side and he has already shown me through his loyalty to Elvira that he will never do anything like this again.'

Jacinta stared at them both for a moment. 'I am and will always be disappointed in your actions, Samuel,' she said, softly. 'But as your brother says, you have many qualities that, if correctly harnessed, can do much good for our people. However, for what you have done, a price must be paid.'

'I'm sorry, Mother,' Samuel repeated gruffly. 'I truly am.' He paused for a moment. 'There is something I can do that might help.'

Jacinta looked at him with an overwhelming sense of disappointment. 'I doubt that,' she said dismissively. 'I doubt that very much.'

Samuel took a deep breath. 'On the way to the Community, there's a tunnel – a shortcut that will allow us to reach the other side of the bank before the river loops back around,' he said.

Carter frowned. 'How do you know the tunnel is still passable? Have you been there recently?'

Samuel gritted his teeth. 'It's where I met with Saul,' he said quietly. 'I didn't know that tunnel existed but he showed it to me and said that he'd cleared the rubble from inside. He used to use it as a base, like one of our outposts, when he did things that he didn't want Frida to know about.'

'What sort of things?'

Samuel paused for a second. 'Saul had been stockpiling any weaponry and ammunition he could find that he might be able to use to break into the Industry. He became obsessed with it and he would search every town and village around here to find whatever he could. You know how the Township feel about guns and violence – there was no way he could do his preparations there. Saul and I have crossed paths before and when I saw him he told me about his plans, I thought, well…' His words tailed off and he looked ashamed.

'You thought you could help each other? He could keep me out of the way while you took the glory defeating the Industry?'

Samuel nodded. 'I don't know if anything's going to be left there but I was hoping I could surprise you with something positive.'

Carter exhaled in annoyance. 'Samuel – is there *anything* else you need to tell me. Anything?'

Samuel shook his head. 'No, that's it.'

Jacinta turned to Carter, ignoring her other son. 'We have very little by way of weaponry here,' she said. 'When you reach the Community, there will be guards and you will need to be able to defend yourselves.' She turned to Samuel. 'This is helpful, but not enough,' she said. 'This does not in any way make up for what you have done.'

'I know,' Samuel nodded, regretfully. 'But once this mission is over, I will take myself into exile as a punishment for this crime. I will make sure that Carter's quest is successful and then I will put myself to good work in the Deadlands or in the Community, helping others to ensure that my existence is not wasteful. I promise you that I will make you proud of me and that my life will be given in the service of others.'

Carter put his arm on his brother's shoulder – he had never seen him so weak and vulnerable.

'Well, some contrition is better than nothing,' Jacinta said, shortly. 'What I want to see from you is the leadership and strength shown by your brother. With no malice, no jealousy and no hatred. You have killed a man – albeit I am sure you will claim that you were doing this to protect Angel and Elvira – but that will remain on your conscience for the rest of your life. You have jeopardised any affinity with the Township and destroyed any potential alliance we could gain with them.'

She exhaled deeply. 'Carter may believe you but I am still devastated that a son of mine could be so devious. Your father would be ashamed of you. Your exile will be your redemption. When you feel you have made us proud of you, you can return home.'

Carter got to his feet and began to walk around the room in thought. 'I can understand your feelings, Mother, I can,' he began. 'But we all have a part to play in what Samuel did and we must all be responsible for our own actions.'

Jacinta looked up at him, surprised. 'What do you mean?' she said curtly.

Carter picked up a book from the shelf and passed it from hand to hand. 'Samuel learned from a very early age that I was special – more special than he was. He has spent his whole life trying to prove to you that he is just as good – if not better – than I am. In the Community, I was never in any danger of survival – I always had food to eat, an incredible education and a place in the world with people who loved me. But I was proud, confident, immature and sheltered from the truth. It can't be any surprise that there would be tension between us.' He furrowed his forehead. 'What Samuel did was a mistake – he didn't mean for anyone to get killed but that's what happened and we need to accept that. His honesty in telling you is just one part of what demonstrates his remorse.'

His mother took a deep breath. 'There are some elements of this I can be responsible for,' she conceded gracefully. 'And I see that now. But you are right, Carter, we must all take ownership for our parts in this and make it right. And Samuel's will begin once this mission is over.'

Carter nodded. 'The threat to our survival is greater from those in the Industry than from each other. Until we have completed our mission, we do not need to share the full details with the people of the Village. We can't afford for them to doubt my brother's commitment and trustworthiness under any circumstances. I – we – need Samuel to overcome them. There is no question about that.'

Jacinta listened carefully to each scene the brothers replayed exactly as it had happened and her eyes glistened with tears when they talked about Elvira and how she had fallen deep into the tunnels within the Catacombs. Samuel explained their capture by the Township and how Elvira had been when he had last seen her.

'When this is done, we will collect her,' said Jacinta, running her hands through her hair. 'I will speak with Frida, she's a good woman and she'll be amenable to our requests – I know they will take good care of her there.' She paused. 'And what of Angel – and of McDermott? Did you find her? Tell me, is there such a thing as Chamber One?'

Carter paused – there were so many details, so much information to share with Jacinta. 'We found it,' he said, his eyes twinkling with pride. 'We found *her*. Inside Chamber One we found Alice Davenport.'

Jacinta whistled loudly through her teeth. 'Alice Davenport,' she repeated. Her face was pale, but her eyes shined bright. 'And is she well? I would never have imagined that she was still alive. We all believed that they had killed her when the baby was born.'

'She is pretty upset,' said Carter. 'And very confused. But she's in good health – or at least she was when we left her.'

'Tell me everything,' said Jacinta with intense concern. 'And then we work out our next steps.'

'We need to work them out soon,' Samuel pointed out, turning to his brother. 'Because from what Carter has told me, the Industry are coming for the Township and then they're coming for us.'

When Carter awoke it was early evening and Jacinta was shaking him hard. The majority of the afternoon had been spent discussing the approach they would take on their return to the Community and how many of the Villagers they could count upon to join them.

'You've had enough time to rest,' she said. 'It's time for you and Samuel to address our people. We have set up the podium in the main communal area – everyone is eager to listen to what you have to say.'

This time, when Carter and Samuel stepped up on to the small stage in the centre of the clearing, there was no sense of the rivalry that had underscored their previous address.

'Thank you for talking to Mother,' said Samuel in his usual offhand manner, but not without true feeling. 'I will make sure we get Isabella back.'

Carter nodded, his shoulders heavy with responsibility. 'I have to,' he said. 'I made a promise to her – and to Ariel – and I won't let either of them down again.'

The people of the Village had crammed into the grassy space – men, women and children carrying small bags, wooden weapons and armfuls of food with them.

'Why have they brought all this?' whispered Carter, as Jacinta organised them into rows so that the space could be most effectively used.

'They've come prepared,' she said with a smile, ushering a group of children into an orderly line. 'In case they are asked to leave immediately. They've been asking about you every day since you left – they all want to help. You just need to tell them how.'

Samuel nodded and looked at Carter and a rare smile crossed his face. 'How many of them do you think we need?' he said. 'You've been out there, you've seen them.'

Carter scanned the crowd, his heart warm with pride for his adopted people. 'All of them,' he said. 'Well, everyone who can make the journey. Everyone has something to offer and this fight belongs to us all.'

When the crowd had settled, Jacinta took her place on the stage and welcomed everyone, her demeanour friendly, yet still serious.

'People of the Village,' she began. 'As you are all aware, some days ago my sons and four of our other brothers and sisters made their way towards the Community to try to understand what their plans are and to search for a way in which we could stop the terrible things that they have been doing to us.'

The crowd were silent, not one person spoke or moved, their eyes firmly fixed on the podium. 'This evening, we will tell you the full story,' continued Jacinta, 'but there are a few things you need to be aware of.'

Carter glanced across at her and then at Samuel as her voice rose again. 'Sadly, we have lost two of our best people – the brothers, Lisa and Aaron.'

Samuel kept his gaze firmly fixed at the floor; Carter could see him shifting uncomfortably as he stood on the other side of his mother.

He took a deep breath, desperately hoping that Jacinta would keep the details of their death to herself as she had agreed.

'They bravely represented themselves against an intruder and saved the lives of Elvira, Angel, Samuel and Carter. When this is over, we will raise a memorial to them and their passion and creativity in field of nutrition. But, in this moment, we will pause for a minute and remember their lives in silence.'

The people of the Village bowed their heads.

'Elvira,' continued Jacinta, 'has been injured and is recuperating with people of the Township that are known to us. They have taken her into their infirmary so that she can recover from her injuries but we should remember that it was her tenacity and bravery that allowed my sons and Angel to enter the Community through the area that is known as the Catacombs, out near Drakewater.'

'The Township?' called one man from the audience. 'I understood that we were to stay away from them – that—'

'Frida and her people have some issues with us, that is true,' continued Jacinta, holding up her hand to stop the man from asking further questions. 'But we had to enlist their help during the mission. You should also know that Angel is safe and in good company.' She handed the stage over to Carter and Samuel. 'I will let them tell you the rest of the story and then you will need to decide for yourselves how you will help them.'

A muted cheer rose from the crowd and Carter gathered his thoughts as he addressed them.

'What I have to say to you is one of the most important things you will ever hear,' he said carefully. 'For many years you have been waiting for a chance to change your way of life and to save the people of the Community.' He paused for a moment. 'That time has now come. I will tell you what we need to do next and you will all have the opportunity to join us, if you wish to.' He eyed the front row of the eager group, one by one, assessing their strengths and weaknesses. 'But first, I need to tell you what we encountered when we went there. When we first entered the Catacombs, we discovered an area – a cell – that you may have heard of, called Chamber One.'

There was an audible gasp from the crowd as the whole clearing hungrily devoured every word that Carter spoke. 'Within that Chamber, we found Alice Davenport.'

The silence was broken only by the soft whistle of the wind through the trees as many hands shot into the air with questions. Carter nodded in acknowledgement, but continued.

'Alice Davenport, as many of you will know, was a revered Scout and the symbol of what the Community believed in – although it was taught in the schools that she sacrificed herself in childbirth to bring forth the next generation. Her martyrdom is what has been the source of compliance within the Community since its inception and the truth about what really happened to her has been hidden for all this time. Alice Davenport was a rebel – and a good friend of my great-grandfather Richard Warren. Her very existence is a terrible threat to everything the Industry has ever taught to their people. Angel is with her as we speak, developing a plan for making this public to the people within the Community.'

Carter paused as his audience ingested the news. Most stood open-mouthed, while others shook their heads in disbelief.

'But there's more,' said Samuel, suddenly, stepping forwards. 'My brother and Alice also uncovered a plan that the current Controller General has to bring an army of people out here to destroy us – people that have been...' he struggled to find the words '...changed in some way so that they will obey only her.'

'We will kill them!' shouted a woman from the audience. 'They have destroyed us and we will destroy them.'

Carter held up his hand, thinking of Isabella. She could be one of them by now, one of Elizabet's experimental military.

'We need to get there before the Industry sends out their new army,' he declared with force. 'These people may not yet have been modified and if we can save them, we will. But we need your help.' He paused for a moment. 'The next stage of our mission will be difficult and travel to the only gate in the Barricades is dangerous. A group of us will go on ahead but we need to ensure that we protect those of our Village who are not strong enough to make the journey.'

There was a mumbling from the crowd. 'But there are thousands of them. We number only a few hundred. Even if the Township joined us, they'll shoot us before we get within a quarter of a mile of that big metal fence!'

Carter shook his head. 'We have help on the inside,' he said. 'McDermott, Angel, Alice – and my son Ariel – will ensure there's enough distraction so that we can enter without being seen. We have no choice but to try to overcome them. Once the people inside know what the Industry are truly like, they will support us.'

Carter kept his voice strong but, inside, he was worried. What if Alice and Lily had been captured? What about Angel and her visible differences? How could he lead these people into what might be a certain death?

He felt the strong reassurance of his brother's arm on his shoulder as Samuel stepped past Jacinta and stood next to him.

'Many of you will be aware that I hated my brother when he first arrived,' said Samuel, his gruff, deep voice full of emotion. 'But since I've got to know him, he's, well, all right.' The crowd laughed a little.

'In the few months he spent with us, he learned to live a different life to the one he's always lived. He taught himself to become a doctor – and a damn good surgeon.' He whipped off his shirt to show the stitches Carter had put in his shoulder after the incident with the arrow. 'And he's the bravest, cleverest and kindest man I've ever met. If anyone can change the course of history, it's my brother, Carter. And I'm the first to stand behind him in this mission.' He coughed a little, sounding almost embarrassed by his emotional oration. 'We have no other choice,' he added.

The people of the Village stood, clapping in appreciation, their faces determined and united in support.

'We leave tomorrow morning before sunrise,' said Carter, with strong determination. 'Now all of those of you who wish to join us, raise your hands.'

Chapter Fourteen

The Family

"What happened to Mama Jescha?"

The voice that floated through the room sounded like that of a young child. Alice lifted her head, eyes red-rimmed and sore, her fingers still intertwined in the gnarled paws of the old woman's, her cheeks wet and shining with tears. In front of her stood a figure, shadowed in the darkness, curling a long flame-like auburn ringlet around her index finger. She watched Alice carefully, her eyes wide and bright. Suddenly, her gaze focused and a serious frown etched its way into her forehead.

'I know you,' she said clearly, her words low and drawn out. 'You're Alice Davenport. You have different hair now and a stupid Industry uniform, but I know it's you. My little girl Lucia said you would come and save us one day. My name is Samita. Where is Carter Warren?'

As she came towards Alice it was clear that she was much older than she initially sounded or looked – perhaps thirty or so, but she still held the stature of a girl much younger, her face open and simple, a little like Jescha's, but with much paler skin and hair the colour of a hot sunset, spindled with golds, oranges and threads of dark red bunched into ringlets that framed her face.

She looked like a character that had been drawn in felt tip pens against a blank wall in an underground station – almost a caricature of the person Carter had told her about. The woman he'd had children with in order to avoid a lifetime in the Catacombs so he could come back and change things for them all: a plan that had not gone well for any of them.

Samita kneeled down next to her own mother and cupped her hand over Jescha's eyes, closing them as she did. Alice sat back, her eyes stinging and a tight lump in her throat.

'She had… she had a heart attack or something,' she murmured, unsure of how to break the death of her mother to the girl. 'I don't really know what happened, I'm sorry… I…'

'Mama Jescha wasn't always very nice to me,' said Samita, her face brightening a little. 'It's sad when people die – good people and bad people – but it's sadder when the Industry is bad to them.' She ran her fingers through the curls of Jescha's hair and then looked at Alice seriously. 'We need to get rid of her,' she said. 'If we leave her here, they will come for her. And also, she will start to smell.'

Alice felt bewildered and confused. As she wiped her cheeks dry, her heart still heavy and her stomach churning, the woman – not more than five feet tall – had already dragged Jescha's body out through the kitchen. There was the click of a door and she heard the thump-thump sound of Samita moving her mother out into the garden. The rain had all but stopped but the air was still damp and earthy. Alice followed her and watched as she bundled the woman into an old brick-built shelter with a corrugated arch-shaped roof.

'Anderson Shelter,' Alice whispered to herself, her thoughts flitting from one experience to another. 'I saw one of those once in the Imperial War Museum…' She remembered that had been another instance of her mother doing some business – this time with one of the curators. They had climbed into the cockpit of one of the aeroplanes in the early morning, before any other guests had been at the museum and Alice had hidden inside the shelter until it had all been over.

She ran her fingers over the brickwork that was covered with a springy damp moss and wet with the rain.

Her granddaughter emerged from the shelter with a curious smile. 'I am sorry your daughter is dead,' she said in a weird staccato voice. 'People used to say that, didn't they? We don't say that now because we know that it is not our fault most of the time.' She wiped her hands on the thin cotton dress she was wearing that didn't look anything like the workwear that most other people had been clothed in.

'Mama wasn't always a good person,' she said, simply. 'She was like most of the people who came first – most of her babies died. Four of them – all before they had their open eyes. She was told she couldn't have any more and that made her sad. She went to sleep in the Catacombs for a while, until they developed medicines for her.'

Alice felt the dull ache inside of her grow. At some point, her daughter had been deep underground possibly just a few feet from her while they both slept.

'Do you know I'm your… grandmother?' said Alice to the woman, not knowing what else to say.

'Oh yes,' replied Samita, narrowing her eyes in an over-dramatic fashion. 'I'm not stupid, just different. But they don't like different here. Different is wrong.'

Alice nodded her head. 'But you know that's not true, right?'

Samita looked at her almost scornfully. 'I'm real smart,' she said. 'Smart enough to know that the drugs Mama Jescha made me take to keep me out of trouble just made me like someone who is dead and come back from the ground – Zombers, I think Lucia called them. She read that in a book. She broke all the rules too. Just like us.'

Alice smiled a little, seeing something of herself in the strange, child-like woman who seemed to have thought nothing of dumping the body of her mother in an old air raid shelter. 'Did Lucia stop you taking the tablets?' she said as they walked back into the kitchen.

The woman stopped and frowned at her. 'I was telling you the story,' she said. 'Don't interrupt with questions until I have finished. Do you understand?'

Alice bit her lip and nodded again, and Samita continued.

'Now I will take you away from this house and back to where you need to go. Arial will be home soon and the nasty Controller Elizabet might be with him so you need to go away.' She pulled her hair back and handed Alice her guard's hat. 'We go to a safe place,' she added. 'And I will come with you. Lily's house. She's one of us too.'

'What about…?' started Alice, but the girl had pulled on a thick shawl and was heading through the door with a large torch in her hand.

The night air had turned crisp although there was still moisture on the ground from the rain that had now stopped. The fresh, dark smell reminded Alice of when she was young, walking through the park at night.

Samita continued the conversation as soon as they were in the covered shade of the wood. 'When she was about thirty, my mother went into the Catacombs,' she started. 'Grandpa Filip said she had to go underground because she couldn't keep her babies alive.' She kicked at a stone that flew through the air. 'They kept dying,' she added.

Alice looked at Samita, horrified. 'Did he actually say that to her? Did he make my little girl go into the Catacombs?'

The woman shrugged. 'A few of the Descendants went to sleep there for a while so that the medics could make better drugs. That's when they started the experiments on the babies.'

'You know about that?' Alice felt her blood run cold. 'How do you know about that?'

'Lucia told me.' Samita looked proud every time she mentioned her daughter's name but then her face clouded. 'I told you not to interrupt me,' she scowled. 'Let me finish.'

'Okay, okay,' said Alice, holding up her hands, fighting back the need to ask a thousand other questions of the woman about how life above ground had been for her family.

Samita looked her deep in the eyes before continuing. 'So, Mama told me that when she was about thirty, she was put underground for a long time, about twenty years. When she came back, Grandpa Filip was even older but he still wanted her to have a baby so he sent her to the doctors down in the old Ship.'

Alice took a sharp intake of breath but said nothing. Samita eyed her suspiciously. 'I was very lucky to have been born,' she said. 'Lots of other new babies were broken and they died down there.' The woman twirled a spiral of hair around one finger and watched as Alice fought back the urge to ask her a question. She thought back to the stories she'd heard from Carter about the babies that were sent out, still alive and gasping for breath into the dark, foetid waste and out into the Deadlands to die.

The wind curled through the trees in the darkness and Alice shivered.

'But I was alive,' continued Samita, 'and so Mama Jescha and me came up here when I was born. But I was different and Mama knew that. She thought that I was like those broken babies and the people in the Industry wanted to have me tested. She made me take drugs every day that she got from the nice professor so I would be quiet and not be difficult. She said if they found out I was different that I would have to go and live in the dark place on my own.' Samita shuddered. 'I don't like the dark place in the underground.' Her fingers moved in patterns on the kitchen bench, large circular patterns that looped in and out in an intricate fashion. Alice waited, watching, until she was ready to speak.

'When I got bigger, the nice teacher came to this house so I didn't have to go to the Academy. She was my friend. But then Mendoza said I had to have babies with Carter Warren so I would be a normal person. I heard her telling Mama.' Samita ground her fingernail deep into the countertop.

'Mendoza?' said Alice. 'Carter's teacher?' She thought back to the little she had heard about Mendoza – that she'd been on the side of the rebellion and a friend to Carter's mother before she'd escaped from the Community.

'She came to Mama,' said Samita, sadly. 'I didn't want to have a baby but they made me have them so I would be like a normal person. Everyone here has to want to have a baby. But I didn't.' Her face flushed dark red and the lines of her mouth straightened in anger. 'But I do love Ariel and I loved Lucia too. She was special like you are. It wasn't the doing it that I minded; it was the babies. I never wanted to have them. But they said I would get sent underground if I didn't. And he would too, because he loved the Lab Girl and he wasn't supposed to. Mendoza told Mama that if I helped him, he would help me when he came back.' She scowled at Alice who was about to speak. 'But he didn't help me – or my Lucia. She got killed.'

Alice sized up her granddaughter Samita. She looked just as Carter had described her: a bright scramble of red hair and sad, doe-like eyes. In the old days, people would have said she was special – and she was, but in a very different way. Her heart sank for the woman who looked so young but had faced so much as a result of what the Community had become. Guilt coursed through her, mixed with an aching sadness and an anger that bit into her like hot iron.

Samita's torch burned bright in the darkness of the trees as they followed the path that wound around the back of the Community. Within half an hour they had reached Lily's house and, when they reached the door, Lily pulled them both inside.

'Where the hell have you been?' Her voice was a mixture of anger and concern. 'And why have you brought her with you – do you know who she is?'

Alice pushed her way past Lily and into the main room. Through what would once have been a long kitchen, a table stood with a white sheet covering it. There were no appliances in the kitchen but on the sheeted table lay Elizabet, her eyes closed but her heartbeat regular. Behind her Alice felt Samita take a sharp breath.

'I hate her,' the woman spat. 'She should be dead too.' Samita moved forwards, her arms raised, but Lily stepped in front of both her and Alice.

'Regardless of what she's done, we need to keep her alive right now,' she said firmly. 'Angel has been working hard to mend her wound and to keep her stable with the medical supplies we were able to bring.' She turned to Samita. 'You shouldn't have come here,' she snapped. 'You know you aren't supposed to be anywhere near here. I told you to keep a low profile.'

'*She* came to *me*,' said Samita. 'I didn't ask to get involved with her, but then she killed Grandma Jescha.'

Lily whirled around to look at Alice with incredulity. 'You killed your own daughter?'

'She had a heart attack,' said Alice, quickly her face moving from angry to sad. 'I didn't kill her.' She looked over at Elizabet. 'How is she?'

'Alive,' said Angel, finishing the wound dressing. 'I've stitched her up and reduced the sedative. We need to decide what we're going to do with her – she's going to wake up soon. She's lost some blood but she'll definitely make it.'

Samita's eyes narrowed. 'Shame,' she said. 'I hate her. It's her fault this all happened. She killed my daughter.'

Lily put her arm on Samita. 'Lucia died quickly,' she said. 'I told you there was nothing we could do. Elizabet got to her before Carter and I did.' She turned to Alice and spoke quietly. 'When Elizabet was training to become Controller General against Carter, her mentor told me that she was more intent on destroying the other candidates' reputations than enhancing her own. When I did some enquiries, I found out from one of the rebels that Elizabet told Lucia that Carter was in the tunnel and that she should go as far as she could to wait for him. She pretended to be on her side. When Lucia was out in the tunnels she must have realised the Industry was tracking her, so she tried to cut the trackers out of her wrists and then—' Lily gulped '—she didn't make it.'

'Izzy was responsible for her death?' Alice asked. 'Does Carter know?'

Lily shook her head. 'The guilt that Lucia went in there to find him would destroy him,' she said. 'But Elizabet knew that if Lucia attempted to cross into the Deadlands, the trackers in her wrists would explode and kill her. Her death in the tunnel would confirm her status as a dissident and damage Carter's reputation. It was just chance that we found her body before the Industry did.'

Alice shook her head. 'That girl has so much blood on her hands,' she said. 'So much.'

Alice told them the story of Kelly and how Izzy had killed her at Barnes's request. Of how the small girl she had once cared for had turned into a strange monster and had murdered her friend, just a child herself, who had been pregnant. When she finished speaking, Alice wiped the tears from her eyes and felt the cold lump in her throat soften.

'We should just let her die,' said Angel. 'Shouldn't we?'

The four women stood at the table looking over Elizabet and glanced from one to the other. Her breathing had stabilised into regular exhalations. Her finger twitched a little, making them jump. Alice remembered what her daughter had told her – about how the girl had been stopped from competing for Controller General and how she had blamed Alice for ruining her life. For a moment, looking at Izzy, she felt sorry for her.

Samita's eyes narrowed. 'I hate you,' she said viciously towards the girl laying on the table. She put her hands out to touch her but Lily brushed them away.

'We need to decide what we are going to do with her,' she said. 'We can't just keep her here. She's supposed to be addressing the Community soon and Ariel is going to be looking for her.'

Alice shook her head. 'We'll leave her here until we can intercept the broadcast – speak to Ariel and tell the people of the Community the truth. Just as we planned.'

'We'll strike tomorrow,' said Lily. 'With any luck Carter should be back by then.'

'Where's Catherine?' said Alice, her eyes unmoving. 'How did she get on with decrypting the data from the Lab?'

'She's upstairs,' said Lily. I have some equipment set up in a spare room there.' She ushered Alice into the kitchen away from the others, her faced concerned. 'I sat up there with her for a while and, well, the look on her face…'

'What kind of look?'

'She cracked some part of the code that had been programmed by Elizabet – it was old code, she said, written in a language that hadn't been used for years and when I asked her about the content of it she shook her head and wouldn't speak about it.'

'And when you pressed her for more information?'

'She said there was more to decode and she wasn't sure she was getting it right because it was so archaic.'

Alice glanced back into the room where Samita sat chatting animatedly with Angel.

'When did you last check on Catherine?'

'About an hour ago.'

Alice looked at her intently. 'You've not been keeping an eye on her?'

'Why would I? She's on our side. She shot Elizabet.'

'Catherine!' Alice shouted loudly up the stairs. She and Lily looked at each other.

'Catherine?'

Alice flew up the stairs, pushing wide the doors of each room. Each one was empty.

'Catherine, where are you?' She searched the upstairs of the house frantically looking under beds and behind the curtains. Finally, in the last room she entered, Catherine was sat on a long bench crouched over a tablet, her forehead crunched in concentration. Relief washed over Alice as the girl looked up at her, concern creasing her face.

Behind them, Alice heard the thump of footsteps on the stairs as Lily and Angel bounded upwards and crowded into doorway, breathless.

'There she is,' breathed Lily. 'You had us all scared there.' Her face broke into a smile but Catherine's remained steadfast, concerned even.

'I *am* scared,' she said. 'Look at this.' She turned her screen towards the group. 'Look,' she said, her eyes wide.

Alice scrunched her forehead and tried to make sense of what the girl presented to them. A pattern swirled across the screen and what looked like an old high-frequency graph flitted up and down in spurts, reminding her of the ancient stereo she had been allowed to keep in her room, that had once belonged to her father.

'Is this what you downloaded from the Catacombs?' she said, squinting her eyes and watching the patterns. 'What does it mean? I don't really see anything?'

'It's not live,' whispered Catherine, looking over her shoulder. 'But you can see it. You can hear it. When she spoke about the others, I never thought she was really telling the truth... I thought she was saying it to scare me... I...'

'Calm down,' said Alice, holding her arm. 'You're not making any sense. I don't understand what you're talking about.'

Catherine's eyes looked wild, unsuited to her usual calm demeanour. Alice felt nervous, remembering the way she had snapped and shot Elizabet. She put her hand on the girl's shoulder.

'Explain to me,' she said slowly. 'Show me what you can see on screen.'

Catherine traced her finger across the graph. 'You see these?' she said, pointing to an array of lines moving up and down the screen. 'These are sound waves.'

'Okay,' nodded Lily from behind her. 'But that's nothing unusual, we know that the Industry monitor chatter from inside the houses through the FreeScreens where the signal is strong enough.'

'No,' said Catherine. 'These aren't from the Community. These sounds have come from outside the Barricades.'

Alice felt her blood run cold. 'Do you think the Industry are listening to the Village, to the place that Carter has gone to? Do they know about our plan?'

Catherine shook her head. 'No,' she said. 'They'd have already captured us if they knew that. This is something else.'

'What do you mean, you thought she was doing it to scare you?' Angel pushed past Lily and looked at the screen. 'What was she saying to scare you?'

'What you can see on the screen are radio waves,' said Catherine, her voice low and shaking slightly. 'They're being transmitted from another facility.'

They all stood there for a moment in silence as the patterns swirled across the screen.

'Another *facility*?' said Alice, finally. 'Do you mean, like this one?'

Catherine nodded her head. 'Just like this one,' she added quietly.

A shrill yell from downstairs broke the stagnant, terrifying silence in the room. Lily grabbed Alice by the arm and dragged her out to the landing.

'Elizabet!' she screamed. They tore down the stairs, their feet slamming onto the wooden steps and launched themselves into the living room to where they had left Izzy laying on the table.

On the floor lay the white sheet that had covered her, tiny spots of blood peppering the fabric. A faint breeze lifted it from the carpet and Alice turned her head. The front door stood open and both Samita and Izzy had gone.

Chapter Fifteen

The Company

As a white sliver of sunrise filtered through the forest, Company Eight, comprising of almost every individual who was fit enough to make the journey to the Community, trekked eastwards through the dense undergrowth. Each person carried with them supplies for the two days it would take them to reach the Barricades and the spot they had agreed with Lily. Samuel and Carter had made their unexpectedly emotional goodbyes to Jacinta, who had remained to ensure the safety of those who had needed to stay.

'Look after each other,' she'd said, somewhat despondently. 'Something tells me that I won't be seeing both of you again.'

Carter put his arm around her. 'If we're successful in what we need to do then we may not be back for some time – but we will send word as soon as we are able to let you know how we are.'

Samuel stepped forward to hug her but Jacinta moved away.

'I need more time, Samuel,' she said, her voice kind but firm. 'I wish you both well, but my focus now needs to be on the people who are here. When you have proved yourself to be the man I always wanted you to be, you can come home. You alone will know when that time is.'

Carter watched as Samuel nodded, a little upset but his strong, gruff nature taking over.

'We'll be back soon,' he said, turning towards the forest. 'We should make it to Woodford Hatch, the old Township, by nightfall and then finish the rest of the journey tomorrow. We'll be at the Barricades at the time agreed with McDermott.'

They walked in groups, Samuel leading the way at the front, with Carter moving between different teams, answering questions and providing them with information about the Community and the people they were likely to encounter.

'The most important element will be personal connection with people,' he said to a collection of men and women towards the front, wielding scythe-like knives. He watched as they deftly cut through the brambles and branches to make a wider path for those following behind. 'We need to be able to appeal to members of the Community and explain to them simply that they have been lied to without invalidating their whole existence.'

'They're a bunch of idiots,' spat one woman with cropped hair as she sliced her knife downwards across a clump of fern fronds. 'We'll overtake them in no time.'

Carter moved amongst the people, listening to their chatter. Each group sounded angrier than the last, their voices thick with resentment and disdain.

'I've been waiting all my life to destroy them,' said one man. 'I lost all my family when they poisoned our water.'

The other man beside him grunted in agreement. 'They'll get what's coming to them,' he laughed. 'I hear we're picking up a stash of guns – there might even be some rifles.' A group to their left cheered and slapped palms with them in solidarity.

A pack of teenagers, barely old enough to fight, held their spears up high, rushing through the trees, whooping, their faces daubed with thick mud and more sharpened sticks tucked into their rope-like belts.

'Kill them!' they yelled, as they darted through the forest.

As the day wore on, Carter felt a nagging worry grow in his chest. He caught up with Samuel who was pouring with sweat as he hacked through the bushes. 'We have a problem,' he said, urgently. 'These people want a war, not to educate.' He paused for a moment to move a branch out of his path. 'They're like you were, Samuel. They hate the Industry – as we all do – but they're confusing the Industry with the people. We need to talk to them.'

Samuel stopped for a moment and used his shirt to mop the wetness from his face. 'They've had a lifetime of seeing these people as the enemy,' he said, his voice curt. 'It's going to take time for them to see the Community as equals.'

'We don't have time,' said Carter. 'This could be a disaster – if we don't get the people in the Community on our side then we'll be destroyed the moment we walk through that gate.'

Samuel gritted his teeth and thought for a moment. 'We'll talk to them tonight,' he said. 'We need to make it to Woodford Hatch before dark or we'll lose half of them before we even get there.'

Carter nodded. 'You're going to need to convince them,' he said. 'They'll listen to you on this one.' They both half-laughed at the enormity of the situation. 'I never imagined in my wildest dreams that I'd be here with you, hacking out the innards of the Deadlands, working out a way to take down the Industry,' he said.

'Nor me,' replied Samuel, stomping down a huge patch of Japanese knotweed. 'Are you scared of going back in there, facing them?'

Carter thought for a moment. 'Not scared, no,' he said, slowly. 'Part of me of afraid of not succeeding – or succeeding but not being able to save Isabella. And my son, Ariel. And Alice,' he added.

Samuel shrugged. 'Remember what Jacinta said the first time we went out there? This is bigger than either of us, bigger than one person and that what we're doing is about the survival of everyone, not just those we love?'

'How long have you been a mouthpiece for our mother?' he said, smiling.

'Sometimes, even though I don't like it and she makes mistakes, she does talk a lot of sense.'

Carter nodded. 'True. And while that place is filled with many people I care about, including my son – and Isabella, it's them I'm fighting for.'

As the late afternoon wound itself up into early evening, the sun cast patchy shadows through the trees and the team found some cool relief in a shaded copse on the outskirts of the area that led towards the old Township. Carter felt a wave of sadness as he remembered that the last time they had been there had been shortly after the death of the brothers.

'Woodford Hatch,' said Samuel, stepping around the battered surfboard and the remnants of broken bottles that still littered the streets. 'This is where they came for him, for our great-grandfather, Richard Warren.'

As the dark shadow of Drakewater loomed to the east, Carter remembered what Samuel had told him about what Leanor had explained while he was being held captive in the Township. About how Richard had given himself to the enemy to save the others. He shivered in the cool evening air. 'We should gather everyone together,' he said. 'There are enough houses here for everyone to get some shelter and they can eat and rest in safety.'

They ushered the groups into Woodford Hatch through the deserted main square where climbing plants had wound themselves around old litter bins and lampposts so that just their eerie shapes remained. This was where they had been, thought Carter to himself – Richard and Alice – when they had fled the Community. He wondered if, generations later, Alice was still the same person that she had been before she had been so bitterly betrayed by the people that she had loved and cared about and how much of her genetics were intertwined with his in the twins, Ariel and Lucia. Even for a person who was used to a non-linear existence, someone who had seen mixed-age generations, the situation was bizarre and unreal. The girl who was so similar to him in age, had lived before the Storms and was the great-grandmother of his children. He shook his head – it all seemed too much to comprehend.

'They're all here,' said Samuel, his boots leaving a thick muddy trace on the brick blocks of the square. 'We should talk to them, like you said.'

Carter shook himself from the reverie and climbed onto a bench. The team of people supporting them stretched out wide; children played with the old pieces of plastic that littered the streets while others held the surfboard high above their heads, marching in time to a strange tune they all seemed to know.

'Hello,' said Carter. 'Hello.' The bustling noise continued until he shouted, loud across the square. His words echoed and reverberated inside his own head and he felt strangely nervous of the crowd he'd spoken to just hours ago – out here they seemed even wilder and somehow less contained.

'Samuel and I must speak with you,' he shouted. 'We want to make sure that we are all agreed on how we will approach the Community and how we can get them to understand what we are trying to do.'

'Don't care!' shouted the woman with the knife. She held it aloft, the blade sparkling in the sunset. 'We just want to kill them all!' A cheer rose up from the crowd and Carter looked at Samuel. 'Get up here,' he hissed. 'You need to deal with them – this is something they will listen to you about, rather than me.'

Samuel leapt onto the bench, quietening the crowd. 'Friends,' he started, loudly, waiting for the group to settle. 'As you know, what we are about to do is very dangerous. But many of the people inside those Barricades are just like us.'

'No, they're not!' shouted a man jumping onto a neighbouring bench. 'They're animals, you've always said that and they need to be taken down!'

Samuel nodded gravely. 'You are right, that *is* what I have always told you. And sometimes we can make judgements about people before we know the whole truth.'

He turned to Carter. 'When my brother first arrived here, I believed he was one of them – just the same as them. The type of person who would cut off our water supply, send drones out to kill our people and try to destroy us.' The crowd roared in agreement, then settled but were still agitated as Samuel silenced them. 'But I was wrong. We were wrong,' he continued.

'Stop right there, Samuel.' The man on the bench turned himself around to address the groups of people below him. 'Just because you've found your long-lost brother and had a change of heart, doesn't mean we have to forgive them for what they've done to us.'

'Yeah!' shouted the woman with the knife. 'My brother disappeared when they attacked Company Five and if they killed him then I'm going to kill them!' A roar emanated from the people around her and she threw her arm in the air, warrior-like.

'And my brother was poisoned when they contaminated our water supply!' screamed a young boy.

'The people of the Community are not the same as the Industry,' shouted Samuel. 'I agree with you – those responsible for causing our Village hardships over the years must be punished but we can't place all that blame on the those who had no part to play in that.' He turned to Carter. 'Many of us, including me and my brother have family inside those walls. Family who don't even know there is a world outside of that toxic compound. There are only a small number of people who are aware of us – our very existence is a secret so that the Industry can prove to their people how powerful they are. They're NOT the only ones who were able to rise up and survive after the Storms – we did that too. We did that without electricity and hospitals and all the technology that they have inside their headquarters. *We* did it without lies and manipulation, without making our people suffer.'

There were a few nods from the crowd as he continued.

One woman put her hand in the air. 'Maybe Samuel is right,' she said, to a grumbling from the crowd. 'Maybe what we've learned over the years about them isn't right either. Maybe both us and the Community folk have been wrong about each other.'

The woman next to her frowned. 'But we *are* right,' she said. '*They're* the ones who've been kept in the dark.'

'What if we're both right and we're both wrong? We don't know exactly what those people in there are like and what they're thinking

– just like they don't know us. It's time we all knew the truth about each other.'

There was an excited rumbling from the crowd and Carter nodded. 'The majority of the people of the Community are innocent,' he started, 'just like you are. In some ways they're worse off as they don't even know what the world outside can offer them. We need to give them the chance to exist alongside us.'

The knife-waver narrowed her eyes. 'But what if they don't agree?' she called. 'Can we kill them then?'

Carter smiled at her gently. 'We will need to give them time,' he said, loudly. 'Many more people are below ground – some of them will have been there since the waters subsided and others, we know, will be open to what we have to say.' He thought of Isabella and the other rebels who had been desperate to leave and change the world. 'But there are others who will be frightened and confused. Can you imagine if your whole world was a few square miles of a city you've never left? That you've always been told that everything outside of the Barricades would kill you?'

The woman shrugged. 'I wouldn't have believed it,' she said. 'I'm not that stupid.'

Carter smiled. 'The people inside are not stupid either,' he replied. 'But the power of the Industry has always been the control of its people through what they present to them. You are the living and breathing proof that what they've been told isn't true.'

The woman shrugged again and pulled her knife to her side. 'But what about those others? The ones who control everything.'

'Those are the ones we need to target,' said Carter. 'But remember, we need to be careful and clever. Our first job is to turn their own people against them – and then we have a chance at succeeding.

Without the Community supporting us, we will be outnumbered very quickly and the Industry will win.'

'We must avoid innocent deaths at all costs,' said Samuel, his voice strong. 'These people are our sisters and brothers and have suffered at the hands of the Industry for long enough. We are there to liberate them, not to destroy them.'

The woman nodded begrudgingly and held her knife up in front of her. 'If anyone comes for me, I'm going to give them a good look at this,' she said, holding it tightly. 'And no one ain't gonna stop me.'

'We all need to learn from each other,' the woman in the crowd who had first agreed with Carter called out. 'Otherwise, how are we going to make this situation any better? We join together with their people to defeat the Industry. Agreed?'

As they settled into one of the upstairs rooms, Carter handed Samuel a packet of food from the large rucksack he'd brought with them.

'You did well up there,' he said. 'I think they understand now.'

Samuel nodded in agreement. 'Hope so,' he said, his mouth full of bread. 'But changing minds and behaviours is a long process.'

Carter laughed. 'It took both of us a while, I suppose. But we're doing all right now, aren't we?'

'Yep,' said Samuel, biting into an apple. 'You're not as bad as I thought.'

Outside in the streets there was the dim flicker of candles and the buzz of quiet conversation as the last of the Villagers crammed into the remaining houses and Carter threw himself down onto a worn bed that he'd covered with old blankets from a cupboard in the next room. Already, Samuel was snoring and exhaustion was beginning to creep into his bones. Before his eyes finally closed, he thought of Alice and her journey, hoping desperately that she and Lily were working closely with the rebels to get together an army. That night, his dreams were filled with terrifying images of hundreds of thousands of people leaping from the top of the tower, screaming and calling his name. He saw their faces – Alice, Ariel, Lucia, Angel and lastly, Isabella. She called his name several times before plummeting into the council gardens below, smashing her head on the rocks that spelled OTHERS.

He awoke in a cold sweat, Samuel shaking him hard.

'Carter, you're dreaming,' he whispered. 'Go back to sleep. They won't all die, I won't let that happen.'

When Carter opened his eyes again, the room was still dark, but Samuel was awake. He handed his brother some water and pushed the remainder of what they had unpacked into the rucksack.

'We leave soon,' he said. 'We need to arrive at sunset and the troops are already restless. Some of them have gone on ahead.'

Carter rubbed his eyes and pulled a shirt over his head. At his side, the knife and gun he kept so close to him glinted in the small amount of sunlight that had started to creep through the early morning clouds.

'I'm ready,' he said, hauling his stiff body off the wooden frame. 'Let's go.'

By the time Carter reached the street, some of the smaller groups had started to congregate at the main square, eager to start the next part of the journey to the Community.

'When we get closer, we'll follow the curve of the river,' said Samuel to a few of the group leaders. 'We won't be following the usual route to the sluice gates, we're going much further south, until we get to the west side of the Community.' He turned to Carter. 'That's what she said, isn't it?'

'Yes,' replied Carter, hitching his backpack over his shoulders. 'We'll need to cross the river. Lily said there's a part that you can wade across.'

'But we go through the tunnel first and collect the weaponry. That's the quickest way.' Samuel took a long drink. 'I'll lead,' he said.

It took them around two hours of trekking southwards to find it but the tunnel, carved into the nearside bank of the Black River, had definitely been used recently. There was a mishmash covering of wooden pallets and metal plates that Saul had barricaded across the front but it was definitely there. A steep concrete slope led down to where it wound a straight path underneath the slow-flowing body of water that ran westwards, just about one hundred metres away from them.

Carter and Samuel sped ahead of the group and down the long slope towards the entrance, pulling off the coverings and tossing them in a heap at the side of the slope. Others ran to join them and, once they'd removed the last of the wooden pallets from the front of the tunnel, they could see that it was just over head height, but pitch-black inside. The large crowd of people behind them had mostly caught up and as many as could fit gathered around them, with others standing on the walkway above.

Questions flurried around as Carter climbed up the bank and held his hands up to silence them. He watched Samuel flare up a wood torch, wound with rags and doused in spirits, and then enter the tunnel cautiously.

'What is it?'

'Where are we going?'

'What's inside?'

Carter held his hands in the air again to stall the questions. 'This tunnel runs underneath the river, which will lead us to the western bank where we can follow the river south and then east, down towards the Community, where we will meet Alice Davenport and Angel,' he said. 'The next part of our journey is likely to be more dangerous – there will be less woodland but at times more buildings that will shield us from anyone being able to see us. Although a good part of this will be out in the open, so you will need to stay alert.'

Samuel emerged from the tunnel, his arms full of weaponry and the torch between his teeth. He pushed it into the grassy mound, the flames dancing and casting bright shadows onto the ground.

'Team leaders come to me,' he shouted, handing out guns to the most responsible individuals known to him – and threw one up the bank to Carter.

'Not loaded.' He smiled and then addressed the crowd. 'These are untested,' he said as the men and women looked at him in surprise. 'They've been gifted to us by a friend and, therefore, you'll need to check they are working, rather than depend upon them right at the moment you need them.'

He beckoned to Carter who slid down the bank and stood next to him. 'Carter and I will go ahead while you have an early lunch. Finish everything you have to eat today as we have a short march and then we'll be crossing the river to the Barricades.'

As they entered the gloom of the tunnel, Carter felt a chill run down his spine. Anticipation and fear filled him but the most important thing was not to show it. Guilt coursed through him for the hordes of people who had started to tramp behind him and Samuel through the tunnel; what fate might await them? Did they have any idea what they had let themselves in for? Were they blindly fighting for what they believed was right? Or did they just want revenge?

They headed directly south, past storm-battered warehouses and broken boats with the river behind them as well as snaking around to their left. Much of the wreckage of the Storms had weathered over the century or so that had passed but most elements were still recognisable from what Carter had read in the books he'd found in Jacinta's house – parts of shop fronts, road signs, clothing and even human and animal bones, although some looked more recent than others.

He glanced across the river every so often and caught the occasional glint of the Barricades far across the water as they walked past the gaps between the buildings.

'Go further inland,' he called out to Samuel and the others leading the groups. 'We need to stay vigilant and keep our eyes out for drones. Although the Community is still a long way across the Black River, we need to get to the far south-west, which means we're exposed here. And we need to go fast – we only have a few hours before sunset.'

Before long the land became patchier, the once heavily populated, busy dockland areas giving way to scrubby parcels of ground dotted with the fallen masonry of once-proud buildings and the occasional signage for bus stops and tube stations.

'How much further?' said Carter to Samuel. 'Lily mentioned that there was an area of the river that was shallower, somewhere we would be able to cross.'

'I suppose we'll know when we see it,' mumbled Samuel, a small stain of blood from his shoulder injury leaking onto his shirt. They

ulled the teams into a side street as a flock of birds skittered above
hem in the sky; both brothers concerned that it had been a drone.

'We must be pretty close,' said Carter, looking behind him as the
rowds limped onwards. 'People are getting tired and it's late.' He cast
is eyes up into the sky. 'The sun is nearly setting.'

'We should head back towards the river,' said Samuel. 'We haven't
ome far enough to miss it, but we need to stay close.'

'Look!' From the back of the crowd came a small boy's voice. Carter
urned to him but he was pointing slightly further ahead. 'Look, it's
he church!'

Right in front of them stood the broken outline of a church, its
pire withered in the sunlight and half-damaged by the Storms. They
eaded towards the river, Samuel wading in, waist deep, carrying his
ag over his head.

'Kaleb, Arya, Olyvia – you all stay here and put people into groups,'
e called back. 'Carter and I will go first and then signal for you to
ome. Stay behind the buildings out of sight if you can. Don't cross
inless we tell you it's safe.'

The others nodded and Samuel headed deeper into the water.
Carter stood at the edge nervously, pushing the Industry's lies about
oxic poisons and monsters from his head.

'It's not the truth,' he whispered to himself. 'The truth will set
ou free.'

The water was cold and, soon, Carter was waist-deep too, the
darkness swirling around his stomach. He took slow steps but hastened
imself to keep up with Samuel who was almost halfway across.

'Come on,' called Samuel. 'It's nearly sunset, we need to hurry.'

Carter nodded, keeping his mouth fully closed as Lily had advised.
The water was faster moving than he had imagined but he was able

to keep his footing on the broken stones that littered the riverbed, rather than having to swim – and for that he was eternally thankful.

When he finally reached the other side, Samuel was sat on the bank, shaded by a bush, swigging from a bottle of water. 'You made it, brother,' he said half-laughing and offering him his hand. He pulled him up onto the bank and they crawled into the brush, out of sight of the Barricades. Carter slicked the water from his hair and took a drink from Samuel, his eyes focusing on the large metal and concrete wall that stood between them and the Community.

'It looks even bigger from the outside,' he said in awe. 'It seems so threatening, formidable almost.' The glinting metal reflected the last rays of the sun across the water. On the other bank, Carter could just make out the people of the Village, sat together in small groups.

Samuel looked back at the wall. 'I don't know what formidable means but if you're saying it's pretty nasty looking, I agree with that.'

They sat there for a while, waiting for the final rays of the sun to set, staring at the sheet metal and stone, shredded with broken glass and rounded at the top with thick barbed wire. Carter remembered being on the other side when he first stepped off the Transporter; watching the mist rise across the top of the Barricades, out into the Deadlands.

'There's the gate,' he said, smiling and pointed across the grassy verge. 'I can see it.' The metallic cobalt-blue door cut into the wall glowed in the sunlight within easy reach of where they sat. They waited a little longer until just a fingernail of red lingered on the horizon before making their way quickly out of the bushes and out towards the gate, beckoning to the others to start their journey across the Black River.

Samuel pressed himself as close to the Barricade as he dared and waited for any sound of movement on the other side. Carter crept

uietly to the door and touched it quickly with his finger. 'It's not
lectrified,' he mouthed to Samuel, who nodded and pressed his ear
gainst the metal plate. But there was nothing.

'Lily,' he whispered. 'Lily, are you there?'

Silence.

They watched as the first of their group crossed the river and bedded
lown behind a small stone building out of sight of the Barricades.

'You sure you got the day right?' said Samuel. 'You didn't lose track
f the time while we were out there?'

'Of course I didn't,' snapped Carter. 'Shut up so I can listen.' He
ressed his ear up against the gate again. 'Lily,' he hissed. 'Open the
ate, we've arrived.'

Nothing.

'She's not coming,' said Samuel angrily. 'We're stuck here.'

'We'll wait,' said Carter. 'She will be here; I know she will. What you
aid to me when we were in the forest about knowing McDermott – she
wants this to succeed as much as any of us. She will be here. Let's take
t in turns to rest and tell the others to do the same.'

The last rays of the sun disappeared across the river as the final group
nade their way out of the water in the darkness. Carter and Samuel
at up against the Barricades, while the others sheltered nearer to the
river bank, at the edge of the floodplain, in the crumbling remains of
he outbuildings. As the moon appeared from behind the darkness of
a wispy cloud, there was the sound of an owl, hooting from the other
side of the wall. Carter opened his eyes wide and there was a rustling
n the darkness. Then it stopped. He looked at Samuel who was asleep.

'Lily, is that you?' he whispered loudly. 'Lily?'

Samuel stirred a little next to him and reached for his gun. The
rustling continued and then, again, it stopped.

'Carter,' his brother whispered, urgently. 'My gun is gone.'

'Lily,' said Carter, this time more loudly. 'You need to let us in, we lost the key.'

'You mean this one?'

There was a shuffling and then, out of the darkness, the familiar patterned face of Frida emerged with the master key in one hand and Samuel's gun in the other.

Chapter Sixteen

The Broadcast

'We need to find her,' shouted Alice, furiously cursing herself for having let Izzy out of her sight in the first place. 'We need to find her NOW!'

Lily paced the room shaking her head, while Catherine sat sobbing quietly in the corner.

'She's going to freeze us,' Catherine wailed. 'She's going to kill us. She will kill my sister and then she'll come for me.'

'We have to get out of here,' said Lily, as she marched past. 'She'll send people straight here; she knows where we are.'

'Stop panicking,' called Angel, calmly. 'She's weak and she can't have gone far. Plus, she has Samita with her. But you're right, we can't stay here for much longer.'

Alice peered through the window, watching the blazing sun arch dark red over the trees. She felt the anger rise and fall inside of her. 'Carter will be back here soon,' she said. 'He'll bring enough people with him to be able help us. But right now, we need to find her.'

'And we need to talk to Ariel,' Catherine sobbed, her hands shaking. 'Aside from Izzy, he's the most powerful person in here and the only one who will be able to help us – if we tell him the truth and that Izzy has taken Samita…'

'You three go and find him. Use the computer thing or whatever.' Alice breathed deeply. 'I'm going after her.' She pulled on the hard Industry uniform cap and military-style jacket. 'I should never have left her. Not then and not now.'

Outside the light was beginning to fade and the air tasted bitter. Alice felt the pounding in her head mirror the banging of her heart inside her chest. She thought of all the places Izzy could have gone. Injured, and with Samita in tow, they would be limited but the place where she had always gone to, even when she was younger, had been Barnes's Lab. The Lab that was now hers. As much as she dreaded entering the Industry building, she knew she would have to make her way there before Izzy herself arrived. She felt sick; a deep nauseating sickness that hollowed out a deep pit in her stomach and made her ache for the days before the Storms.

She instinctively moved north through the trees, every sense heightened as her pace increased. The dank, woody smell and the still, warm heat of the afternoon sun made her skin clammy under the thick material of the uniform and her mouth felt dry. Her mind raced with what Catherine had discovered: radio signals? Messages from another facility just like the Ship? With Izzy escaping she had almost forgotten but now she let the full horror of what might be true sink in. It wasn't until she was deep in the woods and heard the snap of the twig behind her that she realised she was being followed.

'I knew you'd come alone, half-breed council house trash. The others couldn't bear to come with you, could they?' Izzy stood there, a gun in her hand and an ugly grin on her twisting its way across her lips. 'Bored of your bossiness and whining already?' She waved the gun at Alice, her face menacing and angry.

'Where's Samita?' Alice kept her voice calm. 'What have you done with her?'

'Your granddaughter?' Izzy tightened her mouth and aimed the gun at Alice's head. 'She's in a safe place, you don't need to worry about her any more.'

'Have you hurt her?'

'That,' said Izzy, advancing towards Alice, 'is none of your concern.' She stood so close to her that Alice could feel her breath on her face. High in the trees there was the hoot of an owl. For a moment, she thought she could grab the gun from the girl but the dark glint in Izzy's eye told her that she'd already anticipated that move. Alice glanced behind her.

'Don't even think about it,' snarled Izzy. 'You're coming back to the Control Room with me.' She smiled sweetly. 'And don't even think about trying to run – you know I'm the best shot this Community has ever seen.' She turned Alice around and pushed her forward. 'Walk,' she said, pushing the gun into her back.

'You won't kill me,' spat Alice defiantly. 'You need me to prove to the people that I'm a traitor and you—' she laughed with irony '—that you are their saviour.' Alice cursed herself for not being more careful tracking Izzy – the girl had been trained by Filip and by the best in the Industry. Even injured, she would pose the greatest threat imaginable.

'I will kill you if I need to,' replied Izzy. 'You need to remember that you're no longer the great prodigy, Alice Davenport, who took the first steps into the drowned world, intent on saving the human race.' She laughed: a mean, chilling, short laugh. 'You are nothing but a failed mother, just like your own.'

Alice gritted her teeth and tried to remain calm. 'What is it you have against me, Izzy?' She held her jaw strong. 'I tried to take care of you when you had no one else. I wanted nothing but the best for you.'

The girl pushed the metal hard against Alice's skin. 'You took him away from me,' she hissed. 'Filip. He was my adopted brother before the Storms – even before he met you. The one person who loved me and you changed all that. You tried to turn him against me.' She shoved Alice forwards. 'He was never like that before. He changed when you got together with him and came to live with us. You tried to boss him around too. *He* should have been the only person in charge of setting up the Community and instead you had to try to take over. Barnes said that all you cared about was having the power and you didn't care about anybody else. She said you'd try to get rid of Filip – and me – and that you'd betray us all in the end.' Izzy looked calm, terrifyingly confident. 'And Barnes was right, wasn't she?' she added.

The childlike quality of the girl's voice made Alice wince. 'I cared about you,' she said, finally. 'And I cared about Filip, but what was happening wasn't right.'

'You sound like Kelly,' said Izzy, dismissively. 'She wanted to let outsiders into our sanctuary – to bring in their pollution and their old-world ways. She tried to make friends with them and open our borders. You will not ruin what we have planned for the next generation of the Community, Alice. This is much bigger than you'

'You killed her,' interrupted Alice, angrily. 'You killed my friend and Carter's daughter! What is wrong with you? What made you so hateful towards people?'

For a moment there was a silence. A silver moon appeared from behind the trees.

'What could you possibly know about Carter Warren?' Izzy asked sharply. 'Unless he's been here. Unless he's still here?' She whirled around and pressed the gun to Alice's temple. 'I believed he'd been murdered…' It took a moment for the realisation to dawn on her and she rolled her eyes. 'McDermott, of course. She's been a traitor to our people all along.' Her lips tightened. 'She'll die too, of course, when the time comes. As will Carter Warren, if he's still in here.' She primed the gun and dragged it slowly across Alice's forehead. 'You *will* tell me,' she said. 'But for now, Alice, we must say goodbye.'

And then everything in Alice's world turned to a silvery black.

When she regained consciousness, Alice felt a dull thudding ache clouding her brain. Her head throbbed and, as she reached up to run her fingers over the wound, she realised her hands were securely fastened to something and she could not move. She gingerly tried to open her eyes, sticky and scratchy with what she presumed was her own blood but the pain in her head urged her to keep them closed. When she finally brought herself to widen her eyes enough to see the room around her, she found that she was alone, tied to a chair, in the Control Room. The saving grace was that she hadn't been shot – simply smashed on the head with the barrel of Izzy's gun.

A sickness swirled in Alice's stomach as she watched the familiar screens in front of her synthesising data, maps with coloured dots that moved continuously and graphs that charted all elements of the Community. Alice shivered and felt the hollow emptiness in her stomach lurch as she remembered the last time she had been in that same chair, in that same room. Echoes of Filip's words grazed her senses and images of Quinn and Barnes standing over her flashed before her eyes. The hurt and betrayal pained her deeply, shortly before they had cut her baby from her over eighty years before. She shivered; it was happening again, only this time it was unlikely Elizabet would let her live at the end of it and there was no Kunstein to stand up for her.

'You're awake then?' The door to the Control Room ground open and shut again as Izzy strode into the room. She had changed her clothes into a plain white suit with a bright red cravat, her hair braided tightly around her head. She popped two pills into her mouth and downed them with a glass of water. Alice felt her dry throat parch and she swallowed hard.

Izzy placed a glass to her lips and tipped it so that a small trickle of water grazed her lips.

'It must feel just like the old times being in here,' she continued, pulling a gun from her pocket and twirling it around her finger. 'Nothing much has changed, has it? You're still a traitor and I'm still the biggest influence in your life.' She passed the gun from one hand to another and held it towards Alice. 'You left this on the table at McDermott's house – quite careless really, considering that half-witted granddaughter of yours was the only person left downstairs.' She smiled. 'I made it quick for her, I promise.'

Alice glanced around for anything she could use to free herself. 'Jescha told me what happened to you after I left,' she said slowly through gritted teeth. 'It must have been difficult for you – you were just a young girl and I know how hard those expectations must have been.'

Elizabet moved in close to her face. 'You took my brother and then you took my dreams,' she whispered. 'Until you came along, Filip doted on me. He took care of me and he treated me like an equal. And then *you*—' she pointed a finger into Alice's cheek '—*you* took him away from me. He changed.' An angry tear formed in the corner of one eye. 'He changed and it's all your fault. Even *then* I knew you were going to ruin everything for me so I made sure that Barnes knew you were having doubts about the Community.' She pursed her lips in that defiant way that Alice remembered she did as a ten-year-old. 'Barnes didn't like you anyway and thought you were a threat to our society, so it wasn't that hard to ruin everything for *you.* I might have been a child, but you weren't the only prodigy on that Ship.' Her bottom lip quivered dangerously. 'You, Marcus, Kelly… you were all in my way, so I got rid of you. You underestimated me, Alice. You really did.'

Alice sat in a shocked silence. From the murder of her friend, to the division between her and Filip; so much of that was down to the small, excitable young pre-teen with the sweet smile who was often found cartwheeling through her house.

'Wilson wanted *me* to lead the people with Filip,' she continued, unprompted. But Kunstein insisted it should be you because you were older. Because you were *her* choice.'

'You did all this because you were jealous of me?' Alice shook her head in disbelief. 'People *died.* Was this all about you being in control? I didn't do anything to hurt you deliberately.' Her eyes widened. 'People died, Izzy,' she repeated.

The girl's eyes narrowed. 'Don't call me that,' she said bitterly. 'That's a child's name.' She turned away from Alice. 'All of this, it's for a greater good,' she continued, quietly. 'What Filip and Barnes started, I intend to finish.'

'What do you mean?'

The girl looked at her sweetly. 'These people have never really known anything else. There is no one left who was alive before the Storms, but some of them are beginning to get curious. Too many to manage. So, we need to make a change.' She sounded wistful and way older than her teenage years. 'Even those who work for me have begun to lose faith in the way we live our lives. I will be the one who is remembered in history for regenerating our Community.'

'Tell me about the other facility. What is in the north, Izzy?'

The girl's face paled. 'How do you know about that?' she asked quietly, moving across the room and fiddling with one of the screens, her back to Alice.

'So, it's true then?'

In the corner of the Control Room a large spotlight glared a bright fluorescence onto a workstation where large maps projected from screens onto walls. Alice recognised one she had not seen in many years – an outline map of the whole of Great Britain. The land was divided into different patterns and shapes and two whole sections were coloured bright red. One in London and the other further north, towards what she recognised as Manchester. Elizabet snapped a button and the screen faded to black.

'None of that is your business,' she said, coldly. 'Although your presence here will help my people to see exactly what happens to those who are not a part of our Community. What happens to those who fail and betray us.' She paused. 'There were those who have thought that having small groups living outside of our Barricades was in some way acceptable – the "they don't bother us and we won't bother them men-tality", but that doesn't work.' She smiled, a malevolent, dark scratch in her face. 'Barnes knew it and I knew it but we couldn't convince everyone. And the time is now. I will not let anyone stand in my way.'

She ran the palm of her hand down Alice's cheek. 'Even Filip was weak in the end – he was the one who let those tattooed freaks at the Township live in exchange for Richard Warren.' She smiled, distracted. 'He should have killed them all there and then, like Barnes suggested, out he let some of them stay. I remember the day Filip came home with the Warren boy. He was so angry – and Richard put up such a fight. He defended you to the end, Alice. He died for you, you know.' She shrugged. 'I've no idea why – you're nothing but an inconvenience. Always have been, always will be. Even your own mother thought that, didn't she?' Elizabet busied herself at the terminal. 'But that's all in the past – now we need to move forwards. And, for once in your life you are going to be useful to me. You are going to help me to show the idiots out there that the Industry has been too soft for too long. It is time for the new generation, Alice. The new Industry. And I will lead them.'

Alice squirmed in her chair, twisting her wrists in an effort to get free but the ropes were tied much too tightly for her to move. She used all her strength to push her arms up the chair and winced as her skin rubbed up against a gouge in the wood, drawing blood.

She felt sick deep inside her stomach as she watched Izzy delightedly angling screens, switching buttons and adjusting lighting until she was content. The girl hummed to herself as she worked – an unsettling, almost joyful tune from a time before the Storms.

'I thought old world ways were frowned upon,' she said curtly. 'No singing and dancing, no music, that kind of thing. Wasn't that what we agreed?'

Izzy turned and patted her on the head. 'Well done, little Alice, you remembered,' she said with an overly patronising tone. 'Music upsets people and makes them overemotional, doesn't it? And sport makes them violent, and hobbies are a waste of time?' She laughed as Alice's face turned a dark shade of crimson. 'I know, it must be embarrassing to have your words played back to you. But you created this, Alice. This is your fault. And now it's your time to pay.'

Alice bit down on her lip, closing her eyes against the shameful memories. She *had* been a part of this, had set up this world. When she opened her eyes once more, the screens in front of her had changed – one showed Unity Square, where a large group of people had gathered, and another flicked between the various work departments within the Industry headquarters – the Food Plant, the Synthetics Labs and other areas that Alice had never seen before. Another screen captured moving images from the empty perimeter of the Barricades. Alice scanned the crowds for any sign of Lily and the others but there was no one she recognised. The group in the Square looked confused, disorientated somewhat – perhaps even displaced.

There were thousands of them crammed together – more people than Alice had seen since before the Storms. They stood in small clusters that overlapped and spilled out of the square onto the edges of the streets. From where she sat, Alice could not see the detail of the faces but, impossibly, she longed to catch a glimpse of someone she knew who could give her comfort. But unless the camera panned and zoomed, she was unable to see anything other than a mass of thousands of faces that twitched and blinked in the early evening dimness. Her heart sank as she took in the mass of them – each one of them unaware of the lies they had been told and the further untruths that Izzy was about to impart upon them. It some ways it reminded her of the mass rallies she had seen on television in the days before the Storms – the government protests against the failing economy and cruel dictatorships in the months before everything turned crazy. She felt a dark pain rise from deep inside of her.

'Live in three, two, one… Ready to broadcast!' shouted Izzy, triumphant and delighted as a small light at the top of the lens pointed at them glowed green. She pursed her lips into a tight smile and addressed the crowds.

'Good evening, everyone,' she said solemnly. 'My name is Elizabet Conrad and I am your Controller General. Tonight, I will be bringing you a special broadcast from the Control Room and projected live to all of you, whether you are at work or at home and, for this, I have allowed all production to stop.' She cleared her throat. 'Be aware that this is the most important broadcast you will ever hear – this will be the speech that will change the course of history.'

Alice shuffled awkwardly in the chair next to her, desperately trying to edge her hands from underneath the thick rope. She felt the sharp edge of the wood against her skin again, sticky with blood, and edged her arm around so that the rope rubbed up against the roughness. She watched the crowd in Unity Square throw up their arms in jubilation. There were many people there – but not anywhere near as many as she would have expected for such a proclamation.

Elizabet fiddled with the screens and stepped back towards the camera. 'In the short time I have had available to notify you, you should have all received an official warning that this is a mandatory viewing broadcast and, therefore, if you have any colleagues or relatives who are not in front of a screen right now, you should advise them that they have one hour to make themselves available to witness this broadcast.' She smiled sweetly. 'I strongly suggest – no, I *demand* – that you watch together, in Unity Square. There will be no exceptions and anyone who has not been registered as attending this session will be dealt with by me *personally* in the coming days.' The word 'personally' was malicious, malevolent even.

Alice pulled her legs backwards, and subtlety circled her ankles in an attempt to free herself. The chair she was tied to was worn and smooth, no rough edges to drag the rope against, and besides, her arms were tied so tightly she could get no leverage. She glanced across at Izzy, who was smiling broadly and angled the camera towards Alice.

'As you will see, I have with me today someone that some of you may recognise.' She smiled and ruffled her fingers through Alice's hair, making her shiver. The screens around the walls of the Control Room broadcast shocked faces across the Community; there were some who cast a glazed look and others who turned to the person next to them, shaking their heads. A group in one corner of Unity Square started to wave their arms in the air, their faces aghast and shocked.

'This woman,' said Elizabet, slowly, 'is someone you will all have learned about in your schooldays – someone you may have perhaps admired or wished you could have met.' She cleared her throat. 'But today, I can tell you that all you learned about was a lie. Today I can expose her for who she really is and what her contribution to our society was. But you must all be in attendance.'

Alice opened her mouth to speak but, as she did so, Elizabet placed her palm across her lips. 'Your turn to address the crowd will come,' she said, shortly. 'For now, we will focus on the truth of your trial and you will have the opportunity to defend yourself when I have finished giving my evidence.' She turned to face Alice and pulled a chair up opposite her so that they were both side on to the camera.

Alice felt herself shiver as the girl came close to her. 'You're a liar,' she spat at Izzy, her eyes gleaming with rage and her voice shaking with anger. 'You have no right to do this.'

From the darkness of the back corner of the room, an Industry Guard peeled out from the shadows, his weapon trained on Alice as he reloaded another, one-handed and gave it to Elizabet, who put it down on her desk.

'One more word and he will put a bullet through your head,' Elizabet whispered. 'The people deserve to know what a fraud you are and it is the job of our Controller General to expose you.'

As her initial terror at the new threat in the room subsided, Alice's eyes became accustomed to the uniformed figure in the room, his eyes and shape so familiar to her. 'Jayden?' she whispered. 'Jayden Woolcroft – is that really you?' She remembered the overgrown teenager, large and muscular for his age who had been one of the Original Scouts. The boy who had helped her carry the body of her friend Jonah when he had died in the first days after they had come above ground. Now, his eyes looked dark and vacant, the kind, soft tone of them had disappeared and his face looked rough – but empty. Through the dim light, out of sight of the camera, he held the gun firm, his finger resting on the trigger. Alice started to speak but stopped again as he aimed higher, closing one eye to perfect his shot.

Alice tried to think about the last time she had seen him – had it been Kelly's funeral? In the days after she had been killed, he had been kind to her and had visited her in the home she had shared with Filip, but only when she had been alone.

'I should have been there,' he'd said, inconsolable. 'I was supposed to be on duty with Marcus and Kelly when she was shot but Izzy asked me to move some things out of one of the houses. She said it was important – Barnes had told her to ask me.' Tears had rolled down his cheeks. 'If I'd been there with them then it would never have happened, I would have been able to protect her.'

Alice had held his large frame tightly. 'It wasn't your fault,' she'd whispered. 'They had guns and they'd have shot you too.'

Now Alice's eyes burned with anger as she realised how Jayden had been tricked into leaving Kelly alone at the Barricades so that Izzy could attack her. He looked so different in many ways now – his eyes were empty and devoid of emotion but he was still the same, bulky, gentle-looking boy who had been one of the first to explore the world with her and the others. Was there anything she could say to him that would make him remember that they had been friends – good friends – and that they had rediscovered the world together after the Storms? He stared at her, unblinking, his unnerving calmness making her heart beat fast and hard in her chest.

Elizabet narrowed her eyes thoughtfully and poked a bony finger into Alice's chest. Her hands were smooth and childlike; Alice remembered holding them in her own when the small girl had cried when she was much younger.

'Tell the people your name,' said the girl, pressing her finger deep into Alice's chest, making her flinch. 'You may speak to confirm your name only and then—' she turned back to face the screen '—I will expose your story to the whole of our Community.'

Alice swallowed deeply and took a deep breath. 'My name is Alice Davenport,' she said, in a mixture of pride and anger, watching the awe and horror of the faces on the screens in front of her. 'My name is Alice Davenport,' she repeated. 'And I was one of your Original Scouts.'

Chapter Seventeen

The Infiltration

'What the hell are you doing here?'

With no regard for the weapon in her hand, Carter grabbed the key from Frida and wrapped his arms around her in a warm embrace. Samuel eyed her cautiously, his hand outstretched for the return of his gun.

Frida's face held a superior, strong look in the moonlight. She held tight to the gun. 'I believe this belongs to my people, rather than yours,' she said directly, but there was a kindness in her face, tinged with worry.

'How did you find us? Is Eli here with you?' Samuel looked around nervously and then back at the river bank where the remainder of the Village were resting. He considered calling to them for help, but decided against it when Frida spoke.

'Some of my people and I came to help,' she said. 'We could not let you do this alone. We saw you when you arrived at Saul's tunnel – we had just got there ourselves and were about to climb down when we saw you. So then we tracked you downriver. But do not worry, Eli has not joined us.' She shook her head and smiled sadly. 'There was much trouble after you left but those people loyal to me believed that the only choice was to come and help you.' She ran her hand down the side of her face, the moonlight revealing a dark purple bruise. 'There were some ugly scenes,' she said. 'But we have done the right thing.'

'How did you know about the tunnel?' Samuel asked in surprise. 'Saul said that it was a secret.'

'You think I do not know what my husband's activities were?' Frida laughed. 'You take me for some sort of fool? *He* was the fool to believe that he could keep that hidden from me. I knew when he didn't come home that night that something bad had happened to him. Although I did not know what.'

She waved the plastic master key in front of Carter. 'When I went through your bag and found this, I knew it was important and that I should bring it to you.' She placed her hand on Carter's shoulder. 'You risked your life to come and warn us, didn't you?'

He nodded. 'The Village and the Township are in danger,' he said. 'And we need every last person we have, to help change the minds of the people inside these walls. Many of them are innocent,' he added. 'They don't know that there is a life not dictated by the Industry. We have a moral and ethical obligation to help them. Our world needs to be different.'

Frida turned her head to face the river and made a rising and falling sound in her throat, a churring noise, similar to a nightjar. Stirring through the shadows, further down the river bank, appeared several of the people of the Township, the beautiful patterned swirls of their faces illuminated in the silver moonlight. They slunk from the darkness with an almost mythical quality, two at a time, and gathered on the floodplain in absolute silence.

Samuel stood stunned. 'You followed us all the way from the tunnel?' he said. 'All of you?'

Frida nodded. 'My people are expert trackers and marksmen,' she whispered. 'And all of us are joined with you in this.' She glanced at the door, handing Samuel back the gun. 'We should go.'

Carter placed the card against the smooth section of the gate. There was a clicking sound and then a grating and, as both Samuel and Carter drew their weapons and beckoned the people of the Village down at the river towards them, the only remaining official door into the Community opened and let in its first visitors since its installation.

As they passed through the gate, Carter wedged it open slightly with a jagged rock he found half buried in fern fronds at the side of a tree. The Township followed them inside and then each of the Company members filed through silently, their eyes wide with awe as they passed through and into the Community.

'Where do we go next?' Samuel asked Carter. 'This is your territory now.'

Carter squinted through the trees and scrubland towards the main part of the Community, which, by his calculations lay a few miles to the east. Aside from the squeak and buzz of hunting night creatures, there was complete silence and only the light of the pin-prick stars to direct them.

'Spark some torches,' he whispered to Frida and Samuel, his heart thumping in his chest, adrenaline shooting through his veins. 'We're going to Unity Square.'

The rhythmic crunch of twigs and the rustling of leaves underscored the march of the several hundred members of the newly formed Company towards the centre of the Community. Every so often the group paused; a wave of bodies that crouched to the ground in silence as the few night birds that circled through the trees made their way to hunt.

'Is it always this quiet?' whispered Samuel to Carter, nervously. 'I never imagined it would be this quiet.'

Carter shook his head. 'No,' he said. 'The broadcast must be happening now. We need to get to the square quickly and take the stage – explain to them what's been happening.'

'We've seen no one at all so far,' whispered Frida. 'Will they all be at the meeting place?'

'Most of them,' said Carter. 'These sorts of broadcasts are pretty much mandatory and most will have been allowed to leave work to attend in person.' He paused. 'Which means that the Industry Headquarters will be relatively empty – but all the Industry guards and anyone who remains loyal to Elizabet will be in amongst the people.' His face tightened. 'They do that to stop the rebels grouping together.'

'So, are you suggesting that we surround them in this Unity Square and prepare to get killed?' Frida looked at him in disbelief.

'We need to start by reasoning with them, explaining who we are and why we are there. I will address the crowd and explain. They will listen to me.'

Samuel looked somewhat less convinced. 'I hope so, brother,' he said with a tinge of doubt in his voice. 'But what do we do if the guards start to attack us?'

'We retaliate,' said Carter, regrettably. 'There will likely be a circle of guards around the edges. Where we can, we slip through but if any of us get caught, then we should kill them – but with as little noise as possible. We don't want the people of the Community to feel like they are under attack. We will not be able to take them all on.'

'What if…?' Samuel looked at him, a thousand possible questions in the tone of his voice, but both Frida and Carter knew what he was asking.

'Some of us may fall,' said Frida. 'But more of us will if we do not do this. A peaceful approach is our best chance but we must be prepared that this won't end well.'

Samuel nodded and they stood there, each holding their weapons tightly, each of them scared, but feeling more commitment than ever to what they were about to undertake.

They crept onwards, with Samuel, Carter and Frida leading them until they reached a small clearing in the forest.

'How's Elvira?' Samuel asked Frida quietly. 'Is she doing okay?'

'She's fine.' Frida smiled. 'Some of our people stayed behind to tend the sick and to make preparations in case our mission failed.' She shook her head. 'Eli remains convinced that this is not the business of the Township and they will be left unscathed by the Industry.' She smiled. 'The irony is that if we are successful, they will be safe and Eli will be right.'

Samuel touched her arm gently and breathed a heavy sigh of relief. 'I would rather prove that thug Eli right and succeed in what we need to do,' he said. 'And thank you for looking after our friend. It means a lot.' He looked at her carefully. 'What happened when we left? How did you manage to get out too?'

Frida shook her head. 'I don't have much time to explain,' she said cautiously. 'But suffice to say, there was a split amongst our people. There were those who chose to come and support you and a smaller group, including Eli, who opposed us.' She hesitated. 'They threatened us with violence. We had to detain them – they are being guarded until I return and we can determine what happens to them.'

The call of a nightjar interrupted them and they looked upwards into the trees. 'This is the last open space before we reach the main part of the Community,' announced Carter. 'We will need to split into groups and approach from all angles.' He positioned himself in the centre. 'Frida, take half the team to the east and then due north – that will bring you out at the front of the square. Samuel, you go east and then south. After that, you can bring your teams around the edges of the crowd and meet. Tell your people about our plans for the guards and that violence is only acceptable in extreme circumstances; if we can, we need to show that we come to them peacefully. The people must understand that we are not who they have been led to believe we are.'

Frida looked at him quizzically. 'And where will *you* be, Carter Warren?'

'I'm going to try to find Lily. And then I'm going into the Industry Headquarters.'

There was a flurry of whispers in the darkness as they passed the directions back to their teams and Samuel, Frida and Carter bid each other farewell. Frida kissed him on the cheek.

'You're a brave man,' she said finally. 'Without you we would never have known they were planning to attack and none of us would be here.'

'We only have one shot at this,' said Carter. 'If you come into contact with anyone – which is quite unlikely unless the broadcast ends early – surround them and include them. We don't have the resources to explain in detail to each individual person. I'm going to need to interrupt the broadcast and tell them myself.' He paused. 'Don't make a move until you hear from me or one of our rebels – if you can help it.'

Carter watched for a moment as the silhouetted bodies disappeared into the trees, the few torches that they carried glowing like fireflies in the darkness. Guilt wracked his heart – how many of them would die before any of them left the Community? *If* any of them left the Community alive at all.

The night air turned cold as he picked up the pace and started to run southwards towards the old Delaney house where he had last seen Alice, Lily and Angel. His feet pounded on the uneven track of the central path until he reached the broken-down outbuildings of the old village that had once stood there. Two large houses were still intact, set back from the road – one of which he'd been to before. It was the home of his children – Ariel and Lucia. And their mother, Samita.

And in the front room, he could see that there was the flicker of a light on.

The door stood slightly ajar. Carter looked behind him, back towards the forest and then back at the house. He couldn't see any movement but a deep instinct in his stomach urged him to move towards porch area. He pushed the door open and stepped inside.

The room was dimly lit but he could just make out a jumbled shape in the corner of the room that moved slightly as he came closer. He pulled his weapon and approached with caution. A groaning sound came from the bundle that was covered by an old blanket and from one corner he could just make out a flash of blonde hair.

'Ariel?' he whispered. 'Ariel, is that you?'

Carter lifted off the blanket and saw the face of his fifteen-year-old son, gagged, blindfolded and bound, laying on the floor. 'ARIEL!' shouted Carter and desperately pulled at the gag as the moaning continued.

'It was Elizabet,' gasped the boy as soon as his mouth was free. 'You have to stop her, she's gone crazy.' His words were garbled as Carter fumbled with the blindfold. 'She killed Samita! She killed my mother and she would have killed me if there hadn't been someone in the forest.' He gulped back emotion. 'I'm Controller General,' he said. 'But I never wanted to be. Why would she do this to me?'

Carter pulled off the blindfold and put his hand on the boy's shoulder. 'Where is she now?' he asked. 'Where is Elizabet?'

Ariel blinked, tears in his eyes, and looked up at him. 'Carter?' he said, in shock. 'Father, what are you doing here, I thought you were dead?'

Carter shook his head. 'That's what everyone wanted you to believe,' he said.

'You died a traitor, an escapee.' He paused for a moment, furrowing his bloodied forehead. 'You will be arrested,' he said. 'For treason. I should do that myself.'

'That's not exactly true,' said Carter. 'It's a long story and we don't have time for that now. Are you hurt? What did she do to you?'

Ariel stretched out his arms as Carter removed the binding. 'She said she would kill Samita unless I did what exactly she said,' he said, angrily. 'She tied me up and gagged me at gunpoint and then she took Samita upstairs and then I heard a gunshot.' His throat made a sad, guttural, choking sound. 'When she came back down she was alone. I don't think she had any bullets left because when she fired it at me, it didn't work but I was tied up and I couldn't do anything. Then all of a sudden, she stopped. She looked out of the window and her face changed and she made a spitting sound. I think there was someone out there in the woods – then she covered me up and disappeared outside.' His words were stumbling as his voice broke over the story.

Carter pulled him to his feet. 'I think you were very lucky,' he said. 'Did she say anything – maybe about Lily McDermott or where she might have been going?'

Ariel swallowed deeply. 'She said that the Warren-Davenports were the worst kind of people – even worse than the Lab Mades, because even though we are Descendants we're the product of two of the most espicable kinds of creatures.' He cleared his throat. 'When the sound came from outside, she just said "Davenport" and then left.'

'Alice,' said Carter, urgently. 'We need to find her, she's in danger if Elizabet knows that she's here.'

'Alice Davenport is awake?' said Ariel, shocked. 'But I saw her in the Catacombs.' He looked around the room. 'She's in Chamber One,' he whispered. 'I saw her.'

'I know,' replied Carter, pulling the boy to his feet. 'You're lucky to be alive. I need you to come with me.'

Ariel shook his head. 'I can't,' he said. 'What if people see me? I'm the Controller General and you're a rebel. I… I…' he started to stammer, confused and upset. 'I need to find Jescha; she'll know what to do.'

The boy cut a pathetic figure, dishevelled and broken. It struck Carter that most of his family had been murdered. He looked empty and alone. Carter put his arm around his shoulders, remembering how much weight he'd put on being a candidate for Controller General and how much he had thought it had meant to everyone in his entire world when, in the greater scheme of things, it meant so very little at all. It almost felt like talking to his younger self, just a few months ago.

'Ariel,' he said slowly, 'Elizabet is a very bad person and we need to stop her. That's partly why I am here. There are many, many things you don't know about the Industry, the Community and, most importantly, about Elizabet and our family. She caused the death of Lucia, Ariel. Being Controller General won't help you very much at the moment. I know that more than anyone.'

He looked deep into the boy's eyes. 'I know this is difficult, but you're going to need to trust me because I need your help.' Carter's heart ached for the boy, not much younger than himself, who stood there so naïve and delicate. He felt an overwhelming urge to hold him, to tell him that it would all be okay and to allow him to crumble into his arms and compensate for the years of his childhood that he had not been around. But, instead, he released him and pushed back on his shoulders, standing the boy upright until they were the same height.

Ariel bit his lip hard. 'I think she's horrible,' he said, sounding a little childlike and naïve. 'I loved my sister, even though I knew she was a rebel and I tried to protect her in the best way I could. But Elizabet's different. She's not like the other people in the Industry and she was starting to scare me. Some of the things she said I disagreed with and when I told her that she started to threaten me. We won't be able to overcome her on our own; she's too powerful. All the guards are on her side.'

'She scares lots of people,' said Carter, 'but we also have a lot of people here inside the Barricades who are willing to help us. Some of them have travelled a long way to be here – from outside the Community.'

'Outside?' the boy looked terrified. 'But what about disease and their weapons and—'

Carter shook his head. 'There are people on the outside who are just like us,' he said carefully, steadily. 'They are not a threat – at least not to us and to those people who want to live a free life.' He glanced outside the window, thick grey clouds skittering over the last rays of light. 'But we must leave,' he said, finally. 'We need to find Lily and Angel before it's too late.' He paused for a moment, fearing the worst. He had no idea if they were still alive or safe. 'We need to warn them that we're all in danger if Elizabet already knows that Alice is awake.'

Ariel nodded, deep in thought. 'I have to check on Samita first,' he said, finally. 'I know Elizabet would never have let her live, she hated her so much.' He strained his face, pushing back the tears. 'But I have to see her, even if it is just to say goodbye.' He took a deep breath. 'I want to go alone,' he said. 'Don't follow me.'

Carter sat quietly as his son padded upstairs and into the bedrooms. He thought back to the short time he'd spent with the twins' mother at the request of Professor Mendoza and how, in those few moments together they had created the children he had never got to know as his own. A muffled howl from the room above him made his heart sink with sadness – Samita was dead, he had known that already. His son had lost his sister, his mother and so much more in such a short space of time. A strange set of emotions crept over him; guilt at having betrayed Isabella in the first place, sadness at the loss of his daughter, anger towards the Industry and a sliver of fear at how they would fare against the might of Elizabet. He shivered.

'We can go,' said Ariel.

Carter spun around, so lost in his own thoughts that he'd not even heard his son come back downstairs to join him. Carter opened his arms and hugged the boy tightly. 'I'm sorry,' he whispered. 'I'm sorry that all of this happened to you.'

'Let's go,' repeated Ariel, this time emboldened. 'She can't be allowed to do this any longer.' He stood tall. 'Now tell me everything.'

As they ran through the forest, Carter explained many things to his son, first starting with Isabella and ending with Frida. While Ariel was upset, Carter noticed that he tried hard not to show it, wiping his eyes occasionally as Carter explained Elizabet's plans to create a modified army. The boy retched when he heard about the new-borns that had been cast out into the Deadlands. His face turned ashen as

Carter unfolded the story, but an even greater look of determination came over him.

'I will help you,' he said quietly, as they turned onto the concrete track that led to the old Delaney house. 'I will do whatever it takes.'

'We start here,' said Carter. 'But I doubt we'll find anything of use.' He was right – the house was empty, the bloodied tablecloth still scrunched into a ball on the floor. Some of Angel's belongings sat on the kitchen counter, along with Catherine's laptop.

Ariel looked around, his head still spinning from the revelations. 'We have to find her,' he said. He picked up the laptop and then put it down again.

'They left in a hurry.' Carter kicked the tablecloth. 'Someone was injured.'

'That might have been Elizabet,' said Ariel. 'She was in some pain when she arrived here.' He thought for a moment. 'There was something else,' he said, looking desperately like he was trying to remember. 'We had a communication device in our house – Jescha was allowed to have one because of all the trouble with Lucia. The Industry left it with her to report anything urgent that she found.'

Carter felt his heart beat fast. 'Who did she call?' he demanded. 'Think, Ariel, who did she call?' If Elizabet had been able to contact people inside the Industry headquarters then there would be little chance of getting into the building.

'I think she said Jayden,' said Ariel, clearing his throat. 'She told him to come to the south forest urgently. But it didn't sound official, I don't know…' he steeled himself hard and pushed back his fears. Carter felt a surge of pride as the boy nodded, remembering. 'Her voice was strange, the way she spoke to him,' Ariel continued. 'She said the broadcast still had to go ahead.'

'The broadcast,' exclaimed Carter, in horror. 'Of course it's going ahead.' He switched on the FreeScreen and watched in horror as the screen burst into life. His stomach flipped a sick, violent somersault when he saw the still image in the centre of the screen. It was Alice Davenport, her face battered and bruised, tied to a chair in the Control Room.

'Oh no,' he said, the sound of his own voice scaring him. In the top right-hand corner of the screen there was a countdown clock, with just over half an hour remaining. A sign above it stated:

TIME UNTIL LIVE EXECUTION OF TRAITOR.
MANDATORY ATTENDANCE IN UNITY SQUARE.

Carter took a deep breath, trying not to let the panic that filled him take over his body. In the bottom right-hand of the screen, there was a camera overview of the square, thousands of terrified, confused faces glued to the front of the stage, above which was the huge screen.

'There!' shouted Carter. 'Look!' He pointed to the middle, near the front where Ariel could just make out the shapes of three women, huddled together and talking animatedly.

'Would you recognise McDermott?' he said, jabbing his finger at her tiny outline.

'I guess so. I've seen her around the Industry Headquarters.'

'Good,' said Carter, quickly. 'Go to her, in Unity Square, now – and to my friend who will be with her.' He paused for a moment. 'There will be many people there but you will find them. They aren't from the Community and will look... different.'

Ariel looked concerned but determined to help. 'I can do that,' he said. 'I will.'

Carter smiled. 'Tell them about Frida and Samuel and all the people who will be standing on the outside of the square, ready to help them.' He paused again. 'When they have gathered, get them to talk to people, to share about themselves and who they are. There should be no violence. Frida embodies peace and generosity – she should be the first to speak. You should join her after that and tell the people what you know – between you they will listen to you. You need to be brave.'

Ariel nodded enthusiastically. 'But won't she think that I'm with Elizabet? I'm still Controller General. I'm supposed to be the most Industry person there is.'

Carter thought for a moment. 'Say to them *Veritas liberabit vos.* Can you remember that?'

'*Veritas liberabit vos,*' repeated Ariel. 'But why?'

'Because then they will believe you are on our side,' said Carter. 'It means, "The truth will set you free".'

'Aren't you coming with me?'

'No,' said Carter. 'I'm going to get Elizabet. If she's unarmed like you believe she is, then I can take her alive and make her pay for what she's done – and for the terrible pain she has caused so many people. And find out where she's keeping Isabella and how I can save her.'

As they ran through the forest and out onto the open road, Carter felt the rush of adrenalin course through his veins. Whatever they had started could now not be stopped. There were hundreds of them that had breached the Community Barricades and the one piece of evidence that had proved that the Industry had been lying to its people all along, was now exposed. He watched as his son disappeared northwards, to the main body of the Community, towards Unity Square as their paths snaked away from each other again. In his heart, he vowed to himself to become a good parent – or more likely, a good friend to the boy who was only a few months younger than he was. But now, his fight was with Elizabet – and his priority must be to save Alice.

He arrived, breathless, at the building that housed the Industry Headquarters. For all he had said to the teams about peace, there was little to no time left to save Alice and find out where Isabella was. As he stepped up towards the main building, a guard drew his weapon.

'What are you doing here?' he asked, pointing his gun.

Carter narrowed his eyes towards the doorway and picked up his pace. The guard aimed and took a shot that whistled past Carter's shoulder. He took a deep breath and raised his own gun, feeling a deep twinge of regret as he shot the Industry official dead and made his way hastily to the Control Room.

Chapter Eighteen

The Confrontation

Alice ran her tongue across the dry roof of her mouth and pursed her lips together in defiance. She closed her eyes tightly and gritted her teeth in anger. The dark silhouette of Jayden in the corner of the room cast a shadow through into the main body of the Control Room, and she focused on his outline, strong and calm, the gun still pointed in her direction. Elizabet stood in front of her, looking intently into her eyes.

And then, without warning, the girl stepped away, sweat pouring from her forehead.

'It's time.' She glanced across at Jayden who stared ahead blankly, the weapon still pointed at Alice. 'Do not move. Do you understand me?'

The boy nodded, his eyes glazed and unmoving. Alice looked across at him – his bottom lip protruded a little and it seemed as though the very core of him was gone. His shape had changed; the way he held himself was different. And then suddenly, the realisation filled Alice with an icy, terrifying chill.

'You were her experiment,' she said her herself. 'Oh Jayden, I am sorry. She's done it to you.' The boy stared ahead, still and cold with no recognition in his eyes.

'Yes.'

Elizabet pushed her way between them. 'He was – he is – my proof that by modifying the gene and brain function that controls self-determination and rebellion we can create a simple and highly effective army of individuals who will serve the purpose of the Industry.' She smiled. 'No other Controller General has been able to manage this.'

She glanced across at Jayden proudly. 'Your friend here tried to argue with Filip and Barnes when they sent you underground. He tried to get them to release you – said that is wasn't in the Constitution, that they were acting illegally.' She walked across to Jayden and poked a finger into his chest. 'He came down to the Catacombs, demanding to see you – but of course, he was stopped. It was Quinn who injected him but then I brought him back just a few days ago.' A light dangerously danced in her eyes. 'I had been working on some volunteers in my Lab – known rebels – taking samples I could work with and experiment on, and then I remembered he was here. It's your fault, Davenport.'

The boy looked ahead emotionless and a dark, aching responsibility spread through her. Jayden had been frozen not only because of her actions, but because he too had known that what they had been doing was wrong. Her guilt almost overwhelmed her, but for now she had to push it aside.

'You did all that genetic research and all that sampling in the few days since you've been Controller General? That would have been years' worth of the best geneticists' work in the old world.' She shook her head. 'I'm impressed, Elizabet; I knew you were smart but I underestimated you.'

The girl pursed her lips. 'Yes, Alice, you did underestimate me,' she said. 'And you should know that I actually started developing this

Contribution when I was living with you and Filip.' She smiled. 'I remembered everything and reproduced it.'

Alice shut her eyes tightly and for a second, let herself be taken back to the house in Morristown Row that she had shared with Filip, Marcus and Izzy. She thought back to the nights when she had helped the small girl with her cryonics homework and supported her with her studies in the Ship. And the whole time, her almost daughter had been planning to create a genetically modified population that would serve her, Barnes and the others. Her skin crawled as she looked at the girl and her heart burned a rapid fury.

'You…' she started but could not finish. Izzy laughed a little and then fiddled with the dials in front of her, views on the screens within the Control Room. Images of Unity Square, the Academy, the Food Plant and the Industry Headquarters flashed up in front of them. All but Unity Square were empty – most, if not all, had heeded Elizabet's warning.

'That's more like it,' she said. 'Look at the crowds.'

There were hundreds, perhaps thousands, of people packed into every space displayed on the screens. Each face stared intently into the camera, waiting for the broadcast to restart. Izzy checked a separate monitor that brought up a chart on the wall.

'Almost one hundred per cent attendance,' she said, frowning. 'I can't imagine what the few people who are not within a fifty-metre radius of one of these screens could possibly be doing that they believe is more important.' She tutted in an over-exaggerated fashion. 'There *will* be consequences,' she said with artificial remorse. 'But we can't wait any longer.' She clicked a switch and cleared her throat as the broadcast begin again.

'Welcome back,' Izzy spoke into a microphone with a dark smile. 'I see most of you have now understood the importance of this broadcast and have joined me for the occasion.'

Alice flexed her fingers and edged herself as far away from Elizabet as she could but the girl dragged the chair back into position opposite her, facing the main camera.

'As she herself admitted earlier, this is Alice Davenport, and I have brought her here in front of you today to explain to you the truth about what happened to her and who she was in the days after the Storms.' She turned to Alice. 'I will not be expecting you to speak for the duration of my broadcast but you may, at the end, say a few words to the people of the Community explaining your behaviour.' She glanced at Jayden who stood firm in his position. 'Is that understood?'

Alice nodded, her eyes fired with anger.

Elizabet smiled sweetly towards the camera. 'Alice Davenport is not who you all believed her to be,' she began. 'At school, you learned that she was one of the First Scouts who braved her life to give us what we have today. You all remember *her* name, don't you?' The crowds nodded in agreement as she continued. 'But not all of you will know that all of the work, the hard work, was done by my brother, Filip Conrad. He allowed Alice to take the credit because he wanted to save you all from the terrible truth about her. The fact is that Alice Davenport risked our lives and everything we hold sacred within the walls of our Community to elope with a savage boy – Richard Warren – from outside the Barricades. She stole my brother's child, one of our Descendants, still growing inside her womb, and took her into the Deadlands to die.'

Alice shook her head and opened her mouth to speak but as Jayden took a small, but definite step towards her, she stopped.

Elizabet's eyes gleamed as she looked towards the camera, facing the crowds where angry faces glared back. Alice watched as a scuffle broke out in one corner – a man was attempting to address the crowd before a number of others rained blows upon him and he fell to the floor, until the group closed over where he had been and they were calm again. Industry guards held their guns high and aimed towards the crowd.

'My brother, Filip, was forced to go further out into the Deadlands to retrieve her and Warren, in order that our bloodline continue,' proclaimed Elizabet, in a highly dramatic tone. 'They had been planning to raise the child as their own and to return with others to destroy us. And so, Filip Conrad, Ellis Barnes and Quinn Fordham decided to bring the rebels back here to be punished – and to return the child to its rightful home with our family. Davenport was frozen until the child could be born but Warren, unfortunately, was violent and aggressive and had to be killed.'

Alice felt her blood run cold. She had returned of her own accord – but Richard? Had they really gone out into the Deadlands after him? She thought of him and his brother in the village they had called Woodford Hatch. And of the kind gentleness of the people that had accepted her and asked her to stay with them. The anger built inside of her as Elizabet continued.

'You were all told that this creature died in childbirth, but that was a lie. She was kept hidden underground because my brother was ashamed that his first-born child was born to a traitor and a rebel. They lied to you so that you and your families wouldn't be scared. So that you would believe. They didn't trust you to believe for yourselves so they tricked you.'

Alice watched as the people on the screens looked back and forth. She could just make out their faces – angry and disillusioned; the figures jostled irritably and formed small groups, turning on each other.

'Shut up and listen to me!' Elizabet yelled, raising her voice for the first time, making Alice jump. 'Now that I am Controller General, I have decided that it is time for you to hear the truth. The Industry don't want you to know your own history but I am here to be the one who stands for you – and stands *with* you.'

Alice gritted her teeth and glared at Jayden, his hand unwavering and the gun pointed directly at her head. Gently and carefully she started to rub the rope that bound her arms to the chair, finding the notch again. She pushed the rope against it slowly, her eyes firmly fixed on Izzy as she did so.

'*I* stand beside you,' continued the girl, 'as your sole Controller General, along with anyone who wishes to support me. I will bring the truth to you, not just about this thing before you, but about what she was here to do – and who she was planning to do it with. I am here to expose the lies of your history and to recreate our world in a way where you will not be let down again.'

Alice felt the friction of the rope burning her hands but looked straight ahead.

'Someone known to you all breached our borders and brought with him the threat of disease and destruction; he did this because he wanted to avenge what my brother did to his family.' She paused for a moment. 'That person is Carter Warren – who you all believed to have been killed escaping from our Community, just like his father and his great-grandfather before him.'

The girl took a deep breath. 'I have reason to believe that he is here within the walls of our sanctuary somewhere and—' she paused for a moment '—and that his son Ariel – who I have dismissed from his role as Controller General – is supporting these rebels. Warrens and Davenports – every single one of them threaten our existence and we need to eradicate them if we are to survive. We need to kill them all!'

Alice watched as some people in the audience raised their hands in a cheering motion. Others remained still – confused and shaking their heads.

Elizabet moved closer to the camera.

'This is not a suggestion!' she bellowed, angrily. 'This is an order, coming from your Controller General.' The crowd became briefly subdued and most held their heads low. 'The penalties for disobedience will be severe,' she continued. 'Today, I am issuing a compulsory freezing order for anyone suspected of being rebels, associating with rebels or displaying the characteristics of rebels.' She glanced across at Alice. 'This... *thing*... is exactly the type of dissident we will be excluding from our world.'

Alice rubbed her wrists hard and slow against the crack in the chair, her arms burning with the friction.

'We will start again,' proclaimed Izzy. 'Since the Storms, we have achieved many things, but our leadership made many mistakes. I will lead you through this – as I should have done at the start – and our Community will grow into a kingdom. For those of you who are loyal, there will be positions available at my side and for those of you who are not, I will offer a painless exit from this world.'

Suddenly, the screen in front of Alice panned to the edges of Unity Square where a disturbance was beginning to break out. She watched as Ariel, accompanied by a woman, came striding through the crowd with a tribe of people behind them, dressed in bright colours, their rms held high in the air in an act of peace. She began to say something o the crowd in the square, her people surrounding her and her face nimated. Guards faced her, their guns raised.

Ariel addressed them directly.

'Do not shoot,' he shouted. 'I am your true Controller General nd I order you not to shoot. Elizabet Conrad is no longer in charge f this Community. If you listen, I will tell you the truth.'

Elizabet's mouth dropped open in shock as the woman turned around and revealed the intricate swirls of a patterned tattoo that wept from one eye all the way down her neck.

'WHO IS SHE?' she demanded, pushing Alice's chair backwards nd losing her composure. 'What is she doing here?'

'I – I don't know,' mouthed Alice, her eyes flitting to look at Jayden n confusion. 'I really don't know who she is.'

The woman and Ariel started to address the crowd in the square – he people had all turned away from the screen and stood transfixed, while the groups gathered in other areas of the Community began to empty, some running away fast from outside the Headquarters.

Elizabet began to panic, her cheeks beginning to blaze in anger. Listen to me!' she screamed into the microphone. 'I am your Control-er General!' A few heads turned momentarily towards the main screen while other men, women and children formed themselves into groups, facing the tattooed woman who was now up on the stage, while Ariel stood by her side. Two Industry officials had joined her, their guns pointed at her heart and her head.

'What the hell is going on?' whispered Elizabet, her face inflamed. Who is this woman and where did she come from?' She moved over towards the console and pressed a button and mumbled something into the small microphone that was attached to the desk.

Alice craned to hear what she was saying, all the while straining her arms, desperately trying to free them. Then, the screen flickered with movement and she watched, jaw dropping open, as one of the Industry guards turned to the woman, and shot her clean in the back of the head as she addressed the crowd. Her body slumped to the stage and a dark, black pool of blood formed around her. There was a visible, collective intake of breath from the people on the screens. Alice stared at the screen, horrified, but hopeful that the rebellion had begun at last.

*

In the moments after Frida fell, there was silence. A cold, collective silence and then a screaming came from the crowd. Bullets spattered through the air and several people fell, injured or dead. Ariel pulled out his own gun and pointed it at the guard.

'This woman was with me!' he said. 'You follow my orders now, not Elizabet.'

The Industry Guard turned towards him and held his gun upwards. 'You are no longer my Controller General,' he shouted. 'Step down before I shoot.'

'I won't,' said Ariel, turning to the crowd. 'I won't step down because what we have been doing is wrong.' He eyed the guard nervously but continued as other people stepped up onto the stage beside him. 'Everything that Frida said to you is true,' he shouted into the crowd. 'There are people who live outside the Barricades and Elizabet wants to destroy them.' He took a deep breath. 'Elizabet is creating an army, using our friends and family who have been frozen, and she's going to make your lives even worse than they are.' He stood for a moment, watching the guards and the crowd who stood, terrified nd open-mouthed. Small groups had gathered around the fallen, and were tending to them silently. Men, women and children held each other tightly, confused and afraid. Most guards lowered their guns in confusion. Others stood tall, nodding as Ariel continued.

'Friends,' he said, clearing his throat. 'Some of you amongst us have known for a long time that the way we live is wrong – that what the Industry has done is wrong. You were termed as rebels but now I implore you to help me.'

He heard the click of a gun behind him. 'Please,' he said, 'please stand with me to change our Community.' He knelt down next to the body of Frida. 'Don't let this courageous woman have died in vain. For those of you who are prepared to listen now, there will be no repercussions.' He turned and looked upwards at the guard. 'Please, no more deaths.'

*

Back in the Control Room, for one moment, there was a terrifying silence and Alice felt the sickening thump of her heart quickening in her chest.

'KILL HIM!' screamed Elizabet into the camera. 'And I will kill her. Alice Davenport will be executed, in front of you all.'

She snatched the gun from Jayden and turned to face Alice her eyes filled with hatred and anger.

Alice swallowed hard and looked straight at the camera, calm and composed. Then she arched her back and pulled herself backwards.

'The truth will set you free,' she screamed to the people watching in Unity Square and with all the strength she had left within her, pulled her arms back and forwards and destabilised the chair she was tied to, rocking it over so that she fell face forwards into Izzy, sending them both crashing to the floor as Jayden stood still, watching, like a plaster cast of his former self.

The gun skidded across the floor and landed with a dull clunk against a filing cabinet. Alice, half collapsed on top of Izzy and still tied to parts of the broken chair, pulled at her clothes to expose the wound from the gunshot. The girl screamed in pain and pushed Alice off her, weakened by her injury but still able to get enough leverage to move out from underneath her. Splinters of wood littered the floor, and while the girl regained her breath, Alice reached for something, anything she could use to defend herself. She grabbed at the chair leg still attached to her ankle and pulled it free, holding out in front of her. Izzy reached out for the gun and, as quickly as she did, Alice brought the chunk of wood down hard against her fingers. Izzy screamed again and dragged herself across the room towards the desk, pressing the button underneath.

'Get in here!' she screamed. 'Security, get in here!'

Alice threw herself towards the gun and grabbed it as the hammering of footsteps sounded outside the Control Room. She pulled herself upright, at first unsure of which direction to turn or where to fire the gun. She looked towards the door, and then at Elizabet who was fumbling with the back part of the desk, trying to open it.

Alice glanced back at the door and then at Izzy. She put her finger on the trigger and held the gun towards her almost-daughter, who sat cowering under the desk, her broken hands in front of her face, cropped hair inked with blood. 'You wouldn't dare,' the girl whispered. 'My people will destroy you.'

'You don't have any people left.'

A grinding of metal screeched and the door to the Control Room opened. Then she heard a voice she recognised.

'No, Alice, don't kill her, not yet. WAIT!'

But it was too late. Alice pulled the trigger hard and a loud bang xploded through the Control Room.

Carter ran towards her and grabbed the gun, taking her into his rms and holding her tightly. A trickle of blood leaked from Elizabet's nouth as the bullet lodged itself in her skull, her eyes staring blankly head.

'She's gone,' Alice whispered. 'She's finally gone. Elizabet is dead.'

Chapter Nineteen

The Truth

As the faint smell of cordite evaporated from the room, Carter and Alice held each other momentarily, each feeling the beat of the other's heart in their chest. 'I knew you'd come,' said Alice, finally. 'I knew somehow that we would do this together.'

Carter smiled weakly at her. 'It isn't over,' he said, his body suddenly feeling exhausted. 'We need to get back out there and talk to people. Ariel will need our help. And I need to find Isabella.' On the floor under the desk the still body of Elizabet lay curled in a corner. 'I was hoping she would tell me how to find her, if we spared her life.' He felt a dull aching in his chest at mentioning her name and a desperate urge to run through the building searching for her.

A movement in the back of the room caught his attention. Jayden still stood there, his weapon on the floor. He fell to his knees and covered face with his hands. 'Who's he?' whispered Carter.

'An old friend,' said Alice, distracted by the screen. 'Tie him up until we work out what to do with him.' As Carter approached, the boy cowered and started to shake. He tied him up tightly, but gently and sat him in the corner where the boy whimpered silently.

'Come here and look at this,' called Alice. 'Is that your son?'

Carter glanced over at the screen and saw Ariel on the stage in Unity Square, still flanked by armed Industry officials casting a familiar shape that reminded him so much of himself. 'Yes,' he said, slowly. 'That's him. Do you think we should go out there? We need to explain to the people properly and this is not going to be easy.'

'We talk to them here,' whispered Alice, her voice almost unrecognisable. 'It will take us at least a half hour to get there in person.' She felt a sickness rise in her throat. 'We need to hear what's being said out there as well as them hearing us. Turn on the stage microphone.'

Carter fiddled with some buttons on the console in front of them and immediately, the voice of his son, Ariel, filled the room. The crowd looked bewildered – frightened even – and around one hundred Industry guards had their weapons trained on them. The guards themselves looked puzzled, unsure of whose orders to follow.

'Ariel,' said Carter, loudly. 'Let myself and Alice speak. We want to address the crowd. But we would also like to answer any questions from the people.'

Ariel looked around him and then stepped to the side of the stage. He turned to the guards. 'As your Controller General, I order you to lower your weapons,' he said, his voice now confident. 'These people – ours and theirs – come only in peace. There has already been at least one confirmed death, which was ordered by Elizabet – I will not allow any more.'

Many people, especially those in the front rows, were weeping. Alice and Carter positioned themselves in front of the camera. Alice felt her hands shaking, her eyes filling with tears.

'Many years ago, I stood before you on that very stage,' she began. 'To tell your people about the brave new world we were creating. A world where poverty and homelessness would not exist and where

equality for all people would be one of our founding principles.'
She stopped for a moment and looked at Carter. 'But somehow,
this became corrupted by those with power and then changed, and
the different world that we had worked so hard to create became a
Community without music, without art and creativity and where
"otherness" was not tolerated.'

Carter nodded. 'Descendants are no better and no worse than
Lab Mades,' he started. 'We should all have been born equal – our
worthiness in the world determined only by the people that we became.
Instead, the Industry turned us against each other.' He moved in closer
to the camera. 'Look around you,' he said. 'Who are the Industry?'

'I am,' shouted a man at the front. 'I am a technician for the Model
and I'm proud of it.'

'And I'm a guard,' said the man on the stage next to Ariel. 'And he's
more Industry than any of us. If the Industry has done such terrible
things, why is your son one of our leaders?'

'The Industry is a construct,' said Carter, choosing his words carefully. 'Something handed down from generation to generation. We
are all the Community – and we have all been the Industry at some
point in our lives.'

He watched as Ariel bent down and helped Lily, Angel and
Catherine to the stage. Together, they slowly covered Frida's body
with shirts and other pieces of clothing that had been passed along
the rows of the audience, before carrying her away to some privacy.
His heart sank – the kind, peaceful, beautiful person who had saved
Samuel and himself on more than one occasion had lost her life to
help them one final time. He bit his lip hard but he couldn't stop the
burning in his eyes. Then the three of them returned to the stage and
stood shoulder to shoulder with Ariel.

'Each and every one of our Controller Generals across the ages has been chosen because of one key attribute or strength,' said Ariel. 'And that was the ability to keep from you the biggest secrets of our history and to use those to stop many of you from expressing your own thoughts and feelings – to stop you from rebelling.'

'Paradigm Industries has always taken care of us,' called a woman from the front. 'Without them, we wouldn't have survived the Storms – or we'd be living like wild, half-formed savages in the Deadlands. Like her!' She pointed upwards at the stage, her focus clearly on Angel, who stood without her dark glasses, unflinching at the woman, but visibly upset at the death of Frida.

'As our friend, Frida, told you earlier, peace and freedom are two of the most fundamental rights that every citizen of the world should have,' continued Ariel. 'Regardless of how well you feel the Industry have taken care of our physical needs, we have been hidden away from the rest of society and our free will taken away from us.' He stared out across the crowd. 'Amongst us today are many people whose ancestors survived without – in spite of – the efforts of Paradigm Industries.'

Many of the crowd turned their faces to look around the square as Ariel continued. 'They are not enemies – and they are not dangerous or infected with diseases as we have been told for so many years. They are normal people, just like us – with dreams and fears who argue with their parents, who eat and sleep and want their children to have a life that is better than theirs was.' He paused for a moment. 'The difference is that they have always known we exist.'

A shout came through the speaker into the Control Room. 'But Alice was the one that told us there were monsters on the outside. We've all seen it in the videos – she's the one who ordered the Barricades to be built. And then she betrayed us!'

Alice pulled the microphone towards herself and looked into the camera directly. Her voice shook but she spoke earnestly. 'When I first went out into the Deadlands, I was fifteen years old. I had lived a third of my life underground, being trained by the Industry to believe that the world outside would be full of monsters. And when I went there, that's what I expected to see. That's what I thought I saw.' She swallowed hard. 'Friends of mine were killed because they dared to challenge the Industry in those early days and, for a while, I believed the lies I was told. But when I found out at least part of what was happening, I tried to do something about it. You deserve to know more than I did,' she said finally. 'You deserve to know the truth.'

She continued by telling them a condensed version of her story. About her mother and the life she'd had before the Storms. About her time in the Ship and what happened when they had gone above ground. When she came to the part about Kelly, her lips started to quiver, but she worked hard to keep her story factual, truthful. Marcus was especially hard to talk about – the sweet-natured, kind child who wouldn't even hurt the rabbit he'd found wandering on the path. But when she talked about how Filip had started controlling her and how he'd forced her into the Catacombs before Jescha was born, she broke down, tears rolling down her cheeks.

'I didn't even get to hold her,' she said, swallowing the pulsing pain in her throat. 'I didn't get to see her grow up. For me, no time has passed, but she lived a whole lifetime believing I was a traitor. And I wasn't,' she finished defiantly. 'I was just doing what was right.'

The crowd felt silent for a moment and then, from the edges where the people of the Village and the Township stood came the singular clap of one individual applauding. And then another. Like a wave, the sound cascaded inwards until even some of the Community were ringing their hands together in support. Ariel, Samuel, Angel and Lily held hands on the stage in front of them in solidarity.

'Friends,' said Ariel, looking stronger than he ever had, as the din died down. 'There is much more for us all to talk about and many more walls for us to break down. Many of you will remain confused and upset for some time. But as your Controller General, I hereby announce that the Industry as you know it no longer exists as an entity. I urge those of you who wear the uniform to cast it aside and come into work tomorrow in your regular clothing. We will all become one group.' He hesitated for a moment and looked towards Samuel.

'People have died today,' said Samuel. 'One woman in particular gave her life for what she believed in – and that was our friend Frida, who represented a group called the Township. We need to honour her and also to have the Township become a part of this union.'

He looked around at the crowd. 'Could two of Frida's people come up here and join us please? Lukas and Freya?'

The crowd shuffled a little as a man and a woman pushed their way to the front. Samuel and Lily held out their hands to them and they climbed up onto the platform. They whispered something to Ariel who nodded and introduced them to the crowd.

Carter and Alice watched through the screens, both transfixed as the new team on the stage formally introduced themselves and shared a little of the stories of their lives that had brought them to that point. As each person spoke, she and Carter exchanged glances, their hands clasped in a familiar friendship that spanned generations.

'Although I barely know you, I feel like I've had you around me all my life,' said Carter. 'I don't mean just from the videos; it's like you're part of who I am.'

'Well, your children share our DNA,' she said, smiling. 'I'm their great-grandmother – which makes me your...' she thought for a moment. 'Step-grandmother-in-law? I don't know.'

Carter laughed. 'You have a whole new family now,' he said. 'My mother is out in the Deadlands and my brother...'

'That's your brother on stage there, right?'

Carter nodded. 'Yes,' he said. 'We've had our problems in the short time we've known each other, but fundamentally he's a good guy.'

Alice looked at him more closely and smiled. 'I see the resemblance,' she said and then turned to Carter. 'I'm scared,' she added. 'It seems so overwhelming and, yet, so possible. It feels like I'm getting a second chance.'

Carter clasped her hand again. 'I think this might work,' he said. 'You're right – we both might just have another opportunity to make this world a better place. What do you think?'

Alice pressed her finger to her lips. 'It's too soon to hope for anything,' she said. 'There's a lot of work to do – and we still need to work out the psychological effects on those people who have just found out that their whole lives have been a lie.' She smiled. 'But there's a chance, a sliver of a possibility that we might be able to get it right this time.'

As the last of the people on stage finished talking, Alice moved back towards the screen and spoke clearly.

'Thank you for your patience,' she said. 'Tonight must have been confusing and concerning for everyone—' she paused and swallowed hard '—especially for those of you who were close to our friend from the Township, Frida. We are fortunate that others were only wounded and that greater numbers of lives were not lost.'

She saw the guard who had shot his gun hang his head in shame, shaking his head.

'It was an act done under duress,' said Freya, the woman from the Township who had come onto the stage. 'While we are devastated to lose Frida, we know that if peace is possible as a result of our presence here, she will have died a happy woman, reconciled with her time on this earth.' She paused. 'We will take that into account in any justice that we believe needs to be served.'

From the Control Room, Alice nodded in agreement. 'There are many people here who have suffered injuries and injustices – and these must not go unrecognised – but we will discuss them when the time is right,' she said, wearily.

Carter touched her arm gently. 'We need to make arrangements,' he said, but his son had already started to address the crowd.

'My request to the people of the Community is simple,' he said. 'We have many homes here that are not fully occupied and enough food to feed everyone in the short-term – at least until we agree how we are going to work together. And, until then, the Township and the Villagers will be our guests.' He gestured to the crowd. 'Each of you, please take the hand of the person next to you. If they are not one of your own, please bring them into your home here and care for them as if they were your family. Ensure that nobody is left out. Share with them your experiences and make sure they have access to the same facilities that you do.'

Samuel stepped forwards. 'We will meet again here tomorrow morning and discuss the many, many things that we need to. And we will continue to do so until we have created a new world that works for all of us. Please do as Ariel said and make our guests feel welcome.'

A cheer rose from the crowd and Samuel stepped back, a sincere smile on his face.

Carter and Alice watched as the crowd melted from Unity Square in groups – some stone-faced in shock and others deep in conversation with the Villagers or people of the Township.

'They won't all get along,' said Alice. 'This is bound to cause problems for some who still believe in the Industry. And even those who may still believe in Izzy, however despicable we think she was.'

'After everything she did? Really?'

Alice nodded. 'Both her downfall and her death were very public and there will be a lot of questions to answer. We're also asking our people to rethink everything they've ever believed in – and that includes those from the Township and the Village. They've always hated the Community and now they're being asked to become a part of them, to live alongside them, even if it's just for one night. And none of that is going to be easy.'

Carter nodded as the last of the groups left the square. 'You're right. But for tonight, I need to leave some of this to you and the others.' He swallowed deeply. 'I have to find Isabella. I know you told me that she's not in the Lab any more but I know she's still alive somewhere in the Catacombs. I can feel it.'

'How will you find her? She could be anywhere.'

'I know the Model better than anyone. If Elizabet hasn't taken too many precautions, I think I can use it to find where she's hidden.'

Alice shrugged her shoulders. 'You won't wait until morning? If she's frozen then nothing more will happen to her. And someone can come with you then.'

Carter looked at her resolute. 'She's waited for me long enough,' he said.

Alice smiled at him fondly. 'I get it. I just can't come with you right now. I'm sorry, I can't go back down there – at least not yet, it's too soon.'

'I completely understand that. Eighty or so years would be enough or anyone.'

Alice laughed; her first real laugh in what felt like a lifetime. 'I need o get back to the others,' she said, 'to Lily and your friend Angel. And o rest.' She touched the side of her face that was still raw from the ssault Elizabet had waged on her. 'I'll take Jayden with me and see if here's anything that Catherine can do to help him.'

Carter handed her the gun. 'Take this,' he said. 'And stay safe.'

When Alice walked out of the Industry Headquarters, with a hand-uffed Jayden trailing behind her, a small crowd of her new friends ad gathered to greet her. The air was cool and she realised she was hivering. A sense of anticipation overwhelmed her – thoughts of 'rospect House, the Control Room, the Catacombs and the Ship lled her mind.

'We caught a Transporter,' said Samuel, his eyes twinkling, his arm rushing hers. 'How crazy are they?!' He paused awkwardly and then ut his arms around her. 'I'm so glad you're okay and I don't even now you.' He looked around. 'Where's my brother?'

'Carter's gone to find Isabella,' said Alice. 'And this is Jayden; we eed to work out what to do with him.'

'I'll take him to the Infirmary,' said Lily. 'They'll have a better idea.'

Alice shivered again and Samuel put his jacket around her shoul-ers. It was roughly sewn together, made out in the Deadlands and o different to the Industry garments. Something about it was so real nd genuine that it reminded her of before the Storms. She buried her ace in it and began to cry as Samuel took her arm in his and guided er back to the old Delaney house.

*

Carter took the elevator down as far as he could and then followed the corridor to the end of the eastern passage. From there, he took two right turns, doubling back on himself, just as the map on the Model had indicated. There was something frighteningly eerie about the Catacombs at the best of times, but empty and devoid of any guards it seemed like the most haunted place on earth. Carter felt his heart beating in his throat; around each corner he paused, peering back around to check that there was no one following him. With the rooms of thousands of Sleepers surrounding him, he had the distinct feeling he was being watched.

At the end of the tunnel on the left-hand side, he found the unmarked room with a small silver plate on the outside. Trembling, he took the master key from his pocket and pressed it against the wall. The door clicked and he pushed it forwards, stepping inside, the pounding in his chest becoming so loud, it was almost audible. He closed his eyes, daring himself to look, telling himself she would be okay and then he opened them again.

On a small thin bed, on the bottom bunk he found her. Her eyes were closed and she lay still, almost unmoving except for the gentle rise and fall of her chest inside the sleep suit she was clothed in. The rise and fall gave him some hope – she was, at least, alive.

Carter knelt down by her side and took her hand in his.

'I'm sorry,' he said, his voice choking. 'I had to go away but I'm back now.' He rubbed her fingers gently, his heart aching desperately and every fibre of his body wracked with pain.

'I love you,' he managed. 'I love you, Isabella.' The tears rolled uncontrollably down his cheeks, and his chest heaved with regret.

Chapter Twenty

The Resolution

he next morning, the nine of them sat around a large table in the old
Delaney house. Alice, Carter, Samuel, Angel, Ariel, Lily and Catherine
had been deep in conversation about the mechanics of the new Community since just after the sun rose. Freya and Lukas, representatives
from the Township, had also joined them in Frida's place.

'We need to talk about what we're going to do about the frozen
ones,' said Carter, rubbing his forehead. 'There are thousands of
them down there in the Catacombs, including Isabella.' He looked at
Catherine. 'Have you thought about what we're going to do?'

'I've come up with a draft release schedule,' nodded Catherine.
'I can't guarantee that it will work but based on my calculations we
should be able to bring everyone above ground eventually – although
it will have to happen gradually, and over a few years.'

'Do you think she will survive?' Carter spoke softly, his heart
aching. 'After what Elizabet has done to her?'

Catherine's face turned pale and serious. 'I don't know,' she said,
finally. 'From my initial examinations of her in the Catacombs, it
doesn't look like she's suffered any permanent damage but she's with
the medics now who have agreed to undertake further tests.'

She reached across the table to touch his hand. 'The wounds on her body were relatively superficial and it seems that only small tissue samples had been taken. But the medics will need to confirm if there is any other permanent damage.'

'Do you think she'll end up like Jayden?'

Catherine looked uncomfortable. 'I don't think so,' she said. 'But we will need to see what happens when she comes out of the Infirmary.' She looked at Alice. 'I'm sorry that there was nothing they could do for him.'

Alice bit her lip hard. 'Keep him comfortable,' she said, her voice quivering, 'until the end. He was a loyal friend to me.'

Ariel nodded respectfully. 'We only have a few hours before we meet with everyone. What will the next days and weeks look like for the Community?'

'We should establish an interim council,' interrupted Lukas, 'with representatives of each of our factions to enable fairness.'

'It's what Frida would have wanted,' added Freya.

'We have the infrastructure here to help integrate everyone,' said Ariel. 'But do you think the people who have lived in the Village and the Township will want to stay here?'

'Not all of them,' said Carter. 'But not all the Community will want to stay here either.' The others nodded.

'We need to understand what people want before we decide what we give them,' said Alice. 'Involve them in the decision making – use the talent of all the different groups we have here to establish a world that works for everyone. We always need to remember how important that is.'

'And the Barricades?' Angel looked at Ariel. 'As Controller General you have the power to take them down so that nothing divides us.'

Ariel smiled at her. 'We will let the people decide.'

*

While Ariel, Angel, Freya, Lily, and Lukas made their way to Unity Square to meet with the people, Carter, Samuel and Alice took a Transporter to the Industry Headquarters building. The streets outside were deserted, their footsteps echoing as they walked towards the large, forbidding edifice. On the journey, Alice had noticed for the first time the drab uniformity of the city she had started to create before she was sent underground – the houses were identical, all colour drained. It looked like a grey wash had been dumped on the city. More than anything else, it was depressing. Like a compound.

'It's ugly, isn't it?' said Carter, reading her thoughts. 'Until I went outside, I never realised there was so much colour in the world.' He stared up at the sky. 'Life is beautiful and full of so much diversity, but the Industry sucked the soul out of it.'

Alice nodded. As much as the buildings and everything within the Community sickened her, she knew that there was still significant work to do to begin the deconstruction of the culture of fear that had been carefully built over the years since the Storms began. There was a methodical, deliberate structure of lies and deceit and to be able to destroy it, Alice had convinced the others that they needed to first understand it.

Catherine was waiting for them outside the building. Her skin was paler than the others and dark circles had formed around her eyes. She looked exhausted.

'I've made a list,' she said, handing a piece of paper over to Alice directly. 'I've been receiving visitors all night – I thought you should know that there are at least ten people who have expressed a desire to overthrow Ariel and the new council before it has even begun.'

Alice scanned down the list.

'The surnames of most of these people are familiar,' she said. 'There's a Fordham, a Barnes and a Conrad here.'

Catherine nodded. 'Direct Descendants,' she said. 'They believe the Community and their place in the Industry hierarchy is their birth right and they object to the inclusion of outsiders.'

'How do you know this?'

'They've been reported by people in the Community who want change.' She shrugged her shoulders. 'I didn't expect it, but people have been coming to me with information – especially the rebels.'

Carter reviewed the list carefully over Alice's shoulder. 'Should we arrest them? Talk to them?'

Catherine handed his him own copy of the paper. 'None of them took in a guest last night. After the broadcast, they apparently all spent the remainder of the evening together – at one house in the north.'

'We should include them,' said Alice finally. 'I don't want them arrested in the first instance but I do want them to be able to have their views heard; they won't be the only ones who feel that way.'

'They were all high-ranking officials in the Industry,' said Catherine, shaking her head. 'They have a lot to lose. They won't go quietly.'

'Get Ariel to take a team there to see them after the meeting,' said Alice. 'First, we need to understand what sort of a threat they might be, and what else – if anything – was being hidden by Elizabet.'

She had purposely not discussed what Catherine had said to her about the possibility of another facility – before she panicked everyone, she wanted to find evidence herself.

'But the Industry…' began Catherine.

'The Industry was all of us,' said Alice. 'Everyone who was ever part of the original Paradigm Industries died a long time ago. Most of them

own in the Ship.' She paused. 'For decades now, the Industry has
een pretty much composed of normal people, carrying out the rules
hey believed were the only way of doing things.' She stared up at the
uilding. 'But there are some who will still believe in the Industry and
vhat they were about. We need to know who those people are, and
nlighten them – show them the truth. That's what's important now.'

The main entrance was eerily silent. Catherine had already switched
ff the continuous loop of old film that was usually projected on the
arge screens of Alice and Filip entering the Deadlands. Without the
sual bustle of workers coming and going from their underground
hifts the corridors were silent, and totally deserted. When Catherine
ad returned the night before to look for Carter, she'd watched as
n Industry guard daubed thick, red muddy words on the walls in
lowing artistic circles.

VERITAS LIBERABIT VOS

Samuel repeated the words out loud. 'Isn't that the motto of the
Township?'

Alice smiled a little and nodded. 'It is,' she said. 'People finally have the
truth and now they get to choose for themselves what freedom means.'

They started in the Control Room. A semi-circle of dried blood was
the only sign that Elizabet's body had been there, but Alice could feel
her presence in every piece of splintered wood from the chair that lay
shattered on the floor.

'I had her moved,' said Catherine coldly. 'She was taken to the
incinerator in the early hours and disposed of.'

'She deserved less dignity than she was given,' Carter said seriously. 'What she's done to the Community – to all these people – and what she had planned, was despicable.'

Alice shivered as the image of herself tied to the chair in front of the screen flashed through her mind. She pushed all thoughts of Izzy away. 'We have a job to do,' she said. 'I want to know everything there is to know about what constituted the Industry. Catherine, have you had the building searched? Are there any paper records, files – anything that could give us more information at all? A more modern computer she might have used or something?'

'I brought two teams in overnight,' said the girl, despondently. 'Ariel wanted a count of the numbers underground done and an overview of the infrastructure we have here. The teams checked everything. There's very little written down – except the Constitution and the papers Elizabet gave me, but there's nothing there that we didn't already know. There's always been a policy of secrecy – even in the old days – that any information would be verbally passed from one Controller General to another. The rules state that when the information is passed over, the old ruler is frozen and not to be awoken for at least fifty years.'

Alice felt a realisation dawn on her. 'What about the previous Controller Generals? Are they in the Catacombs?'

Carter nodded, beginning to get excited. 'We could wake them,' he said, 'for information – what about Pinkerton or Chess? They might be able to provide more details about what secrets this place is hiding.'

Samuel's mouth turned into a sharp line. 'No,' he said firmly. 'We don't need any more Industry loyalists out here; we still have to deal with the ten council members.'

'It wouldn't make any difference.' Catherine ran her finger over the desk and looked at them sadly. 'The first thing Elizabet did when

he became Controller General was to switch off the support for
ll previous leaders in the Catacombs.' She turned to face Carter.
They're all dead,' she finished. 'She wanted to run this on her own
with no chance of ever being deposed.' She shook her head. 'Ironi-
ally, her plan was the same as yours – to take down the Industry.
but the difference was that she wanted to replace it with something
ven worse.'

Catherine nodded. 'From what I heard from the guards, there's
lot of confusion – some people are still in denial and others are a
ttle hostile. But it was a stroke of genius to bring the people from
he Township here – they are gentle and kind.' She paused. 'They
ave helped to bring everyone together and the order from Elizabet
egarding the public execution of Frida hit everyone very hard. They
re coming together – slowly – but they are coming together.'

Carter felt a glass-like shard pierce his heart. Without Frida's
trength and determination to support them, they would not even have
enetrated the Barricades. 'If her death can at least mean something,
hen it won't have been in vain,' he said. 'She was a good woman.'

Catherine looked at him nervously. 'There's something else we
hould talk about,' she said. 'Something I mentioned to you before.
he others to the north.'

Samuel looked across at her. 'What do you mean?' he said.

Catherine sighed. 'I believe that Elizabet was communicating with
nother facility, just like this one, but in the north somewhere.'

Samuel whistled loudly through his teeth. 'No way!' he exclaimed.
Like, another Community?'

'We don't know,' said Alice sharply, 'but we're going to find out.'
he sat down next to Carter at one of the long tables. 'Do you have
zzy's tablet?'

'Here,' said Catherine, holding a thin computer out towards Carter. 'I've been through as much as I can. The folder containing the information I mentioned to you is hidden but you can find it if you know where to look.'

Carter pulled the tablet onto the bench and projected the screen onto the wall. It was a much older version, nothing like the ones that were used by the Community now. Alice bit her fingernails nervously as he navigated through to the area, directed by Catherine.

'There,' she said as he hovered over a hidden icon that glowed red as the cursor passed by it. 'It's not even visible unless you're looking for it. And there's old-fashioned protection on it, not the bio-readers we use now.'

Carter clicked twice on the icon that flashed a lightning strike shape and a password box popped onto the screen. He turned to Catherine. 'How did you know the password – it could be anything, a code or—'

'*Veritas liberabit vos*,' Alice interrupted softly. 'That's the kind of irony that would not have been lost on her.'

Catherine nodded with a tight-lipped smile. Carter tapped the keyboard slowly, finger by finger and then pressed enter. The four of them sat watching the screen projected onto the wall as a cursor span. And then stopped. A file opened and series of text communications opened up on the screen. Many were over eighty years old but some were from just a few days ago. Alice's jaw dropped wide open and she gasped audibly as she read silently.

FACILITY 1: Calling Facility Two. We have noticed recent activity. Please confirm your status.
FACILITY 2: I am back, Facility One. It's been a long time, but I am back.

FACILITY 1: As am I. Many of the originals here are dead. Is that Barnes?
FACILITY 2: No, Barnes is dead. This is Conrad, Elizabet Conrad.
FACILITY 1: Good to hear from you, Izzy. We are still in operation. Subjects still unaware of experiment. Our work here continues.
FACILITY 2: Keep it that way, I will be in touch.

Alice shook her head. Another facility like the Ship with people underground? Her blood ran cold and her mind raced as she thought about the thousands of people whose lives had been cut short by the industry. By an *experiment*?

'It's near a place that used to be called Manchester,' said Catherine, taking Carter's place and scanning through the old communications. 'It looks like it was built at around the same time as the Ship and had a similar structure – but from what I can see here, it looks like they were less successful than their London counterparts in keeping people live underground and repopulating.'

She scrolled further. 'But there are still some – and from what I can see in Elizabet's notes, she has a route planned on a map using pictures taken by drones.' She placed her finger on the screen. 'This shows the way the land was reshaped after the Storms.'

'There's the Village,' exclaimed Samuel. 'And the Township. She was going to bring her army through there and attack us.'

'She was a girl of her word,' said Alice bitterly. 'She had everything planned.' Her mind whirred as she went over the implications of the new facility. She knew what she had to do. 'Is there a way to print that?' she asked Catherine. 'Onto something I can take with me. Maybe the same way that Lily made that message in the Drone?'

'You're not thinking of going somewhere?' said Samuel. 'Not there? Surely?'

Alice smiled at him tightly. 'There are people there, living underground in the same way that they have been here – maybe for decades – and I have a responsibility to help them.'

'No you don't,' said Samuel, vehemently. 'You need to be here, with us, helping to rebuild the Community, the Township and the Village.'

'But what if they come for us?' Carter put his hand on his brother's shoulder. 'Maybe Alice is right. If exactly the same thing is happening in the north, can we really stand back and let it happen?'

Catherine shook her head. 'It would be a suicide mission. They might have a Barricade just like this one, and guards and…' She started to shake. 'Elizabet always said that she would kill me – and they would kill her if anyone found out that there was another facility.'

'Well, Izzy is dead and things have changed,' said Alice, determined. 'Did anyone else know about this or was anyone else in communication with them?'

'No,' said Elizabet. 'I never even saw any of these messages. A few nights before you arrived, just after she became Controller General, Elizabet needed some information on the Model – numbers of people underground, their mental status and capacity, that kind of thing. She started to brag about how she would be the most successful Controller General ever and how she was going to deal with the rebels and that she knew about those on the outside. She said she was going to ensure our continued success and then she needed me to get her old tablet working and connected to our systems.'

Catherine brushed her hair out of her eyes nervously. 'I told her we had better technology now but she looked at me coldly and said that this was the only machine that could talk to them.' The girl's bottom p quivered. 'She threatened to kill me and my family if I told anyone if I didn't help her.'

'Get everything you can downloaded from this machine,' said Alice, anding up and walking around the room.

'You're really going?' said Carter getting up and going over to her. f you're going, then I'll come with you.'

'No, you won't,' said Alice. 'You have work to do here to help build this place and be there for Isabella when she wakes up. I don't ave any ties here and my work is elsewhere.'

'If he's not going, then I am,' said Samuel, firmly. 'You're not taking em on alone.'

'I don't need you to come,' said Alice defiantly. 'I can handle this.'

'I know you can,' replied Samuel. 'But Angel can represent the illage here and I think you could use a guide. At least for the first art of the journey. I made a promise to my mother that I would do mething to help. And this is it.'

The four of them sat there for a moment, looking at the screen silence.

'That's settled then,' said Carter, finally. 'Catherine, can you get verything ready for Alice and Samuel before they leave?'

'Wait!' Alice turned to Catherine. 'Hand me that tablet, would ou, please?'

She opened it up to the set of messages and read through them gain.

FACILITY 1: Good to hear from you, Izzy. We are still in operation. Subjects still unaware of experiment. Our work here continues.
FACILITY 2: Keep it that way, I will be in touch.

The others watched as Alice began to type.

FACILITY 2: Calling Facility 1.

There was a still silence as they watched the cursor blink on the screen. Nothing happened for a few moments and then, a sentence flashed up before them.

FACILITY 1: Hello Izzy. Welcome back.
FACILITY 2: The time has come for us to undertake the next stage of our discussions in person. I will coming with representatives to your facility in the next few days to discuss. Confirm you will offer us protection and information.

Alice felt her throat go dry as she typed the words. The only sound was the tap of her fingers on the keyboard and then the long wait before the response came.

FACILITY 1: Affirmative. It's been a long time but I look forward to seeing you again. Regards, William Wilson.

Chapter Twenty-One

The Future

In the brightness of the early morning light, the shards of derelict buildings that could be seen across the Black River seemed to sparkle with an intensity and the promise of a hopeful future that neither Alice nor Carter had seen before. They stood there, watching the rise of the sun together in silence, neither speaking but both reassured in the sense of a common purpose.

'You could stay with us,' said Carter, grinning. 'But I know you won't.'

Alice smiled at him and hoisted the large backpack over her shoulder. 'In some ways, I'd love to stay and help rebuild this place,' she said. 'London has always been my home – I've never been anywhere else. But there's work to be done in the north that none of us can just ignore. I need to end this. I need to end it – them – for good. William Wilson was the one who started this – he ran Paradigm Industries in the days before the Storms and whatever answers he has, I need to hear them.'

'We could use your help here. You'd be an inspiration to people.'

Alice looked up at the sky. 'You don't need me. The Community, Township and Village are starting to integrate well, Catherine has a plan to release those in the Catacombs, including her sister, and work has begun to start resettlement work and create transport links between our new communities.' She laughed. 'Ariel has even managed to convince the old Industry hardliners that there will be a place for them in the new council – as long as they can let go of the past.'

Carter smiled. 'I guess it's something we all have to do at some point.'

Alice nodded. 'You must be proud of him,' she said, 'your son. I know I am.'

'We're getting along well. He's more like a friend, a team mate I suppose, than a son. But I do have some sort of paternal feelings towards him. It's strange because we're so similar in age, but we'll get used to it.'

'You only just met, it's going to take time,' said Alice, shaking her head. 'It's weird, though, you're right. Meeting my daughter in her eighties was more than a little unnerving.' They sat gazing across at the church spire and the riverside buildings on the opposite side of the bank.

'So, your mother is staying in the Village?'

'She won't come back here – at least not yet. Elvira is coming, though – a team has gone to collect her and the other sick people to bring them to the Infirmary so she can get more advanced care.'

'I'd like to have met her; Samuel and Angel speak very highly of her.' Alice had wept openly when Carter had told her of Elvira and her escape from the Community. Her head spun as scenes from her past had been replayed from a different angle, seeing the impact of her actions upon others had given her a strangely focused view on her next adventure.

'What's your plan when you get there?'

Alice laughed, the sound echoing across the hills and out onto the Black River. 'I don't have a plan,' she said. 'I've never had a plan – not a real one. And when I have, it's never worked out the way I wanted it

).' She smiled at Carter. 'In some ways, I've been very unlucky – and
others, I feel like the luckiest person in the world.' She took his
hand. 'If I'd never insisted on going back to the flat where I lived, I'd
never have found Richard Warren. And without him, well, none of
this would have been possible. Maybe I'd have lived out my life as a
e with Filip, who knows?'

Carter shrugged. 'I doubt it,' he said, his face breaking into a smile.
You're a lot of things, Alice Davenport, but you're not the kind of girl
who would let someone tell you what to do – not in the long-term.'

They sat in the sunlight watching the imaginary ghosts of the
long-dead evaporate over the Black River and out into the Deadlands. Alice kept her eye focused on Prospect House, the tower
that loomed dark out in the distance. She thought about how she
had been compelled to go there – to search for her own mother
who was now long dead. Of how she had, instead, found Richard
Warren, Carter's great-grandfather and brought him into the story
of her life. And Samuel, the fiercely protective, somewhat edgier
version of Carter.

'Your brother's quite determined, just like you, isn't he?' she said,
nally.

Carter smiled. 'I think he's a bit in awe of you,' he said. 'But he's a
good man and he'll be able to teach you a lot about the type of survival
that you need out here. A different type to that you already know.'

Alice smiled. 'I can take care of myself,' she said.

'I know. And so can Samuel – but together I think you'll make a
great team.'

'I'm glad he's coming,' she said. 'I feel like I've been a long time
without conversation and he's got a lot of interesting things to say
about what happened to the world while I was asleep.'

'Angel will miss him,' smiled Carter. 'They've been friends all their lives. But I think it will do her good to be here. She wants to teach civilisations to the children in the Academy – educating them about life outside. And she's working well with Ariel on the council. Plus, here is where she was born and she's interested to understand whether she has any relatives alive in the Community – maybe even her parents.'

'It's a strong bond, isn't it?' said Alice. 'That between parent and child. It's sometimes complicated and difficult but intriguing. If it becomes damaged, I think it shapes you.'

'It does,' said Carter, staring into the distance. 'Emotions and love in its many forms is what drives us as human beings – I think by trying to break that, the Industry forgot what it is to be human.'

Alice nodded, tears glistening in her eyes. 'I don't even know how to mend what's broken,' she said, 'but I know that I want to make this world a better place.'

'You already have,' said Carter, his arm on her shoulder. 'Just by being here, everything is better. You're the bravest person I've ever met.'

'Take care of this place,' she said, fighting back further tears. 'I may be back one day.'

'It wouldn't surprise me.'

In the distance, they watched as Samuel approached, a large rucksack on his back, whistling tunelessly to himself. Catherine, Ariel, Lily and Angel tagged behind, chatting excitedly.

'You're going to stay here?' Alice said quietly as they came closer, knowing the answer. 'I mean, long term?'

'At least until Isabella wakes,' replied Carter, his face hopeful. 'Catherine has said she can keep her in a cryonic sleep state for the next thirteen years or so. By then, we'll be the same age and we can start again.'

'But what if you…?' began Alice.

'I won't find anyone else,' said Carter, solidly. 'Isabella has always en the love of my life and I can't imagine being without her.' He iled. 'Catherine says even though she's been through a lot that she'll ake it, and so she'll be the last person released from the Catacombs d I can visit her whenever I want. I will be counting the days until e opens her eyes.'

Alice felt her heart ache a little at the earnestness of the teenage y, who was pledging his life for another. She put her arms around m as the others approached.

'Good luck, Carter Warren,' she whispered. 'We will do what we n to keep in touch.'

Carter held her for a moment and then released her to embrace his other as he came to join them.

'Take care of Alice,' Carter said to him, his voice faltering a little. nd take care of yourself. Mother will be proud of you.'

Samuel grinned broadly. 'We'll be back before you know it,' he said. 1ake sure you all keep this place in good order for when we return.'

'We will,' replied Lily and Angel in unison. 'With Catherine nning the Model and organising the release plan we have a lot of ork to do, but we're determined to make a success of it.'

Alice hugged them each in turn and then looked at Samuel. 'Ready do it?' she said.

'Ready as we'll ever be.'

'I'm going to miss you, Alice Davenport,' whispered Carter. 'The 1th will set you free. Don't ever forget that, okay?'

'I won't,' said Alice, her throat tight. '*Veritas liberabit vos.*'

Then, as the sun climbed its way into the sky and glittered gold ross the Black River, Carter watched as Alice and Samuel made their way towards the north entrance and climbed through the hole in the Barricades that had been hacked away by a group of guards. Carter held up his hand and waved and she held hers up in response as the Community fell into the shadows.

She turned to Samuel and smiled as they stepped across the border and out into the Deadlands, following the trail north.

As Alice turned back for just a second, she could just make out the faint silhouette of her friends, Carter, Angel and Lily, watching her as the ghosts of her past disappeared into the sky, and she felt like suddenly, just in that moment, she could begin to live again.

A Letter From Ceri

want to say a huge thank you for choosing to read *The Storm Girl's Secret*. I loved writing every instalment and watching Carter and Alice grow together in their fight to defeat the Industry. If you did enjoy , and want to keep up-to-date with all my latest releases, just sign p at the following link. Your email address will never be shared and ou can unsubscribe at any time – and don't worry, I won't pass your etails on to the Industry…

www.bookouture.com/ceri-a-lowe

I really hope you loved *The Storm Girl's Secret* and if you did, it ould be so great if you could write a review. I'd love to hear what you hink, and it makes such a difference helping new readers to discover ne of my books for the first time. If you haven't yet read *The Rising torm* or *The Girl in the Storm*, the first two books in the Paradigm eries, please do check them out!

always love hearing from my readers and getting their views on he end of the world so please do get in touch on my Facebook page, through Twitter, Goodreads or my website. Together, we can conquer the Industry.

Thanks,
Ceri A. Lowe

 cerialowe

 @cerilowepetrask

 www.cerialowe.com

Acknowledgements

he road to bring Alice and Carter to the conclusion of their journey
as been a long one and there have been many people who have
een there at various steps of the way. Many of them have helped
or hindered) Alice and Carter in some way – Hannah Quinn,
Kerryanne Mendoza, Dorota Filip(owicz), Kristina Kunsteinaite,
Kelly(ie) Walters, Bobbie (Alderney) Macniven-Young, James (Jayden)
Dummer, Iseult (Samita) Murphy, Elvira Lowe and many, many more.

would also like to thank my fantastic editor, Ellen Gleeson, and
he wonderful team at Bookouture, most notably Kim Nash, Noelle
Holton and Oliver Rhodes, for giving me the opportunity to share
hese stories with my readers.

As always, thanks to my friends and family, the Lifelongs, my
choir Sing Out Bristol, colleagues and my random acquaintances
who have provided the inspiration and encouragement to keep going
throughout the last few years – every conversation we have had about
his trilogy has been so incredibly helpful, in one way or another. And
o Formentera, the place that inspires me most.

Thanks to my dad for your support always, and to my sister, Sally.
here are never enough words to describe how amazing you are.

And the greatest thanks and love to my partner, Lara. For every-
hing. For always.

Printed by Amazon Italia Logistica S.r.l.
Torrazza Piemonte (TO), Italy